A GOOD DAY TO DIE

Center Point
Large Print

**This Large Print Book carries the
Seal of Approval of N.A.V.H.**

TOM W. BLACKBURN

A GOOD DAY TO DIE

CENTER POINT PUBLISHING

THORNDIKE, MAINE

For my daughter, Stephanie

This Center Point Large Print edition
is published in the year 2003 by arrangement with
Golden West Literary Agency.

Copyright © 1995 by Thomas Wakefield Blackburn.

The text of this Large Print edition is unabridged. In other
aspects, this book may vary from the original edition. Printed in
Thailand. Set in 16-point Times New Roman type by
Bill Coskrey and Gary Socquet.

ISBN 1-58547-283-2

Library of Congress Cataloging-in-Publication Data.

Blackburn, Thomas Wakefield.
    A good day to die / Tom W. Blackburn.--Center Point large print ed.
        p. cm.
    ISBN 1-58547-283-2 (lib. bdg. : alk. paper)
    1. Large type books. I. Title.

PS3552.L3422 G66 2003
813'.54--dc21
                                                                        2002034836

I am Wovoka. I am the messiah. I am Father and Grandfather. I have been to the Spirit World and I have seen God. Make the dance I will show you and a new world will soon cover the old. The buffalo and the game and your friends and relations who are dead will live again. Do no harm to anyone. Make no quarrel with the whites. You must not fight. Hesunanin *says so. I say so. I am Wovoka. I am the messiah.*

The People
(Those in *italics* are fictional)

At Standing Rock
CHANCE EASTERBROOK ....a freelance newspaperman
BEAU LANE ....a half-breed Hunkpapa Sioux
NORA CRANDALL ....teacher in the Indian Service school
CATHERINE WELDON.......a self-appointed social worker
JAMES MCLAUGHLIN.......United States Indian Agent

LT. COL. DRUM
CAPTAIN FECHET } ....garrison officers at Fort Yates

LT. BULL HEAD
RED TOMAHAWK
SHAVE HEAD } ....members of Agent McLaughlin's Indian Police force
CATKA
HAWK MAN

COL. WILLIAM F. CODY ..."Buffalo Bill"

At Grand River
SITTING BULL ....head chief of the Sioux Nation
SEEN BY HER NATION......one of Sitting Bull's wives

CROWFOOT
JOHN } ....Hunkpapa boys, Sitting Bull's sons

GRAY EAGLE...................Sitting Bull's brother-in-law
SHINING WOMAN..............Sitting Bull's gift to Easterbrook
CATCH THE BEAR...........Sitting Bull's lifelong friend, one of the Hunkpapa "old men"

JUMPING BULL
BLACKBIRD
STRIKES THE KETTLE } ..other Hunkpapa "old men"
CRAWLER
BRAVE THUNDER
SPOTTED HORN BULL

JACK CARIGNAN ....teacher in a U.S. Indian Service school nearby

REVEREND RIGGS............director of a Congregational mission and school nearby

OLD MOON......................a visiting Cheyenne, a Ghost Dancer

In the Nevada Galilee

WOVOKA ....the Paiute messiah

CHARLEY SHEEP ....his uncle and go-between

KICKING BEAR ....High Priest of the Ghost Dance

At Pine Ridge

RED CLOUD.....................chief of the Oglalas

BIG FOOT } ....chief of the Minneconjous
HUMP

GENERAL BROOKE
COLONEL FORSYTH } ..officers of the Pine Ridge garrison
LT. JOHN J. PERSHING

GENERAL NELSON A. MILES.......commander-in-chief, Army of the West

DR. CHARLES EASTMAN
REVEREND COOK } ....members of the official agency family
CAPT. GEORGE SWORD

LT. EBERLE ....press officer at Rushville, Neb.

STELLA CORRIGAN............a settler's daughter

FREDERIC REMINGTON ....artist and writer

The Beginning

The grass is seasonal on the Great Plains. It dies but lives again in yearly rebirth. It is myriad in variety and much of it is not grass at all. Much of it herb and shrub and creeper. Much of it is weed. But the best of it is the grama, for its persistent root and heavy seeding withstands heat and frost and flood. Despite the treacheries of nature, it is self-perpetuating. It survives all but the plow. Left unturned, it will in time suture the scars of even mortal wounds.

So it was upon this watershed of the Bighorn that Old Moon of the Cheyenne rode to The Place. He carried his rifle and was stripped down for the chase as in olden times. But he was not hunting. It was a game he played, a dream he dreamed, a privilege of those who possess no more than memories.

At camp they believed he had prudently ridden away from the Agency to avoid a chance meeting with soldiers and those who had drunk with soldiers. This was the first day of a new year by the white man's count and there had been much whiskey in celebration. There were certain to be sick bellies and sore heads and tempers as short as his own.

Escape was the excuse he used when he rode into these brown-grassed hills, but it was not the reason. Old Moon was making a pilgrimage. He made it often. When summer came again it would be only thirteen years. Scarcely long enough for a boy to become a man, long enough for a nation to die.

The monument was on the hilltop above him. A tapered stone spearpoint aimed at the sun. About its base was an iron fence, already much rusted with neglect. The honor the white man paid even to his own courage was short-lived. Further out, in a space the size of a thirty-lodge camp circle, were scattered wooden stakes where the bones had been found—bones which only a few seasons past were finally gathered into a permanent resting place at the foot of the blunted sandstone shaft.

There should have been nearly three hundred stakes. Old Moon knew the count well. But less than half of them still stood where they had been driven. The graves of the dead did not renew themselves as the grass did.

Old Moon did not ride up the hill. He had been up there once and he remembered. He remembered Cheyenne friends who had fallen there and all the great war chiefs. He remembered Sitting Bull. He remembered that when the shooting was over a young Sioux who was nephew to the Bull was shown a naked body among the fallen soldiers.

"Yellow Hair thought he was the greatest man in the world," a friend said, pointing to the unmutilated body. "Now he lies there."

"Well," the young nephew of the Sioux chief said with much wonder, "if that is Yellow Hair, then I am the man who killed him!"

It was a great *coup*. The white chief Custer had not been recognized in battle with his hair cut short. It was not known those pony soldiers were his or that he was with them. But he had long been a troublesome enemy. It was good he was dead.

The soldiers had made the attack on the great hunting camp Sitting Bull had brought over from the Rosebud. The soldiers had fired the first shots and the war cry of the Sioux had answered.

"Come on! Come on! It's a good day to die!"

It had rung from many throats. Cheyenne, Arapaho, Sans Arc, Minneconjou, Oglala, Santees, Yanktonais, Blackfeet, Hunkpapa. It was a great camp. Perhaps two thousand lodges in all. But not every man fought that day. There was no need nor even room. Old Moon was among those who counted no *coup,* but it was a good fight and a hard one, while it lasted, against an enemy brave to the last man. It made good remembering. What came after did not.

Old Moon failed to touch an enemy. He did not kill. He rode onto that hill only to defend the women and children in his lodge here on the valley floor. All men knew this. But from that day on he had known hatred at the hands of every soldier and nearly every white man who chanced to learn he had been present here that day. And the hatred seemed to grow with the years.

If it was thus with him, how must it be with those more fortunate men who had won many feathers in that fight? Those were soldier graves under that brown grass up there, but the Indian lay buried in them. So Old Moon believed.

He dismounted in the lengthening shadows of this New Year's Day and stuck a twig into the ground. In a split at its top he wedged a tarnished metal button bearing an insignia of the United States Seventh Cavalry, an insignificant trophy in which he had once taken great pride.

Squatting beside this twig, Old Moon closed his eyes. When there is no hope, a man must pray. It is then that the gods are most likely to answer his plea. And it was said the messiah had already come. It was said he was there in the west, beyond the mountains.

I

McLaughlin

Chance Easterbrook's first impression of the agent at Standing Rock was negative. James McLaughlin looked tall because his boots had high heels. He wore his prematurely white hair with the conscious pride of a battle plume. He was brusque in manner. His handsome, aquiline features were arrogant. And the chip on his shoulder showed in his eyes.

"What the hell they think I'm running out here?" the Bureau man demanded. "A public circus? I need a newspaperman on this reservation now like I need another tribe of Indians!"

Easterbrook was aware the conversation was carrying to the outer office and probably the veranda beyond. He thought the unclosed door was deliberate.

"Even one with a commission from the New York *Herald*?" he asked mildly.

"Damned right," McLaughlin snapped. "This is the Dakotas, man. The middle of the Sioux reservations. Not New York—or Washington."

Chance smiled. He had been born and raised on a

Missouri farm. That had been pretty much of a frontier, then, too. The trouble was no one remembered a newspaperman had to come from someplace.

"I know," he said pleasantly. "It's taken me two days on a rented horse to get down here from Bismarck. And I'm not interested in Bureau politics, if that's what's bothering you. It's just that there hasn't been much in the press on the Sioux the last few years. In fact, not since Sitting Bull came back from Canada, surrendered, and settled down here."

"That old bastard never really surrendered and he won't settle down till he's six feet under."

"That's the kind of thing I'm after. Color. How the old days look to them, now. How they're taking to reservation life. Sort of a series on the manumission of a minority, if you like the big words. Believe me, I don't make trouble, Mr. McLaughlin. I only report it."

The agent swung around in his chair and studied Chance thoughtfully. It was a direct enough scrutiny but not particularly disconcerting. Chance pretty well knew what the impression would be. A loose, spare frame, an inch or two taller than McLaughlin, himself. A skin paled down for want of wind and weather in recent years, but a body hard enough for the life he led and kept so by as frequent holidays in the open as he could manage. No such magnificent mane as McLaughlin boasted, but only a little grayed at the temples. No more than ten years difference in their ages, perhaps. McLaughlin might resent that. Some older men did. A polish that might smack of the effete East here but was mostly a matter of a tailored shirt, thin-soled boots,

13

clean nails, and an acquired affection for some of the niceties of life. Nothing to stir hostility. Nothing but what he was, a reasonably successful free-lance newspaperman in search of a story.

"The *Herald*," McLaughlin said slowly. "The Bennetts' sheet. Gets pretty well read in Washington, doesn't it?"

"A few other places, too."

"I'm not interested in other places. We scratch backs out here, Easterbrook. We've got to, to get the job done. I take it you want some interviews. Well it might be arranged. For instance, there's a white woman I had to order off the reservation today. Her name's Catherine Weldon and she's the representative of the National Indian Defense Association. One of those crackpot outfits. 'Lo, the poor Indian!' You know the kind."

"Well enough to tell you they're not my kind of copy."

"I could tell you some things about this woman that might make you change your mind."

"Spare me."

"The trouble with her is she talks. There's no truth to anything she can say as far as facts are concerned, but we've still got troubles. It would be useful to me—and to the Bureau—if she couldn't afford to open her mouth when she gets back to Boston."

"A little professional defamation?"

"Little? Mister, I want her smeared good. And don't try to tell me the *Herald*'s fussy about that."

"I am."

"I see. Well, sir, we've had a pretty lively summer out here. It may get livelier. Under the circumstances, I don't believe I care to expose my Indians any further to the press at this time."

"*Your* Indians?"

"The Sioux bands on these reservations have been assembled by means of the longest and one of the costliest wars ever undertaken by the United States Government," McLaughlin said. "They have been gathered in to be disciplined and civilized for their own good. Until that is accomplished, they are wards of the government and I am the government here at Standing Rock. Yes, sir, my Indians. And your request is denied."

Chance's expression did not change, but he bridled at the tone. He abhorred little tin gods. Particularly if they were on the public payroll. The rights and privileges of the press were deeply ingrained in him besides being the principal tradition of his profession. Like Mother, Country, and certain relationships with women, it stirred blind loyalty and instant defense, even in the most cynical and dissolute men of the trade.

Chance had survived nearly a dozen years and a score of papers by clinging to that faith as stubbornly as any. He had worked his way from copyboy to free-lance feature writer by an absolute conviction he was one of the Lord's anointed, and he did not like to be told what he could and could not do. He shrugged and came to his feet with deceptive transigence.

"All right. But remember I asked."

James McLaughlin was not misled. He raised his voice.

"Lieutenant Bull Head!"

A short-haired Indian policeman among the loungers

in the outer office marched in briskly. His grin was as irritating as the oversize badge on his blue tunic.

"Lieutenant," McLaughlin said, "Mr. Easterbrook is to have every courtesy while he is on our reservation. He is to be permitted to remain as long as he cares and to leave at his own convenience. But he is not to approach any of the camps or to speak to any of the people from them. Is that perfectly clear?"

The policeman saluted smartly and went out. McLaughlin rose and offered Chance his hand.

"Getting late," he suggested affably. "Lieutenant-Colonel Drum is in command of the garrison across the way. I'm sure his aide can put you up in the barracks."

"Thanks for the hospitality," Chance said.

He went out. There were smirks in the anteroom. He supposed the agent had made a point of sorts with the interview. With these office hangers-on, at any rate. But there was one who did not seem amused.

He was a compact man, a little shorter than Chance, a little younger. His skin had the deep color of the sun. His hair was as black as any present. His wide, deep-set eyes were also black or a blue so deep as to seem black. He was well made and would have been unusually handsome but for a curious lack of animation in feature and expression. Chance decided that his Caucasian blood was dominant, then smiled inwardly at the thought. The vanity of race. All men had it.

From the agency veranda, Easterbrook spotted the wire of a telegraph. It led into the compound of Fort Yates, the military post which was, as McLaughlin had said, across the way. He started across at a brisk pace. A

16

newspaperman with access to a telegraph could do a good deal in a very few minutes with even as remote a bureaucrat as James McLaughlin. But he was hailed from living quarters behind what appeared to be a schoolhouse before he had gone more than a few rods.

A woman came out to the unpainted picket gate to meet him. She was quite an astonishing woman. She was well into middle life, handsome, fashionably dressed in a long-sleeved suit with a great collar rolling up from a robust decolletage, and she seemed magnificently impervious to weeds and dust and heat.

"Forgive me," she said. "No secret lasts very long here. Are you Mr. Easterbrook, the correspondent who arrived a short while ago?"

Startled, Chance nodded.

"I am Catherine Weldon. Mrs. Catherine Weldon. I assume Mr. McLaughlin mentioned me—perhaps that he has ordered me to leave the reservation in the morning?"

"I believe there was some mention."

"Naturally!" the woman said with surprising spirit. "This is most difficult, Mr. Easterbrook, but I must know. Did he also tell you why?"

"Perhaps he meant to, but something else came up."

"He will. Quite bluntly, do you intend to mention me or the unfortunate position in which I find myself in your—in your dispatches from here?"

"Should I?"

"I appeal to your sense of honor, Mr. Easterbrook. Personal publicity of that sort will destroy everything I have been trying to accomplish here."

Desperation was very near the surface. Chance responded instinctively but could not suppress curiosity.

"I see," he said gently. "Not for publication, Mrs. Weldon, but what are you trying to accomplish?"

"I am trying to save the life of a great man. Perhaps one of the greatest men of our time. An Indian. I am trying to help him prevent the extermination of his race. And because he is this man's enemy, James McLaughlin is trying to put me to bed with him in the public eye."

Chance could not imagine this woman in bed with anyone. A blanket Indian least of all. The thought itself was preposterous. He was curious as to the motive for McLaughlin's malice but her distress was so genuine he could not question her further. He bowed without quite knowing why.

"My word, Mrs. Weldon," he said. "Not for publication."

"Thank you."

She lifted her skirt from yard weeds and turned back to the door from which she had emerged. Chance was still at the gate, staring speculatively after her, when the half-breed he had noticed in the agency office came up to him. There was no sound. Just a sudden presence.

"I was listening," the man said. A fact, not an apology.

"Back at the office, too," Chance suggested, displeased.

The inanimate features broke into a sudden smile.

"Like Mrs. Weldon said, there's few secrets around here." The Dakotan nodded off after the woman. "You did right with her. She's had a pretty bad time of it. Been staying with Nora—that's the teacher here—when she wasn't down to Grand River. Only one who'd take her in. Even the Indians aren't sure what to make of her. But she's a friend and they understand that, at least. Trouble's been Jim McLaughlin's had her and Sitting Bull all wrong from the start."

"Sitting Bull!" Chance exclaimed involuntarily. "That the Indian she was trying to tell me about? McLaughlin ought to know he couldn't make that stick. The chief's got to be an old man."

The Dakotan's smile widened.

"Fifty-eight. But he still keeps two wives happy. They call him an old man out in the camps, all right, but that isn't what they mean. In Sioux it's a sign of respect, wisdom, experience and reputation. Look at it the way they do, Sitting Bull has been an old man a long time, now."

"I'd like to see him."

"Well it won't be easy, but I'm for hire. Beau Lane's the name."

Chance sized up the man. He had meant to ask McLaughlin for a guide and interpreter. That was impossible, now, but this man did not seem intimidated by the agent. He doubted he could do better, even with official approval.

"For how much, Lane?" he asked.

"What it's worth. I'm not offering for the wage. You want to write about the Sioux and I want to show you some things to write about."

"Fair enough," Chance agreed. "Maybe tomorrow. If the telegraph over there at the post is working, I'll have permission out of Washington by then."

Lane shook his head.

"Colonel Drum may run the garrison but Jim McLaughlin runs everything else, including the telegraph. No white man's permission means anything, anyhow. Not these days. Go rustle yourself some chow and a bunk. I'll mind your horse and see you in the morning after breakfast call."

The Dakotan turned and walked away as though all arrangements were made.

Beau Lane rode openly into the Fort Yates compound leading Chance's horse and a laden pack mare. Chance was angry at his stupidity.

"Why didn't you turn out the post band, too? McLaughlin will stop us the minute he finds out where we're headed."

"He'll try. Actually, he's going to help us get to Grand River. You'll see."

As they rode out of the compound, two Indian policemen reined away from the rack before McLaughlin's office and moved unhurriedly toward them. Lane smiled and turned up a small rise nearby which he called Proposal Hill. At the summit was a broad view of the lazily looping Missouri. The Dakotan gestured for Chance to dismount with him there. The two Indian policemen came close enough to see that no one else was around, then pulled up curiously to wait. Lane turned Chance eastward, looking across the river.

"They call themselves Dakotas," he said, "but that's where they came from, over there—Minnesota, Wisconsin—Michigan. They were driven out by enemies with trade guns from further east. Anyhow, here at the river were the Pearly Gates, and when they crossed it, they were in Paradise. There were buffalo herds all the way to the Rocky Mountains, so they called it their country and claimed it always had been. This happened a long time ago, before horses."

He paused and scuffed up a dry tuft of sod.

"A white man has to be dead to go to his heaven. In the old days, a Sioux was born to his. Remember that, it's important. There's something else I want to show you—"

They stepped around a clump of brush and were confronted by a curious little monument facing the river. It was of plain country rock, scarcely four feet high. It appeared to be a natural formation which at one time might have had its crude representation of a kneeling Indian woman with a cradleboard on her back, heightened by a few licks of some tool.

"Standing Rock," Lane said, "where the Agency gets its name, used to be at a crossing of the old trails above here. White Hair—that's McLaughlin—knew it was important. He got a notion that some of the wilder ones would come into the Agency more often if he moved her down here. But it didn't work."

"What is she?"

"McLaughlin says she's a putrefaction."

"A petrifaction—an actual woman's body, turned to stone?"

"That's what the old ones say. There was another little rock, of a fist-sized little puppy, that also got turned to stone when she did. There were some building going on at the Agency when McLaughlin moved her down here. The dog got mixed up with some other rocks and went into a foundation or something. Nobody ever did know just where.

"Just a little old rock, but they miss it. That's important, too. Something else they once had that's gone and they'll never get back."

Chance studied the crude monument again.

"They actually believe that thing was once alive?"

"It's not important what they believe. When we get into Grand River or any of the other old-time camps you'll be hearing and seeing things a lot harder to understand than this little old lady and her lost puppy. You've got to get them right, that's all I ask. Get them as they are, not the way they look to everybody else."

"Look, Beau," Chance protested. "This series isn't supposed to be a life's work, you know."

Lane shrugged.

"What you do, do right. It's time somebody did."

He led the way back to their horses and eyed the waiting Indians with anticipatory malice.

"Those Metal Breasts want a ride, let's give it to them!"

They rode down the hill. Lane turned directly south at a steady pace. McLaughlin's police followed with no attempt to close up. Chance kept turning to check their position. Beau grinned at him.

"They won't do anything till they can prove we're disobeying orders. It's forty miles to the Bull's camp. They've got all day to make up their minds."

Lane held to high ground where there was no water. He made no stops. Noon passed. Heat increased through the afternoon and Chance could see sweat stains growing on the blue tunics doggedly trailing them. At the onset of twilight, the Dakotan dipped into a swale which brought them to the thicket-fringed course of a small branch. They turned up this some distance before he reined in at water. He permitted the pack mare to remain at the stream but forced both saddle horses back after only a moment of thirsty snuffling.

The Indian policemen bypassed them and came to water upstream. Beau, seeming to take real interest in them for the first time all day, scowled as one turned sidewise in his saddle and relieved himself into the stream from that position. The Metal Breasts laughed and awaited reaction. When none came, they left their ponies at the water and sprawled indolently on the bank. Lane's irritation turned to satisfaction as their ponies continued to drink deeply.

"Dried them out about right," he said. "Been shot at lately?"

He hooked the horn of his saddle and swung up without touching stirrup. His horse took the stream with a high splash and buck-jumped up the other bank. Chance tried to catch the lead-rope of the pack mare. Beau shouted at him.

"Leave be and ride!"

The Dakotan crashed into brush and disappeared. Upstream, the startled Indians broke for their ponies. Chance abandoned the pack mare and gave his horse its head. A willow branch whipped across his face, setting him back hard as he smashed into the brush after his companion.

A moment later he heard the report of a Winchester. Realization that he was the target came hard and would not quite go down. The bullet ripped through undergrowth and sang off into distance. Chance regained his balance and flattened instinctively forward along the neck of his horse.

More shots sounded, closely spaced. Incredulous that this could actually be happening, even in this place and under these circumstances, Chance riveted his attention on the rump of Lane's horse. He shouted protest to Beau but was unheard or ignored.

They came out of the brush onto a smoothly grassed slope. The Agency policemen broke cover at the same time. One fired his rifle again. Chance drew alongside Lane. The Dakotan was transformed, flushed with high, reckless delight. The Metal Breasts shouted angry encouragement to their ponies. Lane exuberantly echoed their shouts and lashed rein-leather across both thighs.

Beau pulled a little ahead as they crested the hill and plunged in a breakneck slide down the wall of a steeply eroded ravine. Loosened boulders bounded ahead of them. Chance leaned to his horse's tail as the animal sledded with hind feet tucked to the fore and haunches burning gravel.

Lane's horse stumbled and went down in a geyser of dust at the bottom of the pitch. Chance tried to check, but he overrode his companion. He looked back. Beau and the horse came up as one and resumed with unhampered stride. He swept past Chance as they leaned into a sharp turn in the course of the ravine. Shouting something, he took the far wall. Chance followed.

They were halfway up when the Metal Breasts shot around the turn. One jumped his horse against the slope. The other reined in momentarily and slanted his rifle upward. Chance pressed his navel hard against the horn of his saddle. The policeman finished emptying his magazine without effect.

They came out onto the grass of the *coteau* again. Chance took Lane's flung sod in the face. Nearly a quarter-mile lead opened up before pursuit reappeared. A dust-caked abrasion on Lane's cheek leaked a red line to his jaw but he was grinning. Chance now understood his stratagem at the creek. The unguarded watering the Sioux had permitted their ponies at the creek was now telling.

At the end of another mile the *coteau* fell away into a wide, sheltered bottom, cut by the meander of a good-sized stream. Beau shouted exultant identification.

"Grand River—!"

I I

Catch The Bear

Fires glowed among lodges silhouetted on the stream bank. A crude log cabin stood close by. A crowd was gathered before it. Lane, still possessed by some wild spirit, rode almost into the front rank at undiminished speed. He pulled up at the last moment in a spectacular halt. Chance managed more soberly and turned his horse over to a boy who trotted out for it.

The Metal Breasts halted warily, two hundred yards out on the darkening grass. Chance moved angrily to Beau but was sharply gestured to silence. The door of the nearby cabin opened. An old man came out. He stalked into full view of the policemen halted beyond the perimeter of the camp. He threw back the blanket over his shoulders, revealing a rifle in the crook of his arm. He flung the weapon to his shoulder in disregard of distance and failing light. Before he could pretend to sight, McLaughlin's men hastily wheeled their ponies and trotted off in retreat.

The crowd laughed approvingly. The old man looked narrowly at Chance and spoke to Lane. Beau answered rapidly. The old man summoned a woman, then went back into the cabin. The woman led Chance and his companion to a lodge and indicated it was for their use. She made a fire for light. Others brought water and presently a small iron trade kettle. When they were alone, Beau removed the cover and fished out a steaming chunk of meat with his fingers.

"Made a good showing, the way we came in and all," he said with satisfaction.

"Like a couple of damned fools!" Chance growled.

"Like a couple of wild Indians," Lane corrected. "That was the idea. You did fine. But I was afraid for a minute you were going to open your mouth and spoil Catch The Bear's show."

"The old faker with the rifle? He couldn't have hit

those confounded, trigger-happy policemen of McLaughlin's with a Hotchkiss battery in that light!"

"Never intended to try. Just a warning that no uniformed turncoats can ride into this camp after anybody. Like he wouldn't have let you come in if those Metal Breasts hadn't been on our tail. But with them after you, you got to be McLaughlin's enemy. If you're his enemy, you got to be their friend. Simple as that. But it was up to the old Bear. With the chief gone, he's responsible."

"Sitting Bull isn't here?" Chance asked, disappointment adding to his irritation.

Lane shook his head.

"The Bull came into the Agency this morning before you were up to ferry Mrs. Weldon and her trunks across the river. Major Mac saw to it that nobody else would do it."

"You beat my tail all the way out here when I could have seen Sitting Bull right there at Standing Rock?"

"He wouldn't have talked to you there, even if the major would have allowed it. Here's different. Be patient. He'll be back directly. Three-four days at most."

"I told you this wasn't a lifetime project! Where do you get this 'major' business with McLaughlin?"

"All agents are majors. Called that, anyway. Goes with the job, I guess."

Lane plucked another chunk of meat from the pot. Chance watched him deftly twist it as it rose to his mouth so that the thin, dribbling juice twined about the unappetizing gray morsel and his fingers without a drop spilling. A nicety, no doubt. This lodge they had been provided with was also a real honor, Beau said. The flooring hide was buffalo. So was the lodge cover. No longer made and could never be again. But the odors of fats and bodies and old smoke were pervasive and the hide flooring was heavily stained. Chance distastefully helped himself from the pot and wiped his fingers on a pocket kerchief which seemed beautifully clean.

A cough sounded outside. Beau grunted invitation. Two men entered with the packs they had abandoned on the creek. They put them against the rear wall and departed.

"Told you not to worry about the mare," Lane said. "Bet we weren't half a mile away from that creek before they were down off the ridges and had her for us."

"They were watching that far out?"

"That's why we had to make it look good when we shook those Metal Breasts. They like a good trick better than any joke. Been more of a to-do over it but there was some kind of a meeting going on over there in the chief's cabin when we came in. Think I better find out what it's about. Mind?"

Chance shook his head. Beau rose effortlessly from his cross-legged position and stepped into the night. Chance stirred uncomfortably, finally slipped off his boot and chafed his foot. The scar tissue of an old wound from a minor hunting accident occasionally set a nerve to burning and could only be relieved in this fashion. A woman then returned for the supper pot and showed displeasure because it had not been emptied. She went away, muttering to herself. Out on the grass orchestral insects built a pervasive symphony. Chance looked about him and shrugged wryly. He had not meant to involve himself so deeply for a few columns of copy.

Beau returned in a few minutes. He sat down by their packs, and began to unlash his own.

"Now what?" Chance asked.

"Not sure," Lane answered. "Seems another visitor came in this afternoon. A Cheyenne from the Tongue River Agency, over in Montana. They say he has an important message for the chief."

He rolled his pack out and began rummaging in it.

"Don't know if this'll work. May get into Dutch with the Bull for trying it when he isn't here. But there aren't many things to hold an old-time council about any more. Don't want you to miss it—if they'll have you."

The Dakotan straightened from his pack with the head of a small, beautifully worked ceremonial pipe of red stone.

"A present," he said. "Bread and butter, sort of. For Catch The Bear, since he's taking the chief's place. If he lets us in, make a lot of giving it to him. But don't say anything. Some of these old-time people speak pretty fair English and understand it a lot better. Easy to make a mistake. Let me do the talking."

As they crossed the encampment, Beau filled Chance in. Sitting Bull had built this cabin at Grand River in white man's style to show he and the Hunkpapas of his own band were sincere in their effort to travel the white man's road. To Major McLaughlin's intense irritation, the wily old chief continually cited this fact at official meeting and public council in rebuttal to the agent's standing charge he was fomenting trouble and urging his people to cling to the old ways.

In the Bull's absence, Catch The Bear was in charge of the chief's household and duties. The hospitality due a visitor from so distant a place as Tongue River, for instance. With luck, equal courtesy to the two others who had arrived this evening. They had been driven here by White Hair's police, who had shot at them many times. Should they not also be received as friends?

Lane stubbed his toe twice against the bottom of the cabin door instead of knocking. It was a much less peremptory sound. The door was opened by a boy with great colorless round dollar eyes. When he saw Chance he darted back in alarm, uttering a deaf-mute's cascade of unformed sound.

"One of the Bull's sons," Beau said.

The old man who had turned the Metal Breasts away with an unfired gun replaced the boy at the door. Neither Beau nor the old man spoke. Chance was acutely uncomfortable, but the old Bear finally stepped back and Beau thrust him into the room.

If the cabin was white man's style without, it was Indian within. Low beams cradled sagging poles and a cross-hatching of wattling which in turn supported the thick sod roof. Wall logs were chinked with wands and clay. Canvas had been tacked over them to a height of about five feet as further discouragement to wind and weather.

There were no chests or cabinets of any kind. Household and personal paraphernalia hung from pegs driven into chinks above the canvas sheathing. Beds were in corners, robes and blanketing on the dirt floor. A simple heating stove, also used for cooking, sat in the center of the room. A kerosene lantern stood on the cold lids. Another was bracketed on the far wall beside a large portrait in full figure of a singularly strong-faced Indian wearing a magnificent feathered warbonnet that trailed to his heels. As he moved deeper into the room, Chance saw a signature near the frame line: *C. S. Weldon.*

In addition to the dozen or so men in the room there were two women, the deaf-mute, and an older boy of fifteen or sixteen. Catch The Bear dismissed this group with a gesture. However, as the older boy reluctantly followed the others to the door, the Bear spoke to him. Flashing the old man a look of intense gratitude, the boy shut the door and hurried back to a place along the wall.

Space was made for Chance and Beau Lane on the edge of a bed beside the Cheyenne, their other guest. Beau nudged him and Chance produced his gift. Unsure of protocol, he first extended the pipe so the Cheyenne might see. The visitor hissed softly in approval. Holding it higher, Chance then exhibited the gift to the rest of the room. Only then did he offer it to Catch The Bear. The old Sioux accepted gravely but with unmistakable pleasure. Rising, he passed from one to another so all might examine the gift more closely.

In the midst of this, with characteristic lack of warning, the scar on Chance's foot began to burn again. The discomfort was acute. His sock came away with the boot and he massaged the cramped flesh gratefully. This diversion seemed to greatly interest all present. Several rose to their feet for a better view, sitting down only when he replaced his boot. But there was no comment.

Attention presently turned to the visiting Cheyenne.

The Indian glanced at Catch The Bear, received a nod from him, and with some apparent reluctance looked directly at Chance and began to speak. For a moment Chance incredulously believed he understood the unfamiliar sibilance. Then he realized the voice was Beau Lane's. The Dakotan was quietly performing that most difficult of interpreter's arts—a running, instantaneous translation.

"I am Old Moon," Beau said for the Indian as he spoke. "I am a Cheyenne, brother to the Sioux. I was with Sitting Bull on the Greasy Grass when we killed Yellow Hair there. I was a proud man that day. Look at me, White Man. Once I was young. A strong warrior. Now I am an old man. Once my people were young, on a young land. Game was plentiful and fat. Now the game is dead and the land is dead. Only a few of us are left. Soon we will also die. These men here are Indian. They know how it is.

"Well, some time ago my heart was heavy with that. On the day the white man says begins the new year, I went back to that place on the Greasy Grass where all of those dead pony soldiers are buried. I made a prayer there. It took quite a long time, but now *Wakantanka* has answered that prayer. Soon we will all have hope again because of a new thing which has lately happened. That is what I have come here to tell my brothers about."

The Cheyenne paused and shook his head.

"I do not think it is for a white man to hear," he resumed disapprovingly. "But these people think that is all right because that other man is with you. So I speak. We heard it at Tongue River from the Arapaho. They heard it from the Shoshone. The Shoshone heard it from the Bannock and the Bannock heard it from the Paiute. Now hear what they are saying. Now the Indian everywhere will have his time. The time of the white man is short."

Chance glanced involuntarily at Lane but Beau's eyes were unreadable.

"They are saying that lately a Paiute many days to the west, beyond the mountains, fell down and died," the Cheyenne continued. "He died and came alive again. He died the day the sun died. That was the day he went to heaven. That was the day he saw the Father."

A very old Sioux against the far wall spoke up.

"If that was the day, Brother, it was a long time ago. This man must have many winters. The sun has only died once in my years and I was a very young boy when it happened."

"Eclipse?" Chance whispered.

Lane nodded to him and the Cheyenne nodded to the old man.

"That is so in the country of the Sioux, Grandfather. The old men say it is the same in my country. But it is different in the country of the Paiute. It is not a year since these things happened. It is said this man has no more than thirty summers."

Catch The Bear rubbed the shine of his new pipe. His eyes narrowed shrewdly.

"You believe in these things? You believe in this man?"

"His own people believe," the Cheyenne answered. "He gave them this dance to make in prayer. It will bring the new world soon, he says. They dance this dance for five days at every change of moon. Now the Bannock are dancing. So are the Shoshone and the Arapaho. We at Tongue River want to believe, too. The words are good."

Catch The Bear said something to the boy whom he had permitted to remain. The boy took an object from a wall peg. Chance saw it was a large crucifix, sculptured brass against polished wood.

"Father De Smet gave it to Sitting Bull, years ago," Lane murmured to Chance.

Catch The Bear held the crucifix so Old Moon could see the tortured figure on the cross.

"Is this the man?"

"It is said so," the Cheyenne assented. "The Father sent him once to the white man. They killed him as you see there. Lately the Father has heard of the troubles of the Indian, so he has sent the same man again. Soon he will send a new earth. An earth like the olden time. The dead will live again. And the buffalo. But no white man. Brothers, that is good dancing!"

Several of the Sioux stirred.

"*Hau! Hau!*" they murmured in approval.

Catch The Bear put the crucifix aside and stood up.

"These words come a long ways," he said, "but they make a good sound in our ears. It would be good to learn there is truth in these things. If there is, Sitting Bull will know where to find it. We will speak again when he is here."

Thus, abruptly, it came to an end. The Indians filed out without the delaying civilized habit of unnecessary farewells. Chance and Lane walked back to their lodge in silence. Even then Chance was content to wait for the Dakotan to uncover embers and feed them twigs for light.

"Where'd it come from, really, Beau? What's behind it?"

Lane shrugged.

"Think they're actually taking to it as hard as that Cheyenne seemed to believe?"

"He is, anyway," Lane answered. "It's a long ride from here to Tongue River, just to peddle a rumor."

Chance shook his head, fighting off a strange sensation distilled of firelight and the fantasy of which he had been a part for a few minutes. A disembodied feeling persisted that he had stepped through some portal in time into an ancient past. Dim echoes stirred in his consciousness like submerged recollections of infancy. He saw Lane was watching him across the fire and he straightened self-consciously.

"God damn it, Beau, you heard it too!" he said. "An Indian messiah. For Christ's sake!"

I I I

Nora Crandall

Sitting Bull, head chief of the Sioux nations, returned to his Grand River Camp in mid-morning of the third day. He sent at once for Old Moon, his Cheyenne guest. The important Hunkpapa men began converging on the sod-roofed cabin. Summons did not come for either Beau Lane or Chance. Beau occupied the time in familiarizing Chance with names and passing faces.

"They're history," he said. "Nobody gives a damn, now, but sometime somebody'll want to know. And you said you wanted to write about them."

Old Catch The Bear came up along the river from the lower end of the camp. His head was thrust forward and he was swinging a little, growling softly to himself and shuffling at the clumsy-appearing gait of his name beast. Chance wondered if the Sioux had any concept of transmigration of the soul, reincarnation in animal guise. If so, this fierce old man was already far along in transit.

The boy whom the Bear had allowed to remain in council with the men came in from the pony herd out on the grass. He entered the cabin as importantly as any of his elders. Crowfoot, Beau said. Another son of the chief. A great favorite.

Gray Eagle came across the river. He was a brother of the Bull's younger wife. A progressive who had a white man's house of his own a little further up on the far bank of the stream. Lane did not like him. Gray Eagle was too close to Bull Head, he said. The same Bull Head who was lieutenant in McLaughlin's police and one of the two Metal Breasts who had followed them out from the Agency. Bull Head also had a house across the river. His wife and children lived there. So did he when he was not on duty at the Agency.

The old men all came to the chief's cabin. Sitting Bull's closest friends and confidants. Members of the

Silent Eaters who had organized to support and defend him at the time of his election on the Rosebud as the leader of all the Sioux and the allies then with them. Now they were the bravest and most seasoned warriors yet remaining to the nation.

Jumping Bull, an Assiniboine who was the chief's adopted brother and closer to him than a blood relation. Blackbird. Strikes The Kettle and a younger man named Chase Wounded. Brave Thunder and Spotted Horn Bull.

"Lot of Bulls," Chance said.

"Used to be a lot of buffalo," Lane answered. "Most of these Bulls come from an old saying, though. How does it go in English? The four ages of man. Baby— Boy—Man—Old Man. In the dialects it comes out Sitting Bull, Jumping Bull, Bull Standing With Cow, and Lone Bull."

He paused, attention sharpening. A green-painted treaty wagon was rolling in from the north. Bull Head, in full Metal Breast uniform, was driving. A young, very attractive white woman was seated beside him.

"Nora Crandall, the teacher at the Agency school," Lane said. "Now I'm going to catch it!"

Nevertheless, he started out eagerly to meet the wagon. Bull Head pulled up near the riverbank under the watchful eyes of several of the younger men who immediately appeared among the lodges. Lane reached up and swung the Crandall girl down. His grip about her waist lingered and she leaned her body against him.

"I could kill you for taking off down here without letting me know," she was saying as Chance came up.

Lane was grinning.

"Figured on getting around to it, directly. Meet Mr. Easterbrook."

Chance liked the level eyes and the firm grip of her hand.

"I've heard of Mr. Easterbrook," she said. "I think Lieutenant Bull Head has a message for you. And I have one for you, Beau. Private, if Mr. Easterbrook doesn't mind."

"Not at all—"

Beau led the girl down the bank toward a thickly grown bend where there were pools and privacy. Bull Head gave Chance a very military salute from the wagon seat.

"Major McLaughlin says this," he announced gravely. "No more bad feeling. Everything is all right, now. You stay here is all right. You go anyplace else on the reservation is all right, too. He will write you a pass. Come and see him some time."

Chance started to speak but the Indian held up his hand.

"There is more. Do not believe everything. Some Indians lie. Do not believe Sitting Bull. Sometimes he makes much trouble. Do not believe everything that man you are with tells you. Come back to Standing Rock. Major McLaughlin will tell you what is true. We will all tell you what is true. We have all good Indians there."

"I see—"

"There is more. You see today I do not have a gun. That was Red Tomahawk with me when we followed you. We did not like to do a thing like that. It is not good for an Indian to shoot at a white man. Even a Metal Breast. We did not like it."

Chance was tempted to tell the Indian how little he had liked it himself but he realized this was a personal statement quite apart from the agent's unexpectedly conciliatory message.

"I have forgotten," he said.

Bull Head nodded soberly with what seemed honest enough relief. He drove on across the river. Chance wandered back into the camp. The council still continued in Sitting Bull's cabin. All others among the lodges remained expectantly quiet.

It was nearly dark when Lane returned with Nora Crandall to the guest lodge. They were holding hands when they bent through the door-flap. The glow of the sun lingered in both. As the girl automatically folded her skirt away from the soot of the fire-stones, Chance noted a smudge of grass-stain upon it.

"What was your message?" Beau asked. "Major Mac buttering you up?"

"Trying, I'd guess," Chance agreed. "All restrictions off. Go anyplace, talk to anybody I want. All sorts of cooperation if I'll come back to Standing Rock."

"Why don't you, Mr. Easterbrook?" Nora Crandall asked earnestly. "Both of you, with me in the morning."

"The major's really put the twist to me," Lane said. "Out and out bribery. Not only what you see here—" he turned the Crandall girl completely around, "—but a good-paying job and marriage-talk, to boot."

"Now, really, Beau," Nora Crandall protested, "it's a lot more than a job. It's a—a position."

"Might be said so, I guess," the Dakotan agreed. "Stock foreman on a ranch that belongs to some friend of the major's missus, over in Minnesota. Even a house thrown in. Anything to get me away from you."

"Away from Sitting Bull and these malcontents!" Nora corrected sharply. "Oh, I'll be honest with you, Mr. Easterbrook. Major McLaughlin does disagree with Beau on some things. As much a matter of Bureau policy as anything else, I think. But he would feel better if he had one of his own men with you while you're on the reservation. A newspaper can do a lot of harm if it doesn't have access to the right set of facts, you know."

"I'm under the impression facts are sometimes disagreeable but they are seldom right—*or* wrong, Miss Crandall."

"The people on these reservations need help, not exploitation."

"Somebody steers him right, that's what Mr. Easterbrook is going to give them, Nora. Help. But that somebody isn't Jim McLaughlin."

The girl turned earnestly from Lane back to Chance.

"Look at him, Mr. Easterbrook. Can't you see what's happening? The more he stays around them, the more he becomes like them. He's even proud of it, I think. Ask him. They're men, he says. But they aren't. They're children."

Chance smiled at her earnestness.

"I've already met a few I'd hate to raise," he suggested mildly.

"It's true," Nora insisted stubbornly. "The first thing any conscientious teacher learns is that all children are

40

born savages. It's a well-known fact the human seed passes through every phase of human history in its development. At birth it has barely reached the Stone Age."

"She is a very smart girl, Chance," Beau said. "And kind of pretty, too, in a pale-faced sort of way."

The girl glared at him and continued.

"By nature a child is self-centered, treacherous, basically cruel. Right is something pleasant, wrong is something that hurts, and justice is simple retaliation. That's as far as morality goes. That's as far as it goes with the Indians, too. But a child develops steadily into a rational civilized adult. The Indian can't. He can't bridge three thousand years in a generation. Beau won't see that. He won't understand that his white blood makes him different."

"Different from what?" Beau demanded with the first trace of anger Chance had yet seen in him. "From those old men over there in meeting with the Bull? I wish I had their wisdom and their guts. I'd be a better man if I did."

He came to his feet and pulled Nora Crandall up onto hers.

"Time I was getting you over to Bull Head's house if his wife's expecting you for supper."

Nora turned to Chance in appeal.

"I've got to get Beau away from them," she said intensely. "Can't you do something, Mr. Easterbrook? Can't you make him see what he's doing to himself?"

"He's a free agent as far as I'm concerned," Chance said. "I'm afraid it's between you two."

Nora reached blindly for the door-flap and left the lodge. Lane followed her. Chance fished for his penknife and idly began whittling at a piece of willow among the twigs stacked for the evening fire. The bark peeled easily and slid off in one piece. The wood beneath was white and sweet. He was amused presently to see what he was fashioning—a woman's body, grossly elongated by the length of the stick. It had a tiny brown knot for a navel.

He tossed it into the ashes among the fire-stones when Beau Lane stooped back through the entry. His moccasins made sucking sounds and the legs of his pants were soaked to the knees.

"Gray Eagle and some on the other side were going to build a bridge here once," he said. "Got Major Mac to draw the plans and the Metal Breasts hauled I don't know how many loads of Agency lumber down. Sitting Bull burned it for firewood all one winter. Said he wasn't too old to wade across the river and when he was he'd use a horse. So I had to carry Nora over."

"She sure wanted you to take that job McLaughlin offered, Beau."

"Would have taken it three days ago. Best chance we've had since we started talking about maybe getting married. Even if Major Mac did rig it up. But I don't like him easing up on you and trying to get rid of me. Not now. Not till the Bull has finished this council and I find out what he makes of that message our Cheyenne friend brought in here. I think the major's got wind of it, somehow. If he's as afraid of it as it seems like, then so am I."

"Afraid—of what?"

"The dance. I don't like them dancing."

"Just some kind of a prayer, the Cheyenne said."

"Sure," Lane agreed. "But just what's a wild Indian got to pray for, really?"

"Hell, Beau, I'm no authority. His immortal soul, I suppose."

Beau shook his head. He hooked his arms about his wet, drawn-up knees.

"You don't understand. Hardly anybody does. It's buried pretty deep, particularly these days. Let me try to tell you how it is."

It was a story the Dakotan knew well. A full recall of men and what they said. Times and people and places. The portal in time opened again but Chance was not obliged to travel far. Only thirteen years.

It was after Sitting Bull had been elected head chief of the Sioux nations and commander-in-chief of the allies who were hunting with them that season toward the forbidden Yellowstone. It was before the warriors of that confederation drove General Crook and more than a thousand soldiers back in rout from the great encampment on the Rosebud.

It was before Custer tried to entrap that same great hunting camp on the Little Bighorn, too. But only a little. There were Terry and Gibbon as well. The sportsmen were all out that season. Every command was hunting Indians and glory.

June, 1876. Sitting Bull's belly was full of useless council and surrendered land. He would hunt again where game was. If there were soldiers, he would fight.

He would not make war but he would keep his country. And he made a sacred vow.

He took four reliable witnesses and went to a private place. There he prayed. For himself, first. A man who did not do so was not honest in his plea for help. Then for his people and those allies who had become his people when they put their trust in him. He also prayed for wisdom among leaders of the white men who plagued him without reason. To sanctify his prayers he swore to hold a great Sun Dance once again and to participate in it himself for two days and nights and to sacrifice a whole buffalo.

So sworn and witnessed, the chief took his companions on a hunt which lasted until he had killed three buffalo. They rolled the fattest of these onto its belly, legs out orderly to the four directions to prop it so, and the head as straight as possible. The lesser animals were left as they fell so that *Wakan Tanka,* the immutable Living Over Every Living Thing, could see a choice of the best had been made.

Easterbrook remembered an often-heard defense of professional hide-hunters and observation-car sportsmen which maintained the most wanton of them were not as wasteful of the buffalo as the Indian. He wondered parenthetically how much a few uninformed encounters with remains of such a ceremony as this had to do with that widespread conviction.

When the chief returned from his hunt, Beau continued, the Sun Dance pole was already up. It was in the center of the camp with Sioux and allied lodges pitched in one huge common circle for the occasion. More than twelve hundred tipis in all. Sitting Bull came forward and announced he would give of his own flesh as well as the Buffalo. Jumping Bull, his adopted brother, did the work. He pricked the chief's arm with an awl, lifted the skin, and cut away a small bit. This was repeated many times, on both arms, until the chief wore a crimson blanket from shoulders to wrists.

It was a sacrifice worthy of the most powerful prayer. All in attendance knew this to be true. That knowledge filled every witness with excitement. These were great doings. Great things must come from them.

Sitting Bull took his place among the dancers with the blood congealing on his arms. He fixed his eyes upon the sun and began to dance. He danced all that day and all that night. Deep into the next day he was seen to grow faint. The Silent Eaters brought him to a place where he might lie down. After a while he revived and spoke. Heralds took his words through the camp.

He had been sent a vision. His sacrifices were known and accepted. His prayers had been heard. A Voice had spoken. The words were of *Wakan Tanka*. He was shown many pony soldiers and a few Indians, falling from the sky. The Voice said, *"I give you these, for they do not hear."*

Everyone knew what the vision meant. Soldiers were coming to them. Soldiers who had not listened all those times when Sitting Bull had said, *"I do not wish to fight."* They were coming up-side-down, which meant all those soldiers and a few Indians would be killed. So the chief would not get the peace for which he had prayed. But was not this a better gift? Many began to sing the victory songs at once. Others thronged to the Sun Dance pole to find their own visions.

"That's the way it was, Chance," Beau said. "Not what you read and hear, now. Who walked away from that hill above the Greasy Grass to say how Custer fell? No white man. That much is sure. Crook said he was ambushed on the Rosebud, too. He said he was out-numbered. But he lied. His scouts knew.

"So did the Ree Indians scouting for Custer. They saw the deserted ground of the Rosebud camp with the dance pole still standing. They told Custer the Sioux were sure of winning. The dance and a vision had told them. White men falling from the sky. That's why I don't like it, my friend. This new dance from the west is travelling too fast."

The Dakotan shivered in his wet clothing and poked among the fire-stones for a surviving coal. He found instead the little half-carved woman of willow, now stained to an effective duskiness by powdered ash. He turned it curiously, shot a sidelong glance at Chance, and resorted to a match for flame.

"I'll go find out who's feeding us tonight," he said when the fire was rekindled.

He ducked out. After a little Chance thought about it and looked for the piece of willow. He finally concluded Beau had built it into the fire.

A woman soon came with the usual supper pot. She was a girl, actually, and Chance had not seen her before. She was young, well-formed, with a shy, singularly sweet and expressive face. The fresh scent of aromatic sage was about her, too subtle to be accidental.

46

Lane did not return. The girl made it plain that Chance was to eat before the pot cooled. Lacking the means to communicate with her, there was little else he could do. To his surprise, she edged up on her knees and joined him. When he could eat no more she put the pot outside for the dogs, closed the entry, and trimmed the smoke-flap as Beau did when they were turning in. She sat beside him again and checked his hand when he would have added more twigs to the lowering fire. He still did not understand until she took something from her sash and extended it to him on her open palm. It was the carved bit of willow.

The Dakotan's continued absence was now explained, and quick anger at him flared. The girl continued to kneel before Chance in mildly puzzled expectancy. He kept his eyes on the fire with a growing desperation which in some wry, self-appraising eye of the mind seemed utterly preposterous.

When light failed to a wink of ash and ember, the girl left her place beside him. He heard her go to his bed and roll it out, leaving Lane's undisturbed. He heard the soft, leathern whisper of her dress as it came off over her head and he knew she had slid into his blankets. He sat a long time as he was until chill drove him to Lane's roll. He pulled a blanket free and put it over his shoulders and leaned against one of the packs.

Much later a spark exploded among the ashes and there was a moment of glow. She lay on her side, looking at him across the lodge with the wide, round eyes of a child. The next time an ember fell apart and he could see, she was asleep.

IV

Sitting Bull

Chance roused to find the door-flap wide to morning sun. His blankets were rolled with feminine neatness. The girl was gone and Lane stood in the entry, a glint of amusement which might have been mockery in his eyes.

"Some host you are!" the Dakotan said.

"Some friend!" Chance growled.

Beau shrugged guilelessly.

"I try. Better rise and shine. The council's over and the chief wants to see you."

"Why me?"

"What you've been waiting for, isn't it?"

Chance got up stiffly, sloshed his face with water, and made himself presentable. When he stepped out into the sun, Lane had vanished again. Frowning irritably, not sure what was expected of him, Chance headed off through the camp toward Sitting Bull's cabin. Quiet still persisted among the lodges but he sensed an even stronger undercurrent of excitement in the stir of morning chores.

Bull Head's wagon came splashing through the ford. The Metal Breast was driving and Nora Crandall was again beside him on the seat. Neither saw Chance as the wagon headed northward out onto the *coteau*. He supposed that's where Lane had gone after delivering the chief's summons—to see the teacher off on her return trip to the Agency—and he speculated upon where the Dakotan had himself spent the night.

Sitting Bull was pacing in the cabin dooryard. A rolling limp from some old injury was quite pronounced. He seemed otherwise robust and in good health. His features were large, strong, agreeable. His face, framed by heavy braids hanging forward under his ears, was unlined. His shoulders were erect and unusually broad. His tall, heavy body conveyed an impression of unhurried strength.

The chief was courteous but showed no particular friendliness as Chance came up. He indicated the cabin and preceded his caller to it. They entered the room with which Chance was already familiar. It was unoccupied except by the deaf-mute boy who had opened the door on the previous occasion. When the boy saw his father he ran forward but halted at sight of Chance and broke into formless sound. The chief of the Hunkpapas listened gravely, as if the full meaning of this gibberish was known to him.

When the youngster quieted, he swept him up into his arms and moved close to Chance. The boy shrank back a moment, then reached out diffidently and struck Chance lightly, somewhere above the ear, with a small, open hand. The chief's arms tightened in a hug.

"You are a white man but he is not afraid," he said. "That is good."

He put the boy down. The youngster ran out into the sun, bursting with excitement. The chief closed the door and crossed to a wall peg. He hung the hat he was wearing upon this. From a crevice in the chinking he took a single feather bound to a wooden pin. He set this at the roots of his heavy braids where they were parted off at the back of his head. The feather stood straight and tall, accentuating the natural dignity of the man himself.

Chance found himself near the portrait he had noticed on his first visit, really an excellent likeness of the chief. He pointed to the signature.

"Mrs. Weldon?" he asked.

"A friend," Sitting Bull said. "Sometimes she came here before all this trouble with White Hair. She painted it then. A gift."

He sat on the edge of one of the beds, and indicated a place to Chance.

"This man you call Beau Lane says you write some things for the white man's newspapers," he continued. "He says many white men read them."

"When they're in a big paper. Yes."

"You write true things?"

"As I see them."

"Good. This will be a straight talk, then. I am also told you have a wound of the foot. Some have seen and say it is so. By a gun?"

"A hunting accident," Chance said.

Sitting Bull smiled.

"I could say it is the same with me—"

He slipped off his left moccasin. The old wound revealed had been a severe one, corrugating the sole from the base of the toes to the heel and drawing it up in an unnatural arch.

"The Winter The War Bonnet Was Torn," the chief

50

said. "We needed horses and were hunting Crows. It was a Crow bullet. That was the accident."

Chance realized what was expected. He removed his boot and sock. The Indian examined the revealed scar with professional interest.

"A good doctor," he observed.

"My father."

"A sign. My father made medicine for my wound, also. Once my father had a Ree wife. Ree medicine is best for the foot. Your father knew of it?"

"I don't think so."

"Well, it healed. It could be said we are brothers because of this. Today we will talk as brothers. A Cheyenne friend has lately brought me a very important message—"

Sitting Bull leaned forward, earnestness lending especial meaning to what he had to say. He skillfully condensed the salient elements of the revelation Old Moon of the Cheyenne had brought to Grand River. Whether by intent or because he had no convictions as yet, he avoided all personal reaction to the claims, prophecies, and reported statements of the messiah supposedly arisen among the Paiutes.

"They say this man's name is Wovoka. He has sent the same message to all the tribes. Everywhere. All the Sioux chiefs have now heard this thing. Red Cloud called a big council at Pine Ridge. The Oglalas there chose four men to go and see if what we hear is true. They have already started."

"To Nevada?" Chance asked incredulously.

"You will hear it differently, but we are not a foolish

51

people. To find truth, a man must go where truth is, even if it is a great distance. I will tell you why. If a man knows what truth is, he cannot make a mistake. Neither can his people. There are many travelers on that road.

"Minneconjou, Sans Arc, Two Kettle—all these chiefs met in council, also. They are wise men. They chose a man named Kicking Bear to go. The Brules on the Rosebud reservation chose Short Bull."

Easterbrook was completely taken aback by this information. Even if it was only partially true, Lane was right. Something of moment was afoot. Quite possibly even James McLaughlin's misgivings were justified. And the relatively simple series he had himself planned might be worked with a little luck into something which could catch the imagination of the whole country. The feelings surged in him that he might be playing into a real journalistic triumph. Whatever the basis in fact or fancy, this rumor of an Indian messiah was the kind of witch's fabric from which great stories were cut. And he was first on the ground.

"Now we have had this council here," Sitting Bull continued. "It has been decided. We also will send two men to the country of the Fish Eaters. Beau Lane and you."

Again Easterbrook could not believe his own ears. The proposal was preposterous, for all the apparent earnestness with which it was made.

"A half-breed and a white man as delegates from the Sioux?" he protested.

"From Sitting Bull's Sioux," the chief corrected. "I will try to tell you how that is. They say many things about Sitting Bull. Much is not so. They say I am the white man's enemy. That is not true. I am only a friend to my people.

"For many years now I have heard what the white man says. I do not like what I hear but I am chief. I do what is said so my people can live. They say to give away this land which is our mother. I am a man. I love my mother. But I say to give away the land so we will not be killed.

"They say to lay down our guns. I am a warrior. I do not know how to put away my gun. But I say we will learn how it is done. That way we will not die—"

Chance was fascinated by the change occurring in the chief as he spoke. His powerful body began to tense defiantly. His pleasing, hypnotic voice began to ring with anger. All trace of earlier humor vanished from his eyes. In its place a dark, metallic glitter glowed over an ancient abyss of cruel savagery. The nostrils of his great, arrogant nose flared widely and the planes of his cheeks flattened with plaited muscle.

Here, suddenly—in this room, now—was the man who had given a whole buffalo and a hundred pieces of his own flesh to his gods. Here was the warrior whose personal exploits had won him each of the commemorative eagle feathers in the long-trailing warbonnet he wore in Catherine Weldon's portrait. He was again the leader who had been elected above all others to supreme command of the greatest intertribal confederation the plains had ever known.

Here was the peerless general who had engineered the Rosebud, the Little Bighorn, and half a hundred lesser battles in a defensive ten-year war which had engaged almost the whole of the United States Army. The man James McLaughlin maintained was the most dangerous Indian yet alive.

Chance knew he now saw Sitting Bull as General Miles had seen him. Crook and Terry and Gibbon and Custer—those who had hunted him and heard that dread cry from the hills:

"Come on! Come on! It's a good day to die!"

"Many times they have seen how it is with me," the Sioux chieftain continued bitterly. "Could I have lived my life in any other way?' I do not like what I hear them say must be done, so I am a troublemaker. I am sad to give up my land and the bones of my dead, so I have a bad heart. I do not find it easy to lay down my gun, so I plot against them. I do not wish to die, so I am an enemy.

"They are afraid of Sitting Bull. They are afraid of the Indian. They will be afraid of him until he is dead. A different God made him, in a different color."

The chief limped quickly across the room and came back with a cigar box containing a number of nameless trinkets. From among these he fished out a curious, dried, blackened something attached to a thread of fine sinew. He dangled it before Chance.

"These were once a man," he said.

Shocked, Chance saw the object could indeed be a set of genitals, severed and cured by some process or accident of time to this desiccated anonymity.

"I cut them from the Crow who killed my father," Sitting Bull said fiercely. "It was a good feeling that day. It would be a good feeling, now. I would cut them from every white man I could find—I would cut them from you in my own house—if it would mean that we could live. But no, that is not the way—"

The fierceness ebbed. The glitter dulled in the chief's eyes. His broad shoulders seemed to droop. The ringing voice softened.

"—The way is to send a white man to the country of the Paiutes. Send him to see this Wovoka who says he is God come back to save the Indian. Send with him a man part Indian who knows the tongue and the way and the thought of our people. Let this part Indian protect the white man and teach him and help him to see all that is to be seen.

"This white man can talk to this Paiute. Then he can come back and tell us how it is. That way other white men will not say Sitting Bull is making bad medicine again. If this Paiute is God and there is a new world coming, white men will not believe these are lies from Indian lips. That is the way it is. They will believe this white man. His tongue is straight. His heart is good. He is not Indian."

The chief put his grisly trinket away and came back across the room.

"Of course, there will be some other things for you to put in the white man's newspaper, too. Maybe they will not believe they are lies, either."

Chance did not miss the shrewdness. Nor could he entirely suppress his own excitement.

"If Beau is willing, I am," he said.

"Good. Tomorrow."

V
Shining Woman

There was increasing stir and movement in the camp, even in the usually lazy midafternoon hours. Personal finery blossomed everywhere like dress uniforms on parade day at a working Army post. Chance did not recognize the extent of the ferment until a little before sunset. At this hour Crowfoot, the chief's son, and his small, afflicted half-brother, arrived before the lodge.

They wore clean cloth leggings without seats. Their buckskin jackets had been hard-scrubbed with clay to a newly tanned look. Their newest moccasins were on their feet. Each trailed a pony on a plaited hackamore, presents for the journey from their father. Crowfoot made the presentation with appropriate dignity. Lane accepted in kind. But the younger boy set up an unintelligible clamor until he was permitted to pass the lead on his pony directly into Chance's hand. Whereupon he strutted off with great vanity.

A parade of callers followed the chief's sons. A few brought gifts. Most came only to sit a little before departing and making room for others. Often there was no greeting, no exchange. Chance began to perceive the pattern for what it was. This was no ordinary journey. At the very least it was a mission of investigation important to them all. It might turn out to be an epochal, even earthshaking pilgrimage. Each wanted to have been present at its beginning.

Chance became fascinated by the degrees of faith and hope represented. It was luminous on some faces. Yet it could not be belief as he understood it. Too little was known. A rumor at best. Yet the surety was there. The Father had not forgotten his children.

There were lesser stages of conviction, too. They ranged down to a supposedly characteristic stolidity which he began to suspect was only apathy. But they came for their few minutes, along with the others. Hedging, perhaps. They could, at least, always claim they had been there.

Gray Eagle came but did not sit down.

"I say this," he announced loudly, arrogant in his importance as the chief's brother-in-law. "This is a bad thing. It will not please White Hair. This Fish-Eater out there makes a bad medicine. Do not go!"

He strode out, leaving an imprint on those present as he plainly intended. Lane blew disapproval through his nose. Others understood his scorn and smiled. Still, some had listened when Gray Eagle spoke.

Catch The Bear came, returning the pipe that Chance had presented to him at Beau Lane's instigation.

"I do not think this man out there is God," the old warrior said. "It is well known God can be a buffalo. Therefore, I think God can also be a man if he wishes it. But I do not think a man can be God. A river does not run up the mountain. Rain does not fly up into the sky."

Catch The Bear extended the pipe to Chance.

"Smoke with this man anyway," he continued. "Find out what is in his heart. Even if he is not God, he may have good thoughts. These are bad times here. Our thoughts are black. We need a new sun."

Some men passed by outside at intervals. They were wailing mournfully. Beau said they were singing. Sad songs, all right. Their sorrows and complaints, sung now so these emissaries within the lodge would remember them and sing them in turn to this man in the west. This was the best way for him to learn how it was among the Sioux. Listening to the unfamiliar, unmusical minors, Chance was amused at the thought of trying to re-render them. He had enough trouble with *Yankee Doodle.*

The procession of visitors thinned out and ceased as inexplicably as it had begun. Sitting Bull's two ponies remained in the dooryard and a small heap of other gifts lay on the floor. Catch The Bear's pipe. A pendant amulet of agate-like stone that had been artistically worked into an excellent representation of a tortoise. An especially potent charm, Beau said. A pair of belt knives, exactly alike. Brothers, as they would be on their journey. Inseparable, bound together by a spell upon the blades. A bone vestlet made in olden times to turn lance and arrow and now possessed of the power to defend its wearer from all harm. They seemed impediments to Chance, of no practical value and a nuisance, as light as they would have to travel. Beau disagreed.

"They're smoothing the way for you," he said. "Trying to make you as much Indian as they can. All the tribes will recognize these things, all along the way. They all believe in charms and spells. They're important, and they will be to you, too."

When the men were all gone, the women came. They brought a supper pot but put it aside. There were other things that were important. Men did not leave a Sioux camp on a long journey without spare footgear. Supplying moccasins was a woman's affair and since this lodge was without women, others had seen to it. Food, too, well-wrapped in small parcels against spoilage, was prepared.

Game was scarce in these days, so they must have pemmican. Ration beef did not dry well and was poor in suet. It did not have the buffalo's fat and hump-oil, even the bones had little marrow. It was the fault of the beef and not of those who had prepared it that the pemmican was not as it should be. But at least they would not go hungry into strange country.

The last of the women was the girl. She waited diffidently outside when the others left. If Beau saw her, he said nothing. She stood there until Chance uncertainly beckoned for her to enter. She smiled, stepped in quickly, and knelt on the flooring robe, putting a thickly folded blanket she carried down before her.

Eyes bright, searching Chance's face for sign of pleasure, she unfolded the blanket. Wrapped within was a fringed buckskin shirt. It was loose-waisted, box-tailed, and as long as a saddle coat. It was without decoration other than the fringe and the more handsome for its simplicity. A pocket, in alteration or afterthought, had been applied in a slightly different leather below the belt-line, where a white man might reach by habit.

Beau arose before Chance could turn to him for cue or speech.

"I'll take the ponies the Bull gave us out to the herd-boys," he said. And from the doorway, "Her name is Shining Woman."

He bent through the flap and was gone. The girl waited expectantly. Chance fingered the soft leather of the shirt.

"Washte," he said, self-consciously expending his Sioux vocabulary at a word. "Good!"

The girl beamed. Lifting the garment, she held it up to him.

Shining Woman—the name fitted. *Washte,* too.

He understood he was to put on the shirt. He would have dropped it over his head and pulled it down over his own shirt but she stopped him. She loosened the but-tons down his chest while his arms were entangled. He disengaged himself and self-consciously stripped to the waist. She looked at his blanched, thinly haired torso with a disconcerting lack of effort to conceal whatever pleasure of flesh or curiosity she took from it.

In his haste to recover, Chance inadvertently reversed the leather shirt. She laughed and tugged it around to the proper way. The garment dropped into place. It fit well and the texture of that softly tanned other skin felt good against his own. Her expectant face was close and there had to be some expression of gratitude. Chance leaned forward and kissed her.

He had some notion the Indian did not kiss by nature. Where practiced he thought it was a felicity learned from white brethren. However it was, Shining Woman had learned well. When their lips met she took hold of him and let her mouth speak. He released her when he could and got to the entry and stepped outside.

The gift ponies were gone from the dooryard but the camp herd was in full view at no great distance and Lane was nowhere in sight. Somehow this time Chance felt no displeasure whatsoever in the Dakotan's absence. He heard twigs break somewhere behind him and turned. Shining Woman had moved the supper pot over and was making a little pyramid of sticks among the fire-stones. She rose and came toward him, hand outstretched. He reached for a familiar breast pocket, then pointed to his discarded shirt. She found a match, kindled the fire, and, set the pot over it.

He spent some time watching evening settle over the encampment. When he stepped back through the entry he dropped the hide which closed it and adjusted the smoke-flap as though in ancient, familiar ritual. Shining Woman was waiting on her knees beside the now reheated pot. She laughed up at him and he dropped to a cross-legged seat beside her. He did not manage with Beau Lane's graceful ease but it was neither as difficult nor as uncomfortable as it had seemed short days ago. He discovered he was hungry.

He took the first piece of meat from the pot without burning his fingers or staining his new shirt. Presently, when she put the leavings of the meal outside, Shining Woman returned to his arms.

As before, she was gone when he awakened, the bed unmade because he still occupied it. Beau was outside with the horses, putting up saddles with the help of several small boys. The sun seemed especially bright, the air especially clear, as Chance stepped out into it.

"Good morning for a ride," the Dakotan said across a saddle.

"Couldn't be better," Chance agreed with conviction.

"Funny what'll bring on a change in the weather like that—"

Beau ducked into the lodge for the packs. When he reappeared he wore a new pair of moccasins and one of the "brother" knives was at his belt. He insisted Chance wear his new finery. Moccasins and shirt and knife and vestlet. Only Catch The Bear's pipe and the turtle amulet were packed away against damage.

They put the Bull's gift ponies on lead from the mare's packsaddle and rode their own horses. No one was about the lodge when they finally mounted up. No men were visible as they rode through the lodges. The women and children were awaiting at the edge of the camp. They shrilled many things which could only be encouragement.

Lane rode through this farewell as though he neither saw nor heard. Chance looked for Shining Woman. Just as real disappointment settled, he saw her standing apart. He rose in his stirrups, lifted his hat, and waved it. She waved in return. The women, noting this exchange, called out approvingly. The girl was still waving when Chance last saw her.

A quarter of a mile up the river, Lane reined in and soberly surveyed his companion. The unfamiliar, almost winged lightness of the moccasins on Easterbrook's feet had a disadvantage and he complained of it. The moccasins were low-cut and his stirrup-leathers twisted across above them, chafing his lower shins at a place usually buffeted by his boot-tops.

"Won't notice, directly," Beau assured him. "They aim to give us a send-off fitting to our chore, Chance. Watch your horse and don't let it spook on you. And when it's over, remember you've seen it. A Sioux charge, with the old Bull in the lead. Just hope nobody ever sees it again—not ever!"

Leading the pack mare and the trailing ponies, Beau turned away from the river up a rounded, shallow depression rising to the *coteau* like the hollow between the breasts of a reclining young woman. They climbed steadily through this for several minutes. Suddenly Chance felt the barrel of his horse tighten against cinch and thigh. The animal flung up its head. With no more warning than this the Hunkpapas came over the rounded summits above them and cascaded downward in a swift, irregular wave, like grass flattening before a dust-devil's wind.

They came down at breakneck speed. Now even Chance could feel the thunder of their ponies. Dust and the wind of passage. Feathers and sashes and lances and rifles. Naked and painted, bronze and brilliant in the sun. Guns banged black powdersmoke punctuation marks into the sky. A staccato yip-yip-yipping which should breed no terror of itself but unaccountably did, perhaps because it was a vocal vestige of some animal ancestry too terrible to remember. And over all the unknown but fearfully recognizable syllables of that defiant cry which was at once an anthem and a creed.

It's a good day to die!

So this was the way it was. The sudden materialization. A panoply of sight and sound which demoralized horse and rider alike, paralyzing training and turning military order into pandemonium. Swiftness, maximum force, and the impact of personal courage which was inhuman in that it was unmeasurable by any familiar standard.

Wagons overrun. Walking soldiers pinned down like prairie dogs caught too far from their holes. Cavalry entangled in its own harness of science and tactic. Splendor and savagery and death.

Superb tacticians, Custer said. *Individual daring. Horsemanship the best in the world, surpassing even the Cossacks.*

The finest skirmishers I ever saw, said Colonel Ford.

The finest light cavalry in the world, reported Crook's staff.

Foemen far more dreaded than any European cavalry, wrote General Charles King.

Good shots, good riders, and the best fighters the sun ever shone on, General Benteen said.

The best cavalry in the world, General Miles remembered. *Their like will never be seen again.*

Who should know better?

They came down on either flank and melted together in the trough of the hollow like synchronized lines of equestrian dancers, then came on pell-mell to split at the moment of collision and flash past on either side, close enough to set a lance. Slowing, they reversed with much good-natured and self-pleased shouting and came trotting back in two single files, one on either side. Sitting

Bull headed one column, Old Catch The Bear the other.

The Bear wore a feathered bonnet without a train and sat a high-spirited horse. The Bull rode a well-kept, fat grey horse, old and a little winded by the run. Only two feathers were in the chief's hair. One was the natural barred gray of an eagle's plume and the other brightly dyed to the color of blood. He looked behind him and smiled in pride. There were nearly a hundred riders in each file and they were all men.

They all rode on together up the draw to where it levelled out upon the vast undulance of the *coteau*. The camp was far behind and below. A little blue breakfast smoke yet hung over it. Sitting Bull looked again at the double file of warriors, splendid in the morning sun.

"You tell that man out there what kind of nation this still is," he instructed his emissaries. "You tell him we want the truth."

At some signal from its rider, the Bull's old gray horse came up in a magnificently trained and posed rear, pawing at the sky. A plumed quirt dangled from the chief's wrist. He flung it high.

"Hopo!" he cried.

The rearing horse leaped powerfully into a full lope. Quickly the entire cavalcade was again in motion, curving back toward the distant camp. Chance Easterbrook and Beau Lane were left alone with their journey before them.

Sometime in midmorning, Chance became aware of something in the pocket of his new shirt which had not been there the night before. Feeling with his free hand, he discovered it was the foolish little wooden image he had idly carved in the Hunkpapa camp, now all carefully wrapped in sweet grass.

He let his fingers close around it and rode for a long time without attention to horse or companion.

V I

The Pilgrimage

From the first day, Lane became an insistent taskmaster. More than distance separated them from the Nevada Galilee for which they were bound, he said. Time also had to be bridged, a lot of time, and they were not going to rush it. Chance pointed out other delegates were supposed to be on the way and would be among the Paiutes long before them. Beau shrugged. There was no difference, they were Indian. They would take their time, too, once they got there, for that was the Indian way. Plenty of deliberation on something as important as religion. Probably palaver till spring.

"All winter?" Chance protested.

"It will take us as long," Beau said, "you'll see. If they don't shut us out when we show up. That's what we've got to keep from happening."

Each day was an endless torrent of detail, seen by the Indian eye and relentlessly forced upon Easterbrook's consciousness. Much of it was fascinating at first but soon began to pall for sheer mass. To the best of the Dakotan's ability to recreate the past, they travelled as the Indian travelled these plains in the olden time. They saw what the old-time people saw, tracks in the dust, wind on the grass, sun on water, clouds on the hills. They ate and slept and talked as the wild ones once had.

Easterbrook had retained a boyhood marvel at nature. Therefore this was in the beginning an expansive experience. But monotony inevitably set in. This was accentuated when he noted that Beau was constantly using more and more words and phrases in the dialects, that the Dakotan fully intended to force a usable command of the Sioux tongue upon him. Chance rebelled at this. Beau merely smiled and reverted wholly to the dialects until Chance reconsidered and resumed his painful efforts.

They rode two hundred and fifty miles by old game trails from Grand River to the Cheyenne Agency on the Tongue. It took them nearly two weeks. Under the eyes of their own agent, the Cheyenne were not as communicative as Old Moon had been in Sitting Bull's camp. They learned only that the Sioux delegation from Pine Ridge had passed through without official knowledge some time before. The Cheyenne had chosen a delegate named Porcupine to accompany their Sioux brethren. This also was without official knowledge.

More weeks passed while they rode four hundred and ten miles by way of the Bighorn into the beautiful valley of the Wind River, where the Shoshone shared a reservation with the Western Arapaho. Here they heard for the first time of the Ghost Dance. Both the Shoshone and the Arapaho freely admitted they were dancing. And they said they were expecting further good word from the west at any time. It was true, they said, God was coming soon.

They rode on into the mountains. Winter was already lowering into the high valleys. Chance reminded Beau that the Shoshone had told them that the combined delegation ahead of them had ridden from Wind River to the railroad and traded their ponies for parlor-car seats. It seemed sensible for them to do the same, but Lane refused.

"Step off a train like you just came through from Chicago—hire a rubber-tired buggy and drive out to Walker Lake—just see how close the Paiutes would let you get to the man we want to see."

A few rods further on, Beau grinned at him.

"Don't worry, Chance. You're shaping up. By the time we get to the Fish-Eaters and start asking questions, you're going to look like you mean it and want the answers mighty bad."

Chance was not amused. He looked at his hands. There were deep weather cracks at the knuckle joints. And he had given up his razor because of painful high-altitude chapping about his mouth and the crowns of his cheeks.

They came out of the mountains onto the windy, arid steppes of the western slope. It was poor country and winter followed them down. Squalls rode the persistent north wind. Morning ice formed and slanting drizzles often pelleted to sleet. The horses thinned and their coats roughened. There were no towns, no lodge-fires, no life. Finally Lane turned southward.

"Won't be long, now," he said.

VII

Fish-Eaters

In full daylight even Beau Lane's adept eyes might have passed over the Indian camp without notice. The makeshift wickiup was dusted with snow and looked like a slightly larger hummock among uncounted others on these sage flats. The one horse was down a few yards away, also covered with snow.

In the deepening twilight Chance happened to see a burst of sparks from the smokeless sagebrush fire within as they spiralled from the smoke-hole. Beau hailed the blanket-closed entry. There was no reply. Beau pushed the blanket aside and they entered.

It was a temporary shelter, poorly made. Brush against a flimsy frame and sheeted as well as possible against wind and snow with blanketing and a small, ragged tarpaulin. The dirt and sparse sod of the floor was beginning to soften and puddle as the fire drew frost from the ground.

There were five children in the shelter, members of two families. They ranged from a girl of eleven or twelve to an infant so congested in the lungs as to sound as if it were dying of strangulation. There were, in addition, an old woman of unknown relationship, the two wives, and their husbands, apparently brothers. All were thin, dull-eyed and apathetic with hunger and a species of mute terror.

A dirty, sadly worn little robe of rabbit skin was

shared by the raling infant and an older child huddled in a small ball at the mother's knee. None of the others had blankets or robes and Chance realized that such as they had possessed had been used to cover the sorry framing of the wickiup.

It was nearly as cold within the shelter as without. There was a lot of ash under the tiny, inadequate fire. Sage burned with bright, hot flame when first ignited but it was a sparse growth and incredible quantities were required to sustain heat for any time. These people were beyond further search for fuel and what they had was nearly gone.

Aside from occupants, the wickiup was barren. No baggage, no utensils, no food. The Paiutes looked at the intruders with no change of expression save that the arms of the mother tightened a little about the sick infant. Chance backed from the entry and Lane followed him.

"Wood," Beau said. "A lot of it. They're freezing."

Chance drew his knife and attacked the nearest snow hummock, freeing the scant clump of sage beneath it. He whacked at the stringy, resilient growth, kicking thicker, longer-burning root burls to the surface where he could. When he returned with an armload of fuel, Beau had opened a pack and flung their tent canvas over the wickiup, effectively covering and sealing most of it but the smoke-hole.

"No room for all of us in the tent but there is in there, if we squeeze. Keep after the wood. I'll mind the stock soon as I've got food on to heat."

He grabbed their own provision bag and disappeared

into the shelter. For a while the struggle for burls and twigs was welcome after the day's chill ride. After a little Chance became aware of the bite of snow underfoot and the blood on his hands from the rasping of the spiny growth. Lane reappeared. He watered the horses somewhere nearby and staked them in the scant lee of the wickiup. Some time later he whistled from the doorway. Chance came in gratefully with his last load of fuel.

The interior of the shelter had been transformed. It was warmed and less drafty. Beau had broken out their blankets and every shoulder was covered. The fire glowed brightly under their biggest kettle and water steamed in the uncharged coffee pot beside it. Tin cups, bowls, the smaller pots—whatever Beau had been able to lay hands to in their gear—had been portioned out to the Paiutes. Two sometimes shared a container in a polite alternation that was strangely in contrast to the avid eagerness with which each gulped down the thick soup when his turn came.

Only two were not eating—the woman and her sick baby. Chance felt her eyes on him as he squatted gratefully near the fire. Lane saw his glance at the baby and shrugged.

"I'm no medicine man."

"Croup, you think?"

"Pneumonia, colic—whatever they get."

"She thinks it's going to die, Beau."

"When Doc McGillicuddy was agent at Pine Ridge, he kept a record. More than half died in their first two years. And those were Sioux. Odds got to be a lot worse out here."

One of the older children, warmed and drowsing, had put down an emptied cup. Lane rinsed and refilled it with boiling water from the coffee pot. He took a small bottle of unlabelled whiskey from the provision bag, poured generously, and handed the steaming cup to Chance.

"Doubt you could drink this water uncut and you look cold."

He was right. The water was brackish to salinity and the raw whiskey was barely proof against it. The woman with the sick child stirred suddenly. Walking on her knees, she forced others to draw up their legs to give her passage. Chance barely had time to put down his cup before he found the infant in his lap. The sweet-sour urinal odor of infancy arose from the swaddling. The stink of sickness and fever and what Chance thought was the smell of death.

"White man's a doctor, a magician, whatever," Lane said quietly. "Pin them down and they all believe that. When everything else has failed. The best thing's to shake your head and hand it back. It dies on your lap, they'll think you killed it, regardless."

Chance nodded but the woman was already crawling back to her place, her face turned from him. The child's breathing was the only sound in the wickiup. He could feel the small body struggle for every breath. Sucking in a deep breath of his own, he was aware of the lingering vapors of his gulp of whiskey in his head and throat. A childhood memory returned. He pushed the cup of toddy toward Beau.

"Tie a stick on the handle for me—"

Lane curiously obliged. Chance eased the blanket in which the child was now wrapped to give him a triangular corner for his purpose. Taking the extended handle Beau provided for him, he held the toddy cup to the fire until its contents boiled briskly. The mother whimpered when he moved the steaming cup close to the child's head and covered both so the vapor was imprisoned. He did this twice more at brief intervals, then sniffed the cup and extended it to Beau.

"More whiskey—"

The Dakotan spilled in a few more spoonfuls and Chance returned the cup to the fire. When it steamed again he replaced it beneath the blanket at the child's head.

"They're supposed to be children of nature," he said, "wilderness lore and instinct to protect them. How do they get in a mess like this?"

"For one thing, they don't get their winter food all packaged, you know," Lane said. "So many tins of this and sacks of that from the country store. Depends on weather, hunting, luck—"

"Luck! Even animals don't depend on that!"

"No? I knew a fellow up in Bismarck who had a good business, a livery. He had a house and a wife and money set by. He got a bad load of hay one fall. Mildew spread to his whole loft and he had to fork it all onto the manure pile and buy a carload at winter prices. His woman had a baby and it died, leaving her sickly. He had to get help in for her and a doctor all the way from Mankato when those in Bismarck couldn't do anything.

"A wet snow came. That mildewed hay out back heated up like it'll sometimes do when it isn't spread out to breathe and it burned down inside for quite a spell, but nobody noticed. You know how a manure pile will steam when frost's on. Finally it caught the stable in the middle of the night and took the works, including some fancying riding stock, in for keep. Excitement got his wife and she died next day. Owners sued for the stock and the sheriff took the house. They finally found him down in the rail yards a while later, frozen stiff and cut in two by a train.

"He was figured to be a smart, honest, upstanding fellow, too. You figure it, Chance. That's luck. Everybody has it, good or bad. For some it runs all downhill."

"Like these poor devils."

"Sure. You know what's happened, as well as I do. There just isn't enough for them all any more. Same as the Dakotas, Wind River, everywhere we've stopped the whole way across. Hunting grounds, game, everything they understand how to turn into a living is cut way down or gone completely. Even government rations are reduced every time Congress convenes.

"These would have been done if we hadn't come along. But what difference does it make? What about when we've gone on? Loafers, they call them at the agencies. Maybe they are. That's what comes of trying to live on empty bellies."

They fell silent. One by one the children in the wickiup fell asleep with the universal ease of the young. Chance grew cramped as he was unwilling to shift the burden across his knees. At a monotonous frequency of interval he reheated the tin cup, occasionally extending it to the silent Dakotan for a fresh dollop of whiskey.

The old woman drifted off as the children had done. One of the men presently turned about so his head rested upon the thigh of the younger woman who was not the mother of the sick child. She put her hand on his face and he fell into heavy sleep. The woman followed soon after with her head bowed like some strangely associated madonna.

Perhaps two more hours passed. Chance thought the breathing of the child on his lap had eased a little but he was aware of his own weariness and accused it for the notion. Suddenly the mother, unasking, took one of the emptied bowls and dipped soup from the kettle. When it was empty, she looked at Chance. He nodded. She filled and emptied it again. Putting it aside, she smiled gratefully and like a puppy in a litter wormed a place for herself beside her man. He took her hand and tilted her chin against his chest. Both slept.

Beau's eyes came back from their sometimes faraway place. He inched across, careful not to disturb the sleepers, and lifted the child from Chance's lap.

"Did it," he whispered. "Going to be all right, now. They know. You better eat—"

He sat back and cradled the sleeping child across his own knees.

When Chance roused the door-cover was raised to a sunny, windless morning. The sick child was sufficiently recovered to be hungrily at breast across the wickiup from him. In a wave of reaction, Chance saw nothing of the madonna in this. A suckling pup, and runty stock at that. A caricature, ugly and embarrassing in its illusion of humanity. Despite its brief occupancy, the wickiup was rank. Chance thought he would sweat it for days. Beau was a fool and so was he. God disposed. Who the hell did they think they were?

The Dakotan had been out early with one of the Paiute men. They returned with a small prongbuck. The old woman went at the carcass knowingly, taking off extremely thin slices of the dark meat at the saddle. Broiled on Lane's ramrod, they quickly rendered to crisp curls requiring no utensils for eating. Chance had great difficulty accepting his share from the old woman's fingers.

The infant was not sufficiently recovered and the rest of the camp was hardly in better shape to travel, although the Walker Lake Agency was at no great distance. Beau did not consult Chance but left what he deemed necessary. Their tent, their utensils and remaining food, half their blankets, the pack mare, and two of the saddle horses. It seemed likely that with these the Paiutes could reach friends or family who could care for them. He and Chance rode out on the Sioux ponies which had been Sitting Bull's gift. Each had but a thin roll of gear at his cantle.

At a mile's distance they pulled up and looked back. The Paiutes stood at the wickiup as they had left them, watching them shrink off against the sky. Something suddenly struck Chance. Except for a frightened whimper from the mother of the sick child, he had not heard a spoken sound from these people, arrival to departure. He commented upon it.

"What's to say, Chance?" Beau asked.

VIII
Charley Sheep

At midday they reached a small ranch, well onto the Walker Lake reserve. The owner was surprised at their interest in what he thought was local legend but told them what he knew of the Paiute messiah. He was some sort of a medicine man who had set himself up in Mason Valley, a day's ride or so the northwest. He had gotten the Paiutes to holding a dance periodically. This played hell with work about the place for four or five days if you had any of them on hire around the full of the moon. He called a hand in from the yard and the Paiute amplified the story readily and with pride.

He said that there was indeed such a man. He was called Wovoka among his own people and Jack Wilson among the whites when he worked for them. He was the Christ, all right. He had been dead and had come alive again. He had been at Walker Lake for a time but now was in Mason Valley where he had many visitors, some from as far as the seas, it was said. Big things were doing up there. A new world was coming and all must be gotten in readiness for it, but it would do no good for white men to look for this *Wanekia*. This was an Indian affair and besides this Christ could make himself so he could not be seen by white eyes. It was very easy for him to do a thing like that.

Pressed by the rancher, the Paiute reluctantly admitted Wovoka had a relation a few miles away who often visited him. An uncle named Charley Sheep who might have influence with his nephew, but he would cheat strangers. The rancher dismissed the Indian. They got the damnedest notions, sometimes. Jack Wilson, was it? He hadn't known before, but he did know the Wilsons. Early settlers out here. Let be like a lot of others if there were only a few wickiups on their land when they took over. Gave them a little work when there was some. Sort of adopted them. Cleaned them up. Taught them a mite out of the Bible, and some English. Usually gave them your name, too. Hell of a lot easier than Paiute.

He said they'd probably get the whole story from Dave Wilson, but it would likely save a long ride to hunt up this uncle. If he was like most of them, he'd tell everything he knew with trimmings for a dollar or two.

Chance and Lane thanked the rancher and rode on. They found Wovoka's uncle in a well-kept wickiup almost in sight of the Walker Lake Agency buildings. He was of the generally stout, inferior stature of the Paiutes and of indeterminate middle age. His eyes were shrewd and he spoke fluent if extraordinary English. He received them warily.

"You come a long way?"

"Sioux country," Beau agreed.

"Only two horses."

"Had more. Some people out on the flats needed them worse than we did."

"I have lately talked to some Sioux. They say it is a

very bad time in their country. But those ponies of yours have iron shoes. How can Sioux ponies have iron shoes in such bad times?"

"We bought them," Chance said.

"Then you are rich?"

"Plenty rich," Beau assured him. "Show him, Chance. The money."

It was a command. Chance recognized it as such. He reluctantly emptied some of the contents of his snap-pouch into his palm. A few of the heavier gold coins were forced out by weight ahead of the silver. It seemed a sufficient display.

"We can make business," Charley Sheep said.

"You know of the Sioux chief, Sitting Bull?" Beau asked.

"A big killer of soldiers," the Paiute agreed.

"We come from him to see your relation and to find out from him what this all is. Our ponies are gifts from Sitting Bull, himself."

The Paiute looked disapprovingly at Chance.

"What kind of Indian would send a white man on Indian business?"

"A wise chief. What a white man sees and tells, other white men will believe. That way there will be no trouble in the Sioux country over your relation."

Charley Sheep thought this over.

"Well, maybe. I was there when this relation died and came alive again. It was the day the sun died. He was dead many hours. His body was cold. We cut it with a knife and it did not bleed. His hand could not be opened or closed. He was not straight where he was lying and

79

we could not straighten him, as it is with the dead after a little while. We built a fire in a cooking pot and put it near his foot. The flesh roasted. We all could smell it. But it did not turn red or blister. It turned brown instead, like rabbit meat on a cooking stick. But there was no mark when he came alive. Do you believe?"

"Not until we've seen and talked to him," Chance said.

The Indian remained silent for a moment, apparently engaged in some inner struggle. Chance doubted it was with conscience.

"Up there where he is at Pine Grove is a very dangerous place," the Christ's uncle said finally. "Many Indians, many nations. They do not like white men. It will take much talk, many presents. Even then I do not know." He indicated Chance. "I could buy this man a woman. Young, very good. Or a horse and wagon. With money that is easy. But this is the Christ, even if he is my relation."

Chance felt Beau's eyes on him. He pulled out his purse again and tossed it down. Its contents clinked enticingly. The Paiute picked it up and dropped it into his sash.

"We will see," he said.

Travel north from Walker Lake was by wagon. Charley Sheep was adamant on that as his passengers were important. All important men rode in wagons. The Christ did so. He had lately been informed that the great chief Sitting Bull did the same. Beau and Chance had to put up with the unsprung discomfort.

Chance had a preconceived notion of a Nevada desert. There was nothing desert-like about the country through which they drove. The Walker River, spending its short and tranquil life between two lakes, meandered through richly grassed, sometimes even marshy bottoms. Above these were gently rising benches that carried off across broad expanses of grazing lands to distant boundary ridges. Before the plow, such a basin must have been a perennial paradise for game. The Sioux had their Black Hills to mourn, the Paiutes had this.

Pine Grove proved to be a meadow on thinly timbered upland. It was sheltered by a steep ridge and commanded a prospect of Mason Valley proper. There were half a dozen all-weather wickiups and some brush day-shelters. But no multitude could be accommodated here and somehow a multitude was what Chance had expected, complete to fish and loaves.

The wagon pulled up at one of the permanent wickiups. Near it was a large circular space in which the earth had been carefully smoothed and every blade and root of growth removed.

"The dance ground," Charley Sheep said. "We had too many people down at Walker Lake. White men even brought their women, so the Christ picked this place. We only come to make the dance and do not tell the white men when that is. That way we keep it for ourselves."

"Wovoka is here?"

"No."

"Look, Charley," Beau said with deceptive mildness, "if you've beat our tails all the way up here—"

"I said it would not be easy," the Paiute protested. "I said we would see. First there are all these people from other countries. This relation is their Christ, too, now. They will have to say it is all right. Then maybe the Christ will come."

He chucked his passengers' possessions into the wickiup and drove off. In a couple of hours he was back, very officious and pleased with himself. He lifted a tule mat from his wagon and kicked it flat in the door-yard of the wickiup. He then brought out several more and methodically spread them in a semicircle back of and to either side of the first. Then he began to heap various goods on the central mat.

There were several swatches of brightly hued materials and more of cheap unbleached muslin. There were three fancy, high-crowned white felt hats and a stack of trade blankets. There was also a basket containing neatly tied bundles of brilliantly black-and-white bird feathers and perhaps half a bushel of oval cakes of something that looked like cheap vermilion hand soap. Except for the contents of the basket, everything was new, of white manufacture, and fresh from a store-keeper's shelf. Chance realized it all had been purchased from his own purse.

Beau Lane grinned at him.

"Old Charley's sure doing his best for you," he said. "I've seen less than that put on the prairie to bribe a whole tribe."

I X

Kicking Bear

First to arrive at the wickiup was Porcupine, the Cheyenne who had made this great journey as the delegate of his people at Tongue River. He did not look at the gifts displayed in the dooryard but came directly to Chance and Lane. When he spoke, Chance was delighted he could distinguish the foreign dialect from the more familiar Sioux. Porcupine had his own explanation for that.

"In this place there is only one tongue," he said. "When Our Father speaks, we understand without the words of others. When we speak, he understands us. Paiute and Cheyenne all the same. It is so with all our brothers here. If there is difficulty, it is because you do not believe. I am told you are from Sitting Bull."

Chance entered the wickiup and brought out the Sioux gifts which were his credentials. The Cheyenne examined them all but was most interested in the buckskin shirt. He turned it inside out to examine the seaming.

"You had a Sioux woman?" he asked.

"What's he mean?" Chance asked in appeal to Beau.

"Just what you think. Better tell the truth, too."

Chance nodded to the Indian.

"I had a woman," he admitted.

"You have also had white women?"

Chance nodded again.

"Many?"

"Some."

"Many?"

Lane was chuckling. Chance felt uncomfortable.

"All right," he said. "Many."

"This Sioux woman—was she different?"

"Now what's he mean?"

"Tell him," Beau said. "Kind of like to know, myself."

"No, she was not different," Chance told the Indian.

"You did not get right up and go to water and wash?"

"No."

"Then in the blanket she was not Indian?"

"No."

Porcupine smiled.

"I will tell you something, Brother. She would tell her sister you were not white."

As though he had made a point of vast importance, the Cheyenne emissary walked back out into the yard and took a place on the semicircle of mats.

Others began coming in. In small groups they joined the waiting Cheyenne. It was all very unhurried. In half an hour nearly thirty men were seated on the mats facing the wickiup. At the end of this time Charley Sheep rose from where he had been squatting near his foreign charges. He spoke rapidly in Paiute, an abjuration of some kind which reminded Chance of the ancient rote of clerk or bailiff.

"The truth, the whole truth, and nothing but the truth, so help you God—"

Charley Sheep sat down and one of the delegates in the semicircle rose. He struck a conscious speaker's stance.

"Hear what Short Bull says," he announced. "I see nothing here to change my mind. I have seen the *Wanekia*. I have heard his words. I believe, and I do not think this is for a white man."

The Indian returned to his place. Another came to his feet. He selected one of the fancy white hats from the goods Charley Sheep had put out.

"My brothers see many things of wonder here," he said. "Many of these things I, Cloud Horse, do not see. I am told the *Wanekia* speaks in a language all understand, but when it happens I hear a tongue I do not know. A Shoshone or a Bannock must say it again to me the way it is said in my own country."

The speaker held the white hat out, crown down.

"The *Wanekia* shows his hat," he continued. "My brothers look into it and see a whole world coming. Buffalo and all the dead Indians. I say let this white man look into the hat. Like Cloud Horse, he will see nothing."

He replaced the hat on the pile of goods and sat down. Others rose in turn, appraised the goods on the mat, and sounded an "aye" or "nay" as conscience dictated. Chance noted that most, although they touched nothing else among Charley Sheep's offerings, managed to finger the oval red cakes in the basket. He realized they were patties of some dried pigment. The stuff came off easily on the fingers and was surreptitiously transferred to cheek or brow as opportunity afforded.

So it went. Another Sioux. A Washoe, a Pitt River, a Ute, and a Bannock. Walapai, Cohonino, Mojave, Pima, Modoc, Navajo, and Hopi. Arapaho, Shoshone, Caddo,

Wichita, and a single aging Delaware. Kiowa, Kansas, Pawnee, and Comanche. Assiniboin, Gros Ventre, Arikara, and Mandan.

All the nations, stating their convictions, approving or disapproving the presence here of the white man from the camp of Sitting Bull. How many of them were represented here?

"Sixty thousand," Beau Lane guessed. "A hundred, maybe. Or even half that again. Who knows the real count?"

Last among them was a Sioux delegate from the southern Dakota reservations. He had waited with ill-concealed impatience for this speaking vantage, and he scorned the stately dignity of his predecessors. He bounded to his feet like a man whose outraged personal dignity could no longer stomach the acquiescence about him. He was not a large or prepossessing man but his harsh, commanding voice communicated irresistibly. Chance knew at once this Indian was a dangerous one.

"What is this I hear?" the speaker demanded. "You have given away your land, signed away your lives. Now you want to give away your God, too?"

He seized a cake of pigment from the basket of offerings and truculently faced Chance.

"I am well known in my country," he said arrogantly. "To Sitting Bull and all the chiefs. I am Kicking Bear, an Oglala by birth and now a Minneconjou chief. I am husband to Woodpecker Woman, niece of Big Foot, also a Minneconjou chief whose name is well known. I am an Indian and I have no love for white men."

Wetting his fingertips with spittle, Kicking Bear

wiped them across the cake of pigment in his hand and traced two fierce vermilion stripes down his face with a single stroke. He jerked his sash around to display a streamer hanging nearly to his heels and festooned with human hair.

"Count!" he challenged. "Some are Indian. The rest are white and they are many. Pony soldiers, White Man. They warm my heart the most."

He streaked more red paint down his hunter's face.

"All white men know of Crazy Horse. They yet fear him when he is already rotted away. He was my uncle. A great warrior with a great medicine. He could not be killed in battle. But they killed him, all right. Hear this! After that fight with Yellow Hair on the Greasy Grass, my uncle heard there was to be no more war. He believed this was true. He had it in his heart to lay down his gun."

The Indian hawked and spat with consummate insolence.

"In this he was not Indian. In this his medicine could not protect him. They said they were having a council at Fort Robinson. They tricked him into coming in. One brave man, alone. At the gate an officer said my uncle should follow him to where they were holding this council. But when he got in there he saw the bars. He drew his knife and fought his way back outside.

"There the officer grabbed his arm and Little Big Man, an Oglala who was his enemy and a Metal Breast besides, caught his other arm. His medicine could not protect him because he had been foolish and came in there, but my uncle had not forgotten how to fight.

"He cut Little Big Man and the Metal Breast let go.

The officer became frightened at this and held on hard. There were some soldiers nearby. One had a bayonet on the end of his gun. The officer shouted to this soldier. I will say his words.

" 'Stab him, quick! Kill the son of a bitch!'

"The soldier tried to put the bayonet into my uncle but he was very excited. The bayonet stuck in the door of the jail. The officer said some other words which are not remembered and the soldier got the bayonet free. He put it several times very hard into my uncle at the back and the belly while this officer and I think some others held him. After that they put him in a room. They had a doctor there and some medicines for soldiers. But not for an Indian. He lay there for a long time, but before he died, he was all Indian again. I will say his last words.

" 'It's a good day to die!' "

He screamed it out with arched chest and great fury. Then his voice dropped and he continued in quiet, scathing bitterness.

"There is a little more. They gave my uncle's father and mother a box to put him in. The box was too small so the soldiers broke his legs to make him fit. They took him away like that on a pony drag, the old father and the old mother, alone. They made a burial scaffold on the *coteau*. They would not tell where. They did not wish him to suffer again.

"In time his mother came to visit my mother, who is her sister. She gave me the small pouch I now wear behind my ear. It is the great medicine of Crazy Horse."

The Indian drew himself up in a long dramatic pause.

"I tell you this, White Man—I tell you this,

Brothers—I say this is the Christ we have here. I will walk in his road. But I will not make the mistake Crazy Horse did. Not even in my sleep. I have his medicine. I cannot be killed or even defeated. I am Indian and I will not take the white man's road in anything!"

Pivoting on his heel, the Sioux strode off. In a few seconds he disappeared beyond a patch of timber. The seated Indians remained motionless until he was gone. They came to their feet, then, breaking up, and most converged in good-natured eagerness on Charley Sheep's offerings. The greatest scramble was for the bundles of feathers and cakes of pigment.

Despite Kicking Bear and other dissenters, the vote was conclusive. As the council dispersed, Charley Sheep climbed into his wagon and drove off. In fifteen minutes he was back with a passenger beside him on the seat.

X

The Messiah

The man who alighted from Charley Sheep's wagon was young, well-fed, quite large for a Paiute. He completely lacked the reserved, arrogant dignity of the plainsmen Chance had come to know. He had a pleasant moon face, an open manner, and a general air of stolid geniality. He wore heavy shoes, a white man's dark suit, and a tall, broad-brimmed white hat such as those in the merchandise Charley Sheep had bought in the settlement.

Chance saw Beau was as disappointed in Wovoka's

appearance as he was himself. It had been a long ride for this, but the Indian delegates were re-seating themselves, hushed and reverent. Those who wore hats removed them. Faith was there. Chance had a wry thought. What right did Beau and he have to doubt? That Other One had been recorded in life long after his own death. The portraits had been painted by those who had missed seeing him in the flesh by centuries. Maybe this was the way it had really been then, too. A pleasant, dark-skinned young man with no particular strength of feature and no overt evidence of brilliance or divine fire. Only a placid assurance of the goodness man could achieve.

Belatedly, Chance rose to his feet and removed his hat. Scowling, Beau self-consciously did likewise. It was the first time Chance had seen his companion uncovered in the open.

"Jack Wilson," Charley Sheep said.

The man smiled and shook hands. Charley Sheep spread a blanket and they sat down.

"I am told you are sent here to find out what I am saying," the Christ said. "Well, first I want you to understand I know everything, even at a great distance. You have been at Tongue River and the Shoshone Agency. You have crossed the mountains and the country of the Mormons. All on horses, like olden times, at a very bad season to travel. I have expected you here for some time, now."

"Bushwah!" Lane murmured.

The Christ smiled, taking no offense.

"Just lately you made a sick child well and gave some horses and other things to some people who were

90

having a hard time of it."

Startled, Beau glanced at Chance. It seemed incredible that news of the destitute Paiute camp could have travelled here so swiftly.

"I saw that," Wovoka continued. "It made my heart glad. Those people were relations of mine. I thought very soon I would have to go there and do something before they died. That is why I have come to see you as you wanted."

He nodded toward the semicircle of emissaries.

"Some of those men think it is not a good thing for me to talk to you. One has already gone away and will not come back while you are here. But you have given them presents. They will not make trouble, now. I hear you have presents for me."

Chance brought out the stone amulet which was actually the only gift he had been commissioned to deliver to the *Wanekia.* However, Wovoka showed little interest in it. Perhaps the turtle talisman did not have the holy place in Paiute legends of the creation that it did among plains people. Or the messiah was merely cannily unwilling to revere something not of his own cult.

What did interest him was the bone vestlet and its supposed protective powers. He rolled it up and would have put it aside with the amulet if Chance had not uncomfortably explained it was not a gift and must be returned to its owner in Sitting Bull's camp. The Christ was visibly put out and surrendered the vestlet with bad grace.

"It is nothing," he said. "I have a small gun for rabbits that could kill a man very easily through that."

He sent his uncle to the wagon. Charley returned with

a plain, crudely cut muslin shirt sewed with sinew.

"I have shown you I know everything," the messiah said. "Now I will show you I can do anything. That is for you to tell those people where you come from."

"Then it is true that you are God?" Chance suggested.

"No," the Indian answered complacently. "But I talk to the Grandfather. He gives me his power."

"The Son, then—the Christ?"

"I am Wovoka." The Paiute pointed to the circle of emissaries. "Over there they call me the *Wanekia.*"

He took a cake of red pigment from his pocket. Moistening his finger, he deftly and artistically traced some simple designs on the muslin shirt. He held it up for his own approval and draped it across Chance's knee.

"Wear that and even a big soldier gun can't harm you. It is better than this old-time thing. I say so. *Hesunanin* says so."

"*Hesunanin—?*" Chance cut in, seized by a sudden thought.

"The Grandfather."

"It's the word I'm after. The first part—hesu—it's the same sound as the Latin word for Christ."

"Latin?"

"The language of the Black Robes."

"I do not speak that tongue, Brother," Wovoka said with some asperity. "That word I got with the milk from my mother's tit. We have near here a very high place which white men call Mount Grant. *Hesunanin* has lived there since a long time before there were Black Robes. Or white men. It is our word and I have been up there many times to talk with him."

He indicated the painted muslin shirt.

"Take it. A present from your friend Jack Wilson. It will protect you. It is holy."

"But I heard there is to be no more fighting," Chance protested.

"That is true. All brothers."

"Then I won't need protection."

"Well, the new time is not quite here and you are a long way from your own country."

Chance was amused. Appearances were deceiving. Whatever else he was, the Paiute was shrewd. Another thought struck him.

"You know of the Mormons?"

Wovoka nodded uncertainly.

"Don't they have something like this? A shirt or gown with symbols on it. Supposed to wear it inside, where it can't be seen. Endowment Robe, I think they call it. Don't they claim it will keep them from harm, too?"

"I don't know about that," the messiah answered easily. "But the Black Robes have some things. I think they must have many enemies to be afraid of. There are these pieces of that tree they nailed the Christ to that other time. Big medicine with them. But it also must have been a very big tree to have so many pieces. And very hard wood to last so long.

"Also, my friend, I hear they have these holy people, men and women, both, who wear clothes made like the cloth they wrapped the Christ in when he was dead. Hoods for the head and hanging to the ground like an old woman's skirt. They put blood in a cup and give meat and say it is the Christ and eat it. But many of them get killed anyway."

Beau grinned at Chance.

"Not getting much of any place, are you?" He rose and faced Wovoka.

"Not many Indians will believe this, but there are lots of white men who are not their enemies. There are lots of white men who are not soldiers or settlers or government men. But they are far away. What the Indian sees and hears and knows to be true doesn't reach their ears."

Wovoka's full lips puckered dubiously. He looked at the semicircle of emissaries. Many were shaking their heads and muttering among themselves. Beau raised his voice for their benefit but continued speaking to their messiah.

"Why would a proud chief like Sitting Bull send a white man to you?" he urged persuasively. "Because this one can reach the ears of those who do not hear. You say a new world is coming. Well, we all heard Kicking Bear speak a little while ago. Even in a new world a man like that will make enemies. Even in a new world the Indian will need friends. Show this white man what you see coming."

Wovoka seemed in communion and it was some moments before he spoke. His eyes kindled and Chance half-expected his voice to climb in pitch like that of a hell-fire-and-damnation preacher stepping into his pulpit. However, the Paiute continued quietly and with obvious earnestness.

"My father Tavibo was a holy man, a prophet. He had many good dreams and did many good things. I learned much from my father. Later I saw all these bad times we have now and I did not like to see my people die. I thought much about it and dreamed all the dreams I could, but it did no good. Then there was this day the sun died. I was frightened and tried very hard to keep it from happening, but I fell down and died, too. While I was dead—and that was quite a long time—I was taken up on Mount Grant to see the Grandfather. There some things were made plain to me.

"A new earth will soon cover the bad things here like new snow covers the tracks and the mud of the old. The good will come with it. The game and the grass and the friends and relations who are gone."

Wovoka paused, frowning a little as though in an effort at verbatim recollection.

"The new world is all Indian. No wars or killing or any of that kind of trouble. All brothers. No sickness or firewater or gold or fences or plows. Only good things of the old time. Games and many children, all happy. All the dead ghosts all come home. Even the old people young and new. That is what I saw up there. All good. No bad in anything."

The Indian paused again. His heavy features slowly formed a broad smile. Chance supposed that upon any but a pagan face the expression could have been considered beatific. He knew the thought was suspect. What he saw before him bordered on the ludicrous. But he found himself leaning forward, listening, waiting intently.

"The Grandfather knows there is not much strength left," Wovoka continued. "There are not many Indians, these days. So he makes it easy, without harm to anyone. A dance to make, holding hands like brothers and sisters. Songs to sing about the old times that are coming back. Good prayers, good thoughts, good hearts toward everyone. But already some white men are saying this is a bad thing. You see this is not so?"

"There's a lot I *don't* see," Chance said. "You say there will be no white men in this new world of yours. How are you going to get rid of them?"

"Not me," the messiah corrected. "The Grandfather. But I did not see that when I was up there."

Chance looked at Beau and decided to risk the direct question.

"An uprising, maybe, when you've got enough of them fired up and dancing?"

"It is not that kind of dance," Wovoka said sharply. "No war, the Grandfather said. Especially with the white man. He was very strong about that."

"You actually think the buffalo are coming back?"

"It is promised."

"And the—ghosts?"

"I have seen them. Many times. Now, when we dance, others see them, too." The Indian indicated the seated delegates. "Most of those people have already seen and talked to their dead friends and relations when they are fainted in the dance."

"And just when is all this going to happen?"

Wovoka's brow furrowed again.

"I think this spring," he said, "and then winter, and then the spring after that."

"A year from now."

"Yes. But I may shorten the wait if these bad times get

any worse."

"You don't seem to be sure about a lot of this."

For the first time the Paiute showed a trace of exasperation.

"When you go back to those Indians who sent you, all this will not come back to your tongue the way you hear it now. I try to remember everything but it is hard to know about a whole world all at one time. When I die some more and go up there a few more times, I will know everything."

Chance smiled at the simple logic.

"When are you going to hold a dance so I can see it?"

Wovoka stood up, wincing a little at a cramp in his legs.

"My friend," he said, "you have come a long way. Coming to this place, you did some good things. Because of that you have seen me. We have had a talk. Now you know what is in my heart. There is nothing more for you here. Those Indians will stay here a while more. I will give the Ghost Dance to them. It is theirs. But I will not give it to a white man. Tell Sitting Bull I will send the dance to him with these people. It will be there soon. I have no more words."

The Indian gravely offered his hand. Chance shook it. The Paiute Christ climbed into Charley Sheep's wagon. The ring of delegates rose stiffly and followed it as it jolted off. The procession strung off into the thin timber like a cortege.

XI

The Gifts of God

Charley Sheep returned with his wagon a little before sundown. He had everything worked out. The journey before them was long. Their horses were at his place at Walker Lake. Also, it was no season to travel by saddle. Besides, they were rich and could afford the fare. If they would leave at once, he would not have to over-drive his already weary team to catch the weekly northbound train at the nearest swing of the rails.

He had two shoe boxes for each. One contained several bundles of black-and-white feathers. The other was filled with cakes of dried red pigment.

"From the store," he explained. "The Christ has a business with this man there. Some of the boys catch magpies for the feathers. Some of the young men go to this sacred place near Mount Grant and make the cakes of paint.

"The Christ takes these things to this man at the store and gets much money for them. This man sells them to all these Indians who want to make the Ghost Dance when they get home to their own countries. Some who have already gone home write and send money for more. It is a good business. These I have brought are presents from the Christ to show you have been to see him. They are very valuable, very big medicine."

Easterbrook and Beau Lane climbed into the wagon. Charlie drove north and east through the hills sheltering

Pine Grove and far out onto the sage-hummocked flats. It was nearly midnight when tire-iron squealed against sand-drifted narrow-gauge rails, lost in the desert.

There was no growth about for fuel, so Charlie gave them a rusty lantern with a red chimney, nearly out of oil, for use as a beacon. He returned Chance's purse, lighter by some ninety-odd dollars. Sure he was dipping the candle twice, Chance returned a ten dollar gold piece. Charlie pocketed it without thanks and drove off without farewell, leaving his passengers huddled on the ties.

For a long time they could hear the receding clatter of the old wagon. Then it was gone. Lane stirred uncomfortably and prodded one of the shoe boxes with his toe.

"Sorry, Chance," he said. "Been a long time, a long way, and a lot of money for some feathers and a box of red mud pies."

"Think that's all there is to it?" Chance asked. "I don't know, Beau. All the delegates who are there, now. That Cheyenne who showed up in Sitting Bull's camp. The ones we talked to at Tongue River and the Little Wind and damned near every place else we stopped. Whatever this Paiute is, he's got a lot of them believing."

Lane grunted wryly.

"He can afford to. Smart Indian. Got a good thing going and he knows it. Peddling this junk and some white hats beats working in a hay field."

Chance was surprised at the Dakotan's bitterness. It was true that Charley Sheep's placid nephew had exhibited little but the faith of others in support of his pretensions. And his petty personal privateering was obvious enough. But it was equally plain he was doing no harm and might well even be benefiting his believers to whatever degree faith was self-rewarding.

Besides, Lane's sympathies had heretofore been so solidly with the tribes in whatever context that Chance had thought he would support Wovoka, if only because the Paiute's Ghost Dance was exclusively Indian and not likely to be stolen by the white man. He felt uncomfortably defensive of his own position.

"Why the sour view, Beau?" he asked.

"Oh, because it's over, I guess. And I reckon I've been a first-class fool. Not that I won't be glad to get back to Nora. That part's been hard enough and will likely take plenty of mending, the time we've been gone and all. There's still a chance, I suppose, that she can talk Marie McLaughlin and Major Mac into another try for that stock job in Minnesota. Be a place for us, at least. But the fact is, what I really hate is to see you wind up and go back east."

Beau paused thoughtfully.

"I believed for a while that something could be made to come of this. Something that would make the whole country open up and look at them as people, just for once. See them for what they are, what they can do if they're given half a chance. I kind of hoped you'd get into it so deep you'd go back to the Dakotas with me and sort of help it along.

"Naturally, you can't, now. Not with what that moon-faced Paiute's given us to work with. Put that in a paper and it'd be laughed off the streets. Worse yet, nobody is going to believe that two-bit faker is their last hope. Their very last."

"Do you?"

"What? Believe in him?" the Dakotan asked with sudden intensity. "You think I'm that big a fool? No matter how much I wanted to, even! Plain enough what he is. But like you said, he's got *them* believing. That's what counts. It's what makes me so damned mad. Isn't worth a busted bowstring and they're bound to find it out, directly. Then they won't have *anything* to believe in. That's the end, then, Chance."

Lane slammed his balled fist down hard on the railroad tie between them.

"Damn that Paiute for going too far!" he continued savagely. "Look what it does to them. What's it now in anybody's eyes but the kind of stupidity everybody would expect from ignorant, superstitious savages. Damn him for claiming he's God!"

Easterbrook leaned over and straightened the gift boxes Charley Sheep had left with them.

"But he didn't, Beau," he said quietly. "And I'm not wound up with the Sioux. Not until my story is finished. I haven't even begun it yet. We'll go back to the Dakotas together. We'll visit every camp we can. If I have anything to say about it, the country's going to know this Ghost Dance for what it is. The country's going to know the Sioux. And I promise you we're not going to be laughed off the streets."

Lane sat there a long time, motionless in the dark. Suddenly he spoke.

"I never asked. What's your first name, really?"

"Chauncey. Present from my mother."

"Funny. Names I mean. Step-father gave me mine, far

as anybody knows."

A star of light winked toward them from the horizon. The rails beside which they sat began to sing faintly. They rose stiffly and lit Charley Sheep's lantern to flag down the train.

XII

Stella Corrigan

It turned out Lane had never ridden the rails before. As they shuttled up a series of little Nevada short lines to the trunk line east, the Dakotan was all over the cars.

Chance had long been intrigued by Beau's mastery of physical habit. Bowel and bladder functioned at his convenience, and abstinence from relief for long periods did not seem to disturb him at all. Chance had once complained. Beau had laughed and introduced him to the Sioux alarm clock. An ingenious matter of drinking the right amount of water before retiring to insure rising at whatever morning hour was desired. But once on the rails, Beau trotted incessantly, wholly fascinated by the toilet compartment.

He borrowed Chance's watch and counted the clicking rail joints beneath the wheels, converting them by some formula obtained from a trainman to miles per hour. And he always whistled disbelief at the result. While Chance hunched on his seat, trying to work up copy from the notes in his journal, Beau talked with everyone who could spare him the time.

They quit the trunk at Sidney, Nebraska, and shunted over to the little town of Crawford, near the Fort Robinson Military Reserve. At this point Lane figured they were about seventy-five miles from the Pine Ridge Sioux Agency and no more than two hundred and fifty miles from Sitting Bull's camp on Grand River.

They took a sheaf of Chance's copy to the station telegraph office and inquired of the station agent about the availability of a livery to take them on to Pine Ridge. The agent handed back the copy. Orders out of Fort Robinson, he said, which had been set up as headquarters for the campaign. The official press office and entry point for the Dakota reservations was at Rushville, another small Nebraska town about sixty miles east. They would have to go on there.

"Campaign?" Chance repeated, startled.

"What you're here for, isn't it? The Sioux campaign—"

Chance saw his own alarm in Lane's eyes.

"There's been an outbreak?"

"Unh-uh," the agent grunted. "They learned better'n that. Except for that damned foolishness of Custer trying to show off out there in Montana a few years ago, they've had their backsides shot off every fight they got into and they know it. So they're playing tame. Letting us spend good tax money feeding and educating them and letting them breed. Giving them all the time they want to go it slow and plan it real careful. Now they're about ready. Live up here along the border and you see it so plain it makes your skin crawl. The Army knows. Washington'll deny it and General Miles'll have you shot for a liar if you say it, but the Army's scared stiff."

"Of what, exactly?"

"What we got within a hundred miles of right here, Mister. More fighting Indians than was ever in one place before. Enough to wipe out the whole standing army of the United States before anybody'd even know what was happening. That's what the Army's scared of. It had damned well better be. That's what's going to happen unless it wipes out the Sioux first."

The station agent eyed his listeners truculently.

"Think I'm pulling your leg? Go out to Fort Robinson and see for yourself. Know what they're doing out there on the q.t.? Pulling in the Seventh Cavalry. Custer's old outfit. All those boys have wanted since the Little Big Horn is some Sioux to shoot at. Sort of wash the blood off the guidons. Thank God somebody's turned up at headquarters with enough sense to give them what they want before its too late for any of us!"

Easterbrook and Beau Lane did not exchange two words on the ride to Rushville. Beau hurried off to find them a rig to take them on north to Pine Ridge. Chance found the military press officer in an untidy hotel room. A Sergeant Eberle, old Army, with graying hair and a ladder of service stripes suggesting a long career of disciplinary setbacks. His tunic was off and he had not shaved in spite of the lateness of the midday hour. He produced credentials, and Chance saw he was on detached duty from General Miles' staff. He carelessly riffled Chance's sheaf of copy. One word caught his attention. He laughed.

"Messiah—that's a new one for them!"

He signed and dated the first page and tossed the sheaf onto the rumpled bed.

"Get it off tonight, military wire," he said. "Courtesy of the Service. Buy you a drink, Easterbrook?"

"Permissible, on duty?"

"On this duty it's mandatory!"

Without picking up his tunic, the sergeant led the way downstairs. Lane had not reappeared. Eberle pointed to a sign over a door across the street.

"Only saloon in town. 'Aksarben'—Nebraska, backwards. Imaginative as hell, aren't they?"

They crossed over and Eberle pushed the door open into a cheerless, unkempt room. It was empty of either trade or service. The sergeant went behind the makeshift bar, took down a bottle and two glasses. He looked closely at the latter, gave them a quick polish with a smudged towel, and came out to a table. He poured them each a full tumbler of whiskey, then took half of his in one prodigious swallow.

"I understand they're moving the Seventh Cavalry into Fort Robinson," Chance remarked.

"Wouldn't know," Eberle said. "Not my outfit."

"There was a lot of talk about trouble with the Sioux over in Crawford when we came through."

"Ah, you know how an army is," the sergeant grunted. "Got to have something to keep it out of mischief."

A girl came into the trade room from somewhere in back. A slattern, young and buxom, with a ready enough appeal to the senses. She watched Eberle replenish his glass.

"Pa see you helping yourself and you know what he'd do."

"Tell him," Eberle suggested.

"He ain't up."

The sergeant looked at the girl and shook his head distastefully.

"You asked me, Easterbrook," he said. "I'll tell you. Far's I know, there isn't any Indian trouble around here and won't ever be again. But if there ever was, I can show you what would be behind it."

He spoke to the girl.

"Stella, draw a beer and come over here."

"Can't."

"Ah, if Orrie's still on the mattress, he won't make it up before dark. What he don't know won't hurt him."

The girl waggled over to the bar and polished out a tankard with the same cloth Eberle had used. Barely cracking the tap to minimize the head, she leaned on one elbow and waited for the tankard to fill. She was watching Chance. Her dress hung forward from her body in exposure halfway to her uncorseted navel. It was not particularly artless. Nor was her smile. When the tankered brimmed she came across and sat closest to Easterbrook.

"You and Orrie came off a farm up by the Line, didn't you?" Eberle asked her.

"Hundred and eighty acres, three mile from the reservation boundary," the girl agreed.

"Like it up there, Stel'?"

"Hated it fierce."

"Why?"

"Damned Indians."

Eberle glanced at Chance.

"They ever do anything to you?"

The girl stiffened angrily.

"You think I'd mess around with one of them?"

"Hell, I don't mean that. Why you hate them. My friend's new around here. He doesn't understand."

"Everybody else sure does. Mostly women they want. Anything, long's she's white. Not for the fun, either. Rip your insides out when they're done. Or cut him up if he's a man so's he's no good, even if he don't bleed to death."

Chance was appalled at the certainty.

"You actually know anyone that happened to?" he asked.

"Pa does. Scads."

"What else?" Eberle asked.

"Good God, ain't that enough?" She turned to Chance. "If you want details, Mister, I'll give 'em to you. Pa's told me plenty."

Chance shook his head.

"Some of the other things you hate 'em for, Stel'," Eberle prodded.

"Well, they're terrible thieves. Anything that ain't nailed down."

"You and Orrie lose anything up there?"

"A mule. They run him into bobwire and he bled out."

"Anybody see Indians with the mule? Tracks or anything?"

"I've told you how it was, night and all. But no old mule's going to run himself into bobwire, is he?"

"Anything else?"

"Ma had a time, once. Before she took to fluxing so bad she'd do up a couple weeks' bread at a batch. Loaves and rolls and the like. You know. This day there was three of 'em walked right in on her, big as you please. Tore the kitchen up looking for sugar and took every pan she'd baked."

"They steal the bread or did she give it to them?"

"Kilt her if she hadn't. And I had to stay in the privy all morning. Afraid to come out. They'd have got me if I had."

"Now there's a terrible picture for you," Eberle said to Chance.

"They catch a woman the wrong time they put sticks or something in her anyway," Stella added in hopeful embellishment.

Chance presumed he looked sufficiently shocked. At any rate, she smiled at him again.

"They just ain't human," she said in summation.

Eberle poured himself some more whiskey.

"Now, sweetie, tell the man. Did the Indians drive you and Orrie off that place up there?"

"Same as. Ma hated it so bad, hard living and being scared all the time, that she just quit and died. Just me and Pa after that. Nobody else around to even see or talk to. Then I got knocked up before planting time and was pretty sick. Pa figured a hundred and eighty acres of that gumbo was too much for a man to look after single-handed and keep the Sioux off, too. So we come down here and set up on the railroad."

"That was when?" Eberle asked.

"Year ago."

"How old are you, now?"

"Sixteen."

"Draw yourself another beer," Eberle said. "And, if you got a little arsenic around, mix up a dose for Orrie. Be a favor to the human race."

Sensing dismissal, Stella looked hopefully at Chance. Seeing no encouragement, she rose and smoothed her dress over her belly.

"Don't get drunk if you figure on coming round tonight," she told Eberle.

The sergeant sloshed his glass full and looked fixedly at it until the door in back closed behind her. He glanced up in half-apology to Chance, then.

"Wondering why I let you in for a peek at that?"

Chance nodded candidly.

"Was a time I was going to be a first-class soldier," Eberle said slowly. "Even made it for a while. Maybe a little too much piss and vinegar for post discipline, but conscientious as an altar boy about one thing. The Army. The God-damned Army. Best fighting force on the face of the earth. Finest fighting men. Guardians of the nation. I believed it, too.

"Then I began to see what it was—what I was. A bully. A lazy son of a bitch, willing to make the big grunt every now and then to coast between. Swaggering around in a uniform that made you closer to a saint than a priest's cassock, and a hell of a lot more privileges. Had any time in the Service?"

"No," Chance admitted.

"Then you probably won't get this. Soldiers ought to

109

have their own language. What I'm trying to say is it finally gets through to you that there's damned little glory and a lot of rot. All the way up. A hunting preserve, stocked with Indians. A hero-factory if there ever was one. Things to be real proud of. Custer on the Washita and Chivington at Sand Creek.

"And politics for favored sons. Man gets two or three stars and he's headed for the White House with the bit in his teeth. Harrison got in because Crook and Miles locked horns over who was to have first crack. Either could have whipped him, hands down. Now Crook's dead and Miles has lost his chance. So he's got to go back to fighting Indians. What the hell else is a busted-ass general going to do?"

Eberle emptied the bottle into his tumbler. He was drunk and it seemed unlikely he could get drunker. But he clung to his point as though it had great value.

"The Indians. Noble foeman, they say. I've fought them and damned if I see that. But we've cut them down and they've taken their medicine. They got to be for peace, now, except for a few die-hards. But they're not going to get it. And this time it isn't the Army. It's these farmers and settlers, leaning on the government. Stella Corrigan and her old man. Aksarben—Nebraska, spelled backwards. Minnesota, if I could say it that way. All around them. Every side.

"Hate, they say. Hell, they don't hate. They're scared is all. And so are the Sioux. Show me two scareds and I'll show you a devil of a fight."

Eberle lifted the bottle again but it was empty.

"Just you remember this," he said thickly. "This time

it isn't the uniforms. This time it's these miserable, land-whipped, snivelling little bastards like Orrie Corrigan. Sitting in judgment! All right, that's the way it's going to be. But you tell them. You tell them, Easterbrook. This time it isn't the Army. Laying his own kid—Christ Almighty!"

The sergeant lowered his head into his hands. He gave no sign of awareness when Chance arose and crossed to the door, letting himself out into the street. Beau was waiting in front of the hotel with a buckboard and driver. He was anxiously looking at the sky.

"Clouding up," he said. "May be a wet drive. We could lay over."

Chance glanced back at the Aksarben and shook his head.

"No," he said. "Let's get to hell out of here."

X I I I

Red Cloud

Rain came, as Lane had feared. The storm blew on to the southeast, leaving the parched land to the northward untouched. They drove the sun down and into the night as long as the moon lasted. Resting a few hours, they set out again at first glow of false dawn and at a very early hour approached Pine Ridge along White Clay Creek. In contrast to the spartan plant James McLaughlin administered at Standing Rock, this southern agency was a considerable community.

The road passed close to a large Oglala camp along the creek. A second was visible in the next bottom to the east. There were many canvas issue lodges in both camps but a great number of permanent structures, too. For the most part these were low-walled, dugout log and sod shanties.

Further along was a clapboard Episcopal church and an extensive trading post at a junction of two roads. West on one of these were the government buildings— barracks, agency quarters, and the like. Beyond the trading post was a substantial hotel. Across from this was an ugly, two-storied house with a tall, peeled flag-pole before it. Their hired buckboard put them down at the hotel. Chance eyed it dubiously.

"All the comforts," Beau assured him. "Can't put visiting congressmen, generals, and commissioners on a lodge floor or in barracks bunks, you know. So they built it with Sioux money. To keep the bigwig guests comfortable while they dicker for more land."

Chance pointed to the flagpole across the road. An oversize national ensign flew at half-mast from its halyards. Lane nodded, wryly amused.

"Red Cloud's house," he said. "The one they built for him when he came in. And Red Cloud's flag. When he's pleased, he flies her high, wide, and handsome. But when he's got a grouch on, down she comes to half-mast till somebody oils up the old man's hurt feelings or whatever. You go feed and freshen up. I'll see if the chief's going to be in the mood for a visit."

The Dakotan started away, then turned back.

"A suggestion, Chance. If they've got hot water,

might do to shave. Your face is pretty well healed up now and they don't trust beards. Think a white man wears them to hide behind."

Chance paid off the buckboard driver and entered the hotel. There was hot water. And an excellent breakfast. He had just finished eating when an Oglala boy came for him. They crossed to Red Cloud's house. Several Indians were on the porch with Beau. They were all short-haired, hatted, dressed in dusty overalls. From a distance they looked like any knot of idlers gathered under a store awning, anywhere down below the Line.

Coming closer, Chance became aware of a difference. The darker faces and uncommunicative eyes, of course. But the footgear struck him most. Most were shoddy brogans of issue style, worn to utter ruin. Some had been helped along the way by slitted surgery calculated to remedy hopeless fit or the discomfort of unaccustomed confinement. Among usually vain people, the shabby footgear was incongruous. The supposition had to be these men had no other choice.

A single, broken-runged kitchen rocker was on the porch. In it an old man with silvering hair and rheumy eyes sat shrunken under a blanket. From the deference of those about him, Chance realized this was the once arrogant Oglala chief who had formerly been the most famous of the war-makers. He felt deep disappointment at the apparent senility.

Chance sensed some hostility in the group about the old man. However, he courteously expressed his pleasure at being in the presence of Red Cloud. The Chief said nothing but another man spoke.

"This Hunkpapa, here," he said, indicating Lane, "tells us you put some things in white men's newspapers. Well, some of our young men read those newspapers. Especially when they talk about Indians. They say everything they read is lies. That is the white man's way, all right. Come to see the truth and make a lie of it."

Another man nodded strong approval.

"One time I went to Washington with Red Cloud," he said. "They showed us there a place where they had some animals in a cage so they could not get out. Everybody came to look at them and called them wild because they wanted to be free again. I think it is like that with us this morning. You have come to look at Red Cloud because he is an old man and this is a very strong cage they have got us in here."

A third man intervened.

"I do not understand all this bad talk," he protested. "Can this man help it if he is a white man? We can't help it that we are Indian. I do not know of any bad thing he has done in these newspapers."

Another man snorted angrily.

"Some men think everything the white man does is good," he charged. "The good white man, they say. The good father. My brother the white man. I will sleep with him. These men are fools. I will hear no more of these foolish words!"

The man who had defended Chance sprang to his feet at this personal affront. His challenger also leaped up with eager malice. Chance saw Beau's quick, anxious frown. But before the quarrel could develop further, the motionless old man in the rocker spoke. His voice was too soft and swift for Chance to follow. The antagonists froze and the group looked out onto the road. An Indian policeman had paused before the house and was looking curiously toward them. After a moment he hurried on in the direction of the government buildings.

The group eased. The two who had been about to quarrel sat down. A man who heretofore had been silent indicated Lane and spoke to Chance.

"We make trouble for ourselves," he said. "This man says you have been all the way to the country of the Fish-Eaters to see this *Wanekia* we have been hearing about."

"That is so," Chance agreed.

"Then I think that is why you are here. To tell us you have seen the *Wanekia* and he is bad. His words are bad. His heart is bad. Bad for the Indian. That is always the way. There is no good for us in anything."

"No," Chance said. "I could say some things about him to you. But I do not know what they would be because I am not sure. But Kicking Bear was there. Short Bull and Good Thunder, too. You know those men. They heard more. They understand more. They are Indian. Now they are coming back. They will be here soon. It is better that they talk about this thing."

"That is true," the man assented, conceding nothing. "I think it is also better you go, now. We will wait for them. We have no more words for you."

Chance thought this was probably the sentiment of nearly every man on the porch. He could feel the weight of hostility. Red Cloud seemed to have lost all interest in his visitors if he had indeed had any in the first place.

He nodded to Lane and started down the steps but paused. A rider turned in fast from the road and alighted angrily in the dooryard.

"Gallagher, the new agent here," Beau murmured.

The man wore shiny cavalry officer's boots. Pants and hat and short-sleeved uniform tunic, all without insignia. He wore a pistol at his belt and carried a short riding crop. Face flushed, he crossed directly to Chance.

"Just what in hell do you think you're doing here?" he demanded.

"Paying my respects," Chance answered, indicating the figure of Red Cloud.

He extended his card case. Gallagher tucked his crop under one arm, flipped the identifications over, and tossed them back.

"On this reservation you pay your respects at the government office, Easterbrook."

"Not until they're earned, Major."

One of the Oglalas behind him repeated Chance's retort in dialect for any who might have missed its bite in English. The agent's color darkened.

"I don't relish incivility, Mister!" he snapped.

"Goes for me, too," Chance said. "I'm a free agent on legitimate business, Major. You saw my credentials. I suggest this might make an interesting interview in print."

Gallagher considered this and irritably slapped his crop against the outseam of his flared pants.

"All right, Mr. Easterbrook," he said grudgingly. "So my back was up. I apologize. But when one of my police came running to report strangers here with the old man and what looked like a fight making up—"

"Sometimes appearances can be deceiving," Chance pointed out. "We're on our way to Fort Yates. I plan to interview every head man I can along the way. We cleared with the military at Rushville. I hadn't supposed Bureau clearance would be necessary as well."

"No," the agent said. "No, of course not. The Bureau is solely concerned with its responsibilities to the Indians. Can I be of any assistance to you?"

"I think not, Major."

The Bureau man hesitated a moment longer, looking for a graceful exit, then turned back to his horse. He rode out of the yard at a jolting trot, sitting so poor a saddle there was no dignity left.

There was a stir on the porch. The old man in the rocking chair had thrown back his blanket. He stood up. The metamorphosis was startling. At full height Red Cloud was a little stooped, but all sign of senility had vanished. In its place was a secret mirth and the light of an unholy shrewdness.

"I like those words you made there just now," he told Easterbrook. "That man is a very bad agent. He is also a coward. These men will now show you how some more things are with us. Then you will come back. We will eat. After that there will be some horses for you and some other small things. I also want you to take presents to my brother, Sitting Bull, and some other chiefs if you will be visiting their camps."

The old man and most of the others withdrew into the house. The two men detailed reappeared with a shiny new light spring wagon with narrow-tired wheels and tandem seats with cushions and upholstered backs. It was Red Cloud's wagon and the two Oglalas believed it had been given to him by the President, himself. Beau and Chance climbed in and they drove off on a local tour.

They saw the same parched fields they had noted behind Nebraska settlers' fences, the sorrier here for evident neglect in addition to the general drought. It was explained that for two summers, now, commissioners and other government officials had been long weeks on the reservation, negotiating for more Indian land. Each time all men had been required to come in to the councils, leaving their fields untended when they most needed attention.

Chance had a different opinion. The real trouble, as in the Nebraska area he had seen, was that this simply was not growing country. The first official improvidence had been Bureau insistence upon breaking the hardy, richly grassed native sod with a plow.

They saw a pony herd on barren pasture. Chance was genuinely shocked. Shedding out of winter hair, the animals were gaunted down to apathy. Scarcely one in a dozen was fit to ride. It was not like the old days, the Oglalas agreed. There had been ponies by the thousands, then, fat and fast. But when they came in and gave up their guns, a soldier chief had taken the ponies, too. He sold six hundred of them to settlers who came onto Sioux lands for that purpose. They could pay as little as they wished.

But there were not enough white men to buy all the ponies, even then, so the soldier chief drove two thousand more out onto the *coteau* and shot them there. The bones could still be seen. The Government agreed to pay some little price for all those ponies but it had never been done. Now only these yonder were left.

There were a few head of beef in the issue corral. Reserved for the residency and staff, the Oglalas said. These remnants were fleshless. Texas through-beef, trailed up in the fall at twelve hundred pounds or so on the hoof and so credited on the ration rolls. But at ration time they weighed less than eight hundred pounds at kill. And no allowance for the difference.

Each year the treaty allowance was cut, too. The Oglalas did not remember how much but Lane did. The previous year the Pine Ridge bands had been allocated eight and a quarter million pounds. This year he understood they had received less than four million. Congress had been thrift-minded at appropriation time, although treaty terms remained unchanged. Why not? No voting constituency was involved. As some believed, the white man had discovered it was easier to starve the Indian than to kill him in battle. The graves in a mission cemetery bore out the charge. A large proportion were small and so new no growth covered the mounded, reddish-gray earth. In the olden days, the little children did not fight.

When they returned to Red Cloud's house the old man had dressed in a black undertaker's suit and a white shirt with a string tie. But he wore the most beautifully quilled moccasins Chance had yet seen and a quilled buckskin band about his brow. He proudly took them across to the hotel dining room.

Like most old men, Red Cloud talked much of his

youth, when white men were unknown to him and he to them. The goodness of that old life shone in his faded eyes.

"They say sometimes that Red Cloud is unreasonable," he told Chance. "But that is not so. I know only truth. I feel only truth. I look at you and I see a good face. I know that you are trying to do some good things. You come here and eat with me and try to make talk in my language. You do not yet have many words but it makes a man feel good to hear even a few words of his people on another man's tongue. I know you are a white man but I do not call you an enemy. I cannot call you friend but I do not hate you. I have known a few others like that but they are not many."

The old man shook his head with what Chance believed to be genuine sadness.

"You have the blood of your people. I have the blood of mine. You—one man—have done nothing to us. You have nothing bad to remember. But I have had bad things done to me and I cannot forget. I would forget if I could to save my people. I would make them forget. But that cannot be done. We are men and we remember.

"This hate did not grow in our hearts. It was put there. There is nothing I can do about it, now. There is nothing you can do. I want to hear what Kicking Bear and those others say when they come from visiting this *Wanekia*, but I am an old man and many believe me wise. Hear what I say. I do not believe God can do anything, either. Not even if he changes the color of our skin. The remembering will still be there. The hate will not die."

That ended the discussion but the mood changed as

they were leaving the table.

"There is something that I want to ask," Red Cloud said to Chance. "Sitting Bull has a white woman—this is so?"

Chance understood but did not know how to answer. Beau made it no easier.

"Mrs. Weldon," he volunteered.

"That is the one," the chief agreed. "I know of her. Sometimes lately she has written me letters about the Indian. You have seen this woman?"

The question was still directed at Chance and he reluctantly nodded.

"She is a good woman—good for a man, I mean?"

There was no escape. Chance tried to meet the directness with honesty.

"Some men would think so, I believe—when they were through with wanting only girls."

Red Cloud grinned impishly.

"Does he sleep with her?"

"The Bull? No. No, I don't think so."

"Aiee!" the Chief chuckled in glee and slapped his thigh. "And they call me an old man!"

XIV

Big Foot

Red Cloud did not appear in the morning but his flag had been hoisted to the peak of the pole before his house. Some Oglalas brought up ponies, a packet of gifts, a grub sack, and some worn trail gear. There were thanks and farewells. Chance and Beau Lane rode out of Pine Ridge. Their coming seemed to run ahead of them. Wherever they met Indians, they were offered salute. *Kola*—friend.

Fifteen or twenty miles out they stopped at a little store on the banks of Wounded Knee Creek. Mousseau, the half-breed trader there seemed also to know of their approach and inquired about the Paiute messiah. They gave him the same answer they had given the Oglalas. Wait for the return of the Pine Ridge delegates.

The trail across the Badlands began a little north of Wounded Knee. The country progressively became more broken and desolate. They dry-camped on a high bench from which they could look out across the valley of the White River into a distant gut of erosion and improbable silhouette which slanted northeastward across their course. The low angle of the sun accentuated the extremes of this vast trough. A place once shunned by the Sioux as the abode of evil spirits and certain misfortune.

Beau said this was no longer true. As tribal territory had been reduced, several bands had explored in the Badlands. They had found an occasional oasis of grass and water. The Dakotan pointed out the truncated landmark of Castle Butte and tried to single out a lesser eminence for Chance. It was, Beau said, an almost completely separated headland at the upper end of a sheer mesa and was remarkable for dependable springs of good water, grass on its flattened top, and extreme inaccessibility.

The Stronghold, the Sioux called it. Those who had

been there claimed it could be defended by a brave few against a multitude. White men did not know the country in there at all. Few had even heard of the mesa-top refuge.

The next day they gradually descended into the desolation they had seen from the dry camp. It was a lifeless, silent place Chance found eerie and depressing. They crossed it and came to a high escarpment of violently eroded bluff which Beau called the Badlands Wall. Scaling this on badly blown ponies, they camped again in friendlier country. On the third afternoon they approached Chief Big Foot's camp on Deep Creek in the valley of the Cheyenne River.

Despite lengthening distance, word was before them here, too. A Minneconjou party rode out and escorted them with considerable ceremony to a lodge vacated for their use. Water was fetched. Food was sent. Heralds went through the camp, announcing their arrival. Presently they were summoned to the chief's lodge.

Big Foot was a lean, somewhat stooped man with a round head and his hair done in a fine pair of old-time braids. He had undistinguished, kindly features. Although physically better preserved, he seemed to be about Red Cloud's age. Chance tried to observe protocol but, in entering and seating himself in the crowded lodge, he gathered he made some error in custom. Big Foot put him at ease at once.

"This man has lately been at Red Cloud's house and before that to many far places, many other lodges," he announced. "He has learned many things and cannot be expected to remember how they are all done. If he does not know how they are done here, we will not see."

Chance thanked him and presented a gift from Red Cloud. When opened it proved to be a fancifully japanned tin of hardball English candies. Chance instantly divined the source, a tribute Red Cloud had received from some eastern donor. The wily old Oglala had known the effect such an exotic gift would have upon a less experienced recipient.

The tin circulated until all, including visitors, had sampled the candy. When each cheek was pouched about a hardball, Chance passed a tuft of magpie feathers and a cake of red pigment to Big Foot.

"The *Wanekia* sends you these things," he said. "They are big medicine with him. Soon your relation, Kicking Bear will be here. I was asked about this Paiute at Pine Ridge. I told them there I was not Oglala and did not know how this thing might be for Oglalas. Well, I am not a Minneconjou, either. It is best you hear the news from Kicking Bear."

There was a moment of disappointed silence. Then an old man near the door spoke.

"Those are wise words. White men have told us about God long enough. I will wait."

He rose and stepped outside. Others followed. Only two or three remained by special privilege. Big Foot spoke to Chance.

"I understand you also make this visit to find out some things," he said. "Well, I have some special trouble, here. I have been to Washington and saw the Grandfather and those other people there. I am known to be a friend of the white man. But lately when I call the agent down the river Father, my people spit at me. When I say the white man is our brother, they say their bellies are empty. I say the white man means us no harm and these people say there is much sickness and the little children die. I believe in what I say but what they say is also true. It is a bad thing when all of his people are not with a chief."

"You think it is the white man's fault you can no longer handle them?" Chance asked.

"Well," the old man said, "on all these other reservations there is a school. But there is no school here. I cannot teach these people to follow the White Man's Road. I can hardly find the way myself. It takes a school to learn all these new things. I asked the agent and he said he would make us a school.

"I went back to my people and told them the white man could not fill their bellies. There was no more beef in the corral and no more food in the Agency warehouse. I told them the white man could not make sickness go away. There was no medicine and no more doctors. The white man could not make our land Indian again. It was already buried by the plow. But the white man would give us a school and that was good.

"The bad hearts among my people looked and said, 'We do not see a school.' That was spring. They looked in the summer and said, 'We do not see a school.' I went to the agent and he said, 'Soon there will be lumber.' Then it was winter and spring again. Now it starts to be summer another time and there is no school. Lately it makes the agent very angry when I speak of it."

The Minneconjou chief shook his head in honest

perplexity.

"I do not think a school will make one Minneconjou white. Not for the lives of many old men, I think. But it is a thing the white man could give us. It could be made with the Sioux money they keep in Washington. And it is a thing I promised my people. It would keep my word strong with them.

"If I do not keep my word strong, how long can I be chief? How can I keep them from doing the bad things they sometimes talk about? Does the white man want enemies that he does not keep his promises to friends?"

"He's telling it straight, Chance," Lane said in English. "I don't mean about the school. First I've heard of that. But about himself. He's one of the real progressives. Done his level best since they came in to the reservation to keep them on the straight and narrow. And it hasn't been easy. Minneconjous are a wild lot. You remember Kicking Bear."

Chance nodded, remembering well, indeed.

"I'm not a government man and maybe it won't do any good," he told the chief, "but I'll write your agent and send a copy of the letter to his chief in Washington. I'll write up your story in the newspapers so all white men know of it. I'll do anything else I can. You tell your people that."

"No," Big Foot said sadly. "The only thing I can tell my people is to take them to a place and say, 'See, there is that school I have been talking about.' Then maybe they will listen to me again."

He pried up the lid of his present from Red Cloud and offered the cannister to his guests. Both were obliged to take another piece of the venerable candy.

"You say you do not wish to talk about this *Wanekia*," the old man said, frowning with concern. "You say to wait until Kicking Bear comes home. Kicking Bear's wife is my niece. The camp of his band is nearby. He is my relation, but sometimes there is trouble between us. He does not like my road. I do not like his. I think I am afraid of this *Wanekia* if it is Kicking Bear who brings him to me. I would like to hear some things about this man so I will know what is to be done when my nephew comes home."

Chance glanced at Lane, who nodded support of his own inclination.

"All right," he agreed.

"Is this man a ghost?" Big Foot asked.

"No. But they believe that he died and came alive again. They call him the Christ, out there."

"That is like that old-time man the Black Robes talk about."

"The same man, they believe. But come back this time to save the Indian, not the white man."

"That has a good sound. Do you believe it is true?"

"No."

"Do you believe in that old-time man—the other one?"

"Not exactly the way the Black Robes do."

"I see," the chief said thoughtfully. "Do you see anything bad in all of this?"

"I saw no harm in everything I saw and heard."

"Nothing in it to make trouble with the white man?"

"Not if you hold Kicking Bear down," Lane cut in.

Big Foot nodded, smiling wryly.

"I think he has holy water for blood," he said.

"Holy water?" Chance repeated.

"Whiskey," Beau translated.

X V

The Silent Eaters

They went down the Cheyenne River to Touch The Cloud's camp. This chief was Big Foot's natural brother. He had once been nearly as dominant in Sioux affairs as his name indicated. He was, unfortunately, absent when they arrived. Issue day was at hand and he had gone on down to the Cheyenne River Agency. They left a packet from Red Cloud for him and some magpie feathers and a cake of holy paint.

A short distance below they entered the camp of Hump's band. Lane said this old warrior had been there when the Great Encampment had elected Sitting Bull chief of the Sioux and their allies. He had been on the Rosebud and the Greasy Grass, too. Chance much wanted to meet him but Hump had also gone down to the agency to stand in line and draw his rations like the least householder among his people.

Chance was angry at this policy of mandatory begging. These were proud men. He doubted if human history had produced any more proud. He thought this pride among their leaders did duty among these people for a whole lexicon of more articulate laws and moralities. As he understood it, there was little restraint or force of law among the Plains Indians except the unwillingness of their leaders to undertake or approve anything detrimental to their personal self-regard.

The crushing of spirit had a whole history of precedent in dealing with conquered peoples. But not on this continent and in this time. A difference had been proclaimed in America, a dedication to human dignity. And the Declaration of Independence documented it in as sonorous a collection of title and phrase as existed in the Anglo-Saxon tongue. Yet those who wrote the Indian treaties had deliberately stipulated, *"Rations shall in all cases be issued only to the head of each individual family."*

Every two weeks, on a day dictated by Bureau caprice, they had to make a pilgrimage to their respective agency for the pittance without which the proudest of them could not survive. The heroes and the sages. The head men and the chiefs. They were so much more than heads of families. They were quite literally the fathers of their nation. There could be no doubt the humiliation was intentional.

Lane suggested waiting a day or two at Hump's camp or a detour on down the river to the agency so Chance could meet the missing leaders. However, as they drew closer to their point of beginning, impatience increased. They struck off across Cherry Creek and took the old Sioux trail straight for Grand River.

As they approached Sitting Bull's camp they found the country as burned and barren as it had been at Pine Ridge and in Nebraska. The winter had not been kind and there was little spring rebirth.

Coming in from the south as they did, they passed

within a quarter of a mile of Lt. Bull Head's house. Children in the yard saw them and ran inside. A man appeared and used glasses to be sure of identity. By the time they reached the ford across into the encampment, Bull Head was in uniform and saddled up. He crossed below them and took the road to Fort Yates at a long lope.

"Major's Mac's express," Lane said. "Wish he'd waited. I could have sent word to Nora, too."

Others had also seen them. The children were first. A boy broke from among them. He was displeased with the Oglala pony Chance rode. It was not the gift pony from his father that he had personally presented to this traveller on departure. He did not shout as his companions did, but only because he could not. Sitting Bull's deaf-mute son John had grown much taller through the winter and spring.

With the boy trotting proprietarily at Chance's stirrup, they came to the women. Chance looked hard and hungrily at Shining Woman as they approached, shaken at his own quickening. He had not remembered her correctly, as he had thought he had, during the long months of absence. He had been, as the men would say, a long time on the prairie—a long time without a woman. But it was not all that. She was beautiful. So was the welcome in her eyes, in every line of her body.

He leaned far over in his saddle when he reached her. She held up her cupped hands expectantly. Before all these eyes he dropped into them the crudely carved, dark-stained little effigy which, to the Nevada Galilee and back, he had kept as close to him as Kicking Bear kept the powerful talisman of Chief Crazy Horse. Shining Woman smiled and Easterbrook knew he could have returned with nothing that would have pleased her more. She turned and ran lightly before them, leading the way to the door of the same lodge they had occupied before. Beau smiled a little.

"Good to be home," he said.

It was an especial generosity on the Dakotan's part. Forty miles yet separated him from Nora Crandall's school at Standing Rock.

The familiar interior of the lodge was immaculate. Chance realized this Indian girl, this gentle woman, had kept it so through all these months in daily readiness for this homecoming hour. It pleased him that this leathern lodge in this faraway place among an almost unsurmountably alien people did indeed feel like home. He wanted time with this soft creature. He wanted it at once. But a messenger arrived upon their heels, summoning them to council. And unique in his experience thus far, they were advised supper would precede it.

"Big doings, then," Lane said. "A meeting of the Silent Eaters."

Easterbrook was not certain of the term. Beau explained as they washed and made ready.

The warrior societies were the elite in any Dakota band. Among the Hunkpapas the most coveted membership had always been in the Midnight Strong Hearts. They had initiated Sitting Bull before he was twenty.

Later he had served them as a sash-wearer for a long time.

Only two men could hold this office concurrently. The

sash was a strip of cloth worn off the shoulder so that it trailed the ground. In a fight these two chosen ones were sworn not to retreat. They were supposed to pin the end of the sash to the ground with a lance and remain in place until the battle was won. Around these islands of courage, others could reform. Like standard-bearers with the troop guidon.

It had been the Midnight Strong Hearts who had put the Bull up for head chief at the time of the Great Encampment. About twenty of them later formed a special and more elite club to watch over and talk about important tribal affairs. They were in dead earnest and banned the frivolities of other societies. No songs and no jokes at their supper meetings. In time Sitting Bull came to rely upon them as his cabinet.

"All old-timers, now," Beau said, "what's left of them. McLaughlin calls them the Bull's bodyguards. Shows how much he understands when it comes down to it. Mind your manners, Chance. That's who we'll be eating with tonight."

They went up along the creek bank with Shining Woman watching them from the door-flap of their tipi. A large skin lodge had been set up behind Sitting Bull's double cabin. It was so situated that from the dooryard the cabin and the camp were excluded. Nothing could be seen but the unmarked bench rising to the trackless expanse of the *coteau*. The old men were already gathered when Chance and Beau Lane arrived. They were seated without greeting in places reserved for them. Women commenced to serve with soundless efficiency.

Even among the Silent Eaters, the Sioux did not take

food without sound, purely out of common courtesy. How were cooks and hosts to know appreciation without a decent smacking of the lips and grunts of relish? But during this meal there was no talk. Only after the last of the food and the women were gone did old Catch The Bear speak.

"We have here now this man," he said, indicating Chance. "I tell you, Brothers, I think we made a mistake about him when he first came here. Later we sent him away a white man to do certain things for us. We hear now that he intends to do more things, make many words. Some of them are already on the way. We hear also that now he is home and speaks to us, many of his words will be in our tongue. I think he has come back a Sioux."

Chance knew how hard this was for this fierce, intransigent old man to say. He could say simply that he did not love the white man but what he meant was an unrelenting hatred as deeply rooted as his own soul. He could not forget, even for an instant, that Chance Easterbrook had a white skin. To find any friendliness in the face of this was an immense effort. Chance inclined his head.

"Uncle, you honor me," he said.

Beau handed him the laden blanket they had brought with them. He took the Bear's pipe from it and handed it to the old man.

"You wished us to smoke with this man we saw but that did not seem to be done in his country."

"They are not Indian there?" the Bear asked.

"They are Indian," Chance assured him. "This man came to us. We made a good talk. He seemed to speak straight. But we did not smoke."

"That is not the way," the Bear insisted. "I think this man has learned too many things from the white man."

"I think that may be a little true, Uncle," Chance agreed. "Some of the things we saw and heard I think he learned right out of the Black Robes' Medicine Book."

"That is the Christ?" Sitting Bull asked, speaking for the first time. "But you call him 'this man.' He is alive, then?"

"He is alive."

"He makes water and gets hungry and sleeps with a woman?"

"He is a man."

"But he has been dead?"

"It is believed so."

"That is foolishness," Sitting Bull said flatly. "A man that is dead cannot come alive again. And there would be wounds or some marks of sickness. Did you see them?"

"We were not permitted to look. But I think some others believed they did."

"It is foolishness," the chief repeated.

Chance looked at the solemn ring of faces. This was the report they had so long awaited. He thought of others he had seen, other councils he had attended. Other questions he had answered. A curious sense of deep responsibility pressed in on him.

"No, Father," he said quietly. "I think it is hope."

He reached into his pouched blanket and brought out the old-time bone vestlet which had been lent to him for his journey.

"I told this *Wanekia* how this old garment had made my road to see him safe," he said. "He did not think much of that. Just the same, he wanted it. He understands medicine very much. When I would not give it to him he said he would make me a shirt with stronger medicine."

Chance took out the crude, ochre-painted muslin shirt Wovoka had given him. Sitting Bull examined the garment.

"Trade cloth," he said disdainfully. "Very cheap at the Agency store. And a clumsy woman made it."

"This man said that *Wakan Tanka* made it."

The chief finger-traced the designs on the shoddy material.

"A child paints better than this in the mud."

"Just the same, he says it is a holy shirt."

Sitting Bull shrugged and tossed the shirt back. Chance brought out the boxes of magpie feathers and the cakes of pigment which Charley Sheep had given them.

"These are other holy things with this man. They are used in this Ghost Dance and the singing he teaches them there. He sends them to his friends—his children, he says—in the lodges of Sitting Bull's people."

The chief looked at the gifts a long time, turning them in his hands.

"We hoped for good news," he said. "I do not know what kind of news this is you bring. You said this thing this man has is hope. What kind of hope? To see the ghosts of our dead coming back? To see the buffalo again and the old earth we used to know? I do not see how that can be. But I am chief and it has been a long time now since my children have had any hope in anything. I do not see how all this will do anything for them, but we will try it. You will show us how to do this dance they make."

Chance shook his head.

"This man said the dance was an Indian affair. He would not show it to me because I was a white man. Kicking Bear and those other Sioux were there. He said they would come here soon and bring you the dance."

"Well," Sitting Bull said, "we can wait a little longer. You have come a long way. You have been a long time without a lodge of your own. We keep you from sleep."

Abruptly, the council was over. There was a bright moon outside. Beau pointed out that fresh horses were available. Fort Yates was but six or seven hours away. Chance probably had a wagonload of mail waiting at Standing Rock.

The Dakotan laughed, then, at his companion's stumbling reluctance. The mail could wait. He knew that. But he could not. Ration day was due at the agency. Tomorrow many wagons would be heading north. Chance could find a ride on any of them. But it had been too long since he had himself seen Nora Crandall. He called to an Indian acquaintance and moved off with him into the darkness.

Chance returned alone to their lodge. Shining Woman had made up a bed and was kneeling beside a low fire. Stiffly, careful of error, he told her he was glad to see her and was acutely conscious of what a masterpiece of understatement that was. She was delighted his speech had meaning in her ears. She asked him if he was hungry or wished to sleep. He shook his head. A delayed panic of shyness flared over realization they could now communicate so easily. Chance kissed her and this passed.

The words came after that in such a rush he could only follow by fragments and leaps of conjecture. She laughed when he put fingers to her lips to slow them. Later she touched his own face with her fingertips as the blind do that which they cherish or hold in wonder. She moved closer, with little flexings, like a warming kitten. He drew her down beside him.

X V I

Ration Day

Chance secured a place on Sitting Bull's wagon. The exodus from Grand River was general. Although the occasion was an often repeated one dictated by Bureau ration policy, there was an excited air of big doings and high expectation. Chance had the uncomfortable feeling he was a champion of sorts—that the Hunkpapas expected to see him in notable and victorious combat—although he could divine no cause for it.

The Bull's wagon was no more than some springy planks laid lengthwise across the racks of the running gear to serve as bed and body. Chance was offered the place of honor in front, at the chief's elbow. Catch The Bear, Crowfoot, the older son, and the elder of the Bull's two current wives rode behind.

There were a dozen other wagons strung out in casual cavalcade. Horsemen—men, boys, and some of the older girls, ranged back and forth along the file with considerable high spirit and dust. The flexible, unfastened planks of the wagon took up jolt better than patented springs could have done. However, the planks shifted at a sharp pothole and the edges of two, in a shearing action, bit Easterbrook savagely across the buttocks.

His roar of anguish and butt-clutching leap to the ground appeared to be the funniest things that had ever happened in the Dakotas. Sitting Bull pulled up and laughed without restraint. Catch The Bear lay upon his back on the planks, holding his belly and gasping for breath. The old woman shrilled delightedly. Crowfoot mimicked the hurt bellow and that sent them all off again. When they saw Chance was sore as hell, their delight grew. They halted passing riders and sent this great God-damned joke racing both ways along the string of wagons.

Chance went behind some brush and took down his pants. He found a welt across his beam but no real damage. The old woman took a roll of burlap from beneath her, peeled off a gunnysack, and stuffed it with grass. Chance gingerly mounted this cushion and found it welcome. The Bull drove on.

"Like that hurt you had just now, I seem to make white men angry when that is not in my heart," he said. "One time we had some High Hats here to see why we did not want to give them more land. They held a big council. They looked around. They said we were children, crying to the Grandfather because we would not look after ourselves.

"Well, I am known as a good talker in council. Because they called us children, I called my people children, too—my children. That was when the High Hats got angry. They said I was not chief. They said Red Cloud was chief. They said John Grass and Gall were chiefs because White Hair had made them so.

"I was a little angry, then, too. I made this signal. No word. Just this little signal with my hand. My children all stood up and walked out of the council. Those High Hats came a long way to speak hard to a man who was nothing."

The Bull smiled.

"So you see I am father to everyone here. Some time ago, when it was decided you would go to see the *Wanekia,* Beau Lane came to me. He said you were a long way from your country. He said those were long nights with you, among strangers. I know how that can be.

"Before this, one of my cousins had trouble in his lodge. He had an old wife who had sickness in her joints so she could not do much work. At this same time there was a woman in another lodge whose husband had been dead many years and she had lately married another man. The trouble there was this man wanted her daughter, also, and a woman does not like to sleep in the same bed as her daughter. Because I was chief I had to help all those people.

"I had my cousin marry this other woman's daughter, so there would be no more trouble with the woman's husband. The new wife helped the old wife and my cousin was kind to them both. That was all good until the grippe came very soon after. The old wife and my cousin died. The young wife was alone and her mother's husband was after her again. But she would have no man.

"Soon you rode into our camp with Beau Lane and those Metal Breasts shooting at you. Big doings. Like old times. This young woman saw you. She forgot your skin was white. They say it could be seen in the way she looked at you when you did not even see her. Naturally, I knew about this, too. That is a chief's affair. So when Beau Lane came to me about it, I sent this Shining Woman to you. See how it is? Even you are now one of my children."

Chance was astonished at the complexity of the intrigue but he contained himself.

"Father, I am grateful."

"Yes. Of course I am not always so lucky in these things. You know the one we call Woman Walking Ahead?"

Chance had not heard this Sioux appellation before, but in a nation where a woman's place was a good dozen paces or so behind, it was not hard to guess to whom it was applied.

"Mrs. Weldon?"

"I do not understand that one," Sitting Bull said. "She has a good heart. She sent me letters and a little money. She came to Standing Rock. She could write letters with my own words in them, which is very hard for me to have done. She said she wished to come live in my house."

The chief paused and looked wryly over his shoulder

at the old woman on the planks behind them.

"That gave me some trouble. She took the other room in my cabin which is not the room where I sleep. She painted that picture of me you saw. She gave me this—"

He fumbled out a heavy chain with a little golden bull on the end of it.

"She cooked a little and washed sometimes and made things clean. She read from some books about old time white chiefs. I was surprised to hear there were some pretty big wars in which white men killed each other, just like it used to be with us. I think that was before the white man came here and found the Indian to fight.

"Well, White Hair said she was making a wild Indian out of me again. He said some more lies about her and sent her away. I came and took her across the river. I think you were here then."

"I got into Fort Yates the night before she left."

"Yes. Well, while you and Beau Lane were gone, she came back. She said she did not care what White Hair said or did. He was my enemy. She would protect me. I had no other friends. Her place was here with me. Those were kind words. After a while I thought about her lying in there in that other room without kind words from me. I went in there and turned back the blanket. That was a mistake."

"I imagine," Chance agreed.

"It was a very noisy talk they had in there," Catch The Bear said with enjoyment. "We could hear some of it very plain in that other room."

"I do not know about that woman," Sitting Bull continued in honest perplexity. "She has a young boy with her now, her son, so she has known a man before. I do not think it was that. I think it was that I am Indian. I think she did not want dirt between her legs."

Chance saw the dark glint in the chief's eyes.

"I do not know," the Bull repeated. "White Hair came and made her leave the reservation again. Now she stays on another woman's ranch up there across the Cannonball where he can do nothing about it. And she writes letters about all she is trying to do for me in Washington. No good has come of that. Maybe White Hair is right. Maybe what she does is a bad thing."

The old man shook his head and they drove on in silence.

McLaughlin was not at Standing Rock when the Grand River cavalcade arrived. He had left with his wife earlier in the day. Personal business at Mandan, it was said. On his orders, the ration issue was postponed until his return. It was not known when that would be. The Indians did not care for this but they had no choice. Sitting Bull's party went grumbling down toward the river where some friends were already encamped.

Easterbrook tried to locate Beau and Nora Crandall. The school and the quarters behind it were both locked. No one seemed to know where they were. He crossed over from the Agency to Fort Yates. Colonel Drum had a thin packet of mail which McLaughlin had left in his care. It contained two vouchers from the *Herald*, so at least the beginning was recorded.

Colonel Drum seemed to have no interest in Easterbrook's activities or whereabouts in recent months but was cordial enough to offer quarters, a bath, and the pick of his own locker for a change of wardrobe. Chance accepted. Later he was amused that while he was still in his bath the post barber arrived. He suspected this afterthought did not so much reflect hospitality as the sorry state of his appearance on arrival.

Sitting upright in a straight chair, he luxuriated in a shave but on whim altered the barber's intention with his hair. He asked for a trim, only, leaving it long as it had grown during the nearly a year since his arrival in the Dakotas. Dressing for supper, he saved Drum's pressed uniform blouse for a later occasion and put Shining Woman's buckskin shirt back on. Wearing it, the hair did not seem such a folly. The colonel made only one comment when he came to table.

"Who do you think you are, Buffalo Bill?"

Later they had brandy in Drum's quarters. As a result, Chance awoke considerably after mess-call in the morning with a dry mouth and somewhat of a head. By the time he had washed and dressed, only one officer and two civilians remained at table. Chance gathered from self-introductions that the officer was a Captain Fechet, a company commander in Drum's skeletal garrison. The younger civilian was Jack Carignan, teacher at a government school somewhere down near Grand River. The elder was a Reverend Riggs who had something to do with a Protestant mission in the same general vicinity. Like the Indians, they had come in for the excitement of issue day and they also grumbled at the delay caused by McLaughlin's absence. Chance was grateful when they finally went away and left him with his coffee.

In time he finally forced himself to step outside. At this still early hour the sky was a hard blue bowl arched in concentrating reflection over a brassy and merciless sun. Even shadows were poor shelter.

No Indians were about but he could see a small camp of visitors at the base of Proposal Hill. They had loosened the skirts of their lodge covers and rolled them up the poles a distance of three or four feet, leaving ample space for any moving air to pass through. The occupants of the dim interiors looked comfortable in spite of the lethal heat.

Chance thought that these primitive shelters, so often scornfully used as symbols of the unreconstructed aborigine, were in fact the most highly developed living quarters—in terms of efficiency and adaptation to the rigors of the Dakota climate—as the region would see for a long time. No military clapboard or settlers' soddy could approach them for comfort, sanitation, and ease of maintenance.

Jack Carignan and the Reverend Riggs were lounging on the veranda of the Agency residence, making themselves comfortable in the absence of the McLaughlins. They beckoned him over.

"Too damned hot for a white man," Carignan said.

This seemed to cover the weather and talk lagged. Directly there was a stir in the compound. Indians began moving in from all quarters. They were unhurried, gathering by little groups, but steadily filled the area before the Agency warehouse. Sitting Bull's party arrived. As befitted their rank, they took a place before the locked warehouse doors. A Metal Breast trotted hastily across to Fort Yates. He returned in a very few minutes, running at Colonel Drum's stirrup. Lieutenant Bull Head came out of the Agency office to meet the officer.

"What is it?" Drum demanded. "What do they want?"

"Their rations," Bull Head told him.

"No issue till Major McLaughlin returns. They know that." Drum raised his voice to the crowd. "Go back to your camps. I don't know when the agent will be back. Maybe tomorrow. We'll shoot the big gun at the fort when he's ready to open the doors."

Sitting Bull came through the crowd, a respectful lane opening for him to the head of the colonel's horse.

"You do not understand," he said pleasantly. "Some of the people were saying it is no good to wait like this. Some of them were saying we are not dogs to stand around, scratching our fleas, until White Hair throws us some scraps. They were saying that all those things there in the warehouse are Indian, bought for Indians with Indian money. We are here. White Hair is not. Some of these people were saying the thing to do is break down those doors and take those Indian things which belong to us and go home. Maybe if we do this White Hair will stay home next time and not make us wait."

Lieutenant Bull Head started to translate but Sitting Bull stopped him, indicating there was more.

"This is bad talk, of course," the chief continued. "But it might have come to something except for a man in our camp who said he had a sign. He said that when the sun got as high as it now is, we should all come over here. He said that at this time White Hair would come back.

Today. Not tomorrow or some other time. This is a very wise man. He has good signs. That is why we are here."

Drum impatiently heard out the translation.

"Sign!" he snorted. "Poppycock! Who is this man?"

Sitting Bull soberly touched his own chest.

"Me. I saw the sign. And it saved some bad trouble, I think."

Drum darkened with exasperation but before he could explode, a fresh stir ran through the Indians. Trailing a plume of dust in from the north, a light wagon was rolling down the hill behind the warehouse. James McLaughlin was driving. His wife was beside him on the seat.

Easterbrook had never witnessed a ration issue before. It was a good deal more orderly than he had expected. It was, in fact, a good deal more orderly than made sense. Names were called off in alphabetical progression. The Metal Breasts who were reading off and checking the rolls and McLaughlin and everyone else on the official side of the long, trestled table before the warehouse knew what the proper order should be—what it had always been.

When a camp was set up, each lodge had its place. It did not change. When many bands camped together, the same order held. Divisions and tribes and nations the same. When men spoke in council, all knew who was first and who followed. In accord with ancient custom, they were lined up now by bands and head men and families as was natural to them. But they were being called up Bear before Bull and Running before Sitting.

Each call was an affront to the man whose rightful place it was. That was White Hair's way.

Chance walked down closer with Jack Carignan and Reverend Riggs. He saw the portions parcelled out were affronts, too. Catch The Bear came when summoned, leaving his uncalled chief's side with dark displeasure. They put down a green-mottled side of bacon and with a cleaver struck off a three-inch strip weighing a pound or so. There was no lean exposed in the cut and the gray-white fat sweated noisomely in the sun.

They took a grocer's scoop and poured perhaps two pounds of gravelly beans into a little mound beside the bacon. To this was added a paper sack containing half a peck of flour and another a third filled with unground coffee. Lists were consulted and the Bear was informed he had overdrawn at previous issues on sugar, salt, and baking powder and so was entitled to none. Also, as was well known, the beef allowance had all been slaughtered some time ago, so none was available. And there was no soap.

The Bear took an old, greasy flour sack from beneath his summer blanket and scooped his rations into it. He put the sack back on the table and made it known he wished to trade with White Hair. McLaughlin was summoned from within the warehouse. Catch The Bear indicated the sack.

The Government said its contents were enough to keep a man and his family from going hungry for fifteen days. If this was so, they must be very valuable, worth much money. But the Bear was not hungry for that food today. It did not suit his belly. He had once been a good hunter. That was the food his belly craved. Game would make his children strong again. He would trade White Hair all this for ten cartridges to fit his rifle. He drew his massive, brass-framed old Winchester from beneath his blanket.

"You know the rule," McLaughlin said angrily. "No hunting on this reservation. You know you're not supposed to bring guns in here on ration day, too. Show up with that rifle again and I'll have it broken over a wagon wheel. Move along and let the next man have his turn."

The agent thrust the sack back to the old Indian. The Bear took it. He walked a few paces away from the table. Here he threw the sack to the ground, exposed himself, urinated upon it, and walked away. With scant control, McLaughlin turned back into the warehouse.

The dispensing of Government bounty continued. The man who should have been the first called was the last summoned. When he heard Sitting Bull's name, McLaughlin reappeared.

"When is your obstinacy going to stop?" he demanded of the Bull. "Do you know what the penalty is for cheating the government?"

The chief said nothing. McLaughlin kept his voice high so it would carry to all.

"Every issue you claim a ration for a boy named Crowfoot."

"Yes," the Bull agreed. "He stands right there. He is my son."

"I know that," McLaughlin snapped. "I also know he is supposed to be in school. He's supposed to be in Mr. Carignan's school near you there on Grand River."

"I do not like the government school. That is something you know. For some time now my son goes to that man's holy school on Oak Creek."

The chief pointed to Reverend Riggs.

"The Congregational School is twelve miles from your camp," McLaughlin said. "Ours is only three. What kind of foolishness is that?"

"It pleases me," the Indian said.

"It doesn't me. I want him in the government school."

"He is not your son, White Hair."

"I won't argue with you. There'll be no ration for him as long as the Reverend Riggs is feeding and housing him."

Jack Carignan stirred beside Chance.

"I wish Jim wouldn't bear down so hard," he said.

Reverend Riggs nodded. "He ought to know by now that Sitting Bull is the last one of them that it'll work on."

The chief shrugged at the agent's ultimatum.

"He will eat, White Hair. He will live."

The Bull turned from the table, starting to walk proudly away, empty-handed.

"Wait a minute!" McLaughlin ordered. "I want all these people to hear this, too. They tell me you claim you had a sign I would be back here this morning. I'm sick of your signs and revelations and prophecies. I'm tired of you continually hoodwinking your own people. What really happened is that my wife and I didn't get to Mandan as we intended. We stopped last night at Cannonball school. Mrs. McLaughlin didn't feel well this morning, so we turned back from there. One of your friends saw us turning around and brought you word. That's what your sign amounts to."

"No one visited my camp this morning, White Hair," the Bull said quietly. "Many of your own people were there and can tell you this was not so."

McLaughlin ignored him.

"You keep putting on airs but you're no different from any other Indian. I want these people to understand that, once and for all. They say you predicted months ago that we would have a dry summer this year, no rain for a long time. What kind of a prediction is that? Any child knows that when we have a dry winter here, we're bound to have summer drought. Anybody with an ounce of sense knows there'll be no rain now until late fall."

Sitting Bull looked a long time at the agent and at Colonel Drum. The chief smiled and with great dignity walked out to an open space in the center of the compound. He sat down in the dust there, cross-legged, and began to sing quietly to himself. The Indians in the yard also sat down where they were, silent and expectant.

McLaughlin wiped his perspiring face with a bandanna. He signalled Drum and they retired into the warehouse. After a little the ration clerk and guarding policemen also sought the cooler air of the big shed. The chief continued to sing.

In this brilliant, brassy flood of midday sun with the ugly, prosaic background of the Agency buildings, something eerie settled over Standing Rock, as though the little stone woman and her puppy on Proposal Hill had come alive. Presently, Easterbrook saw something he did not believe.

Because they remained in the warehouse and the Indians in the yard made no sound which might have warned them, the agent and the commandant and the others in the big shed did not see the fleece of cloud arise over the northwestern horizon. They did not see the tall, beautiful thunderhead that built above it and marched swiftly down across the *coteau.*

Their first warning was the hard rattle of great drops of rain on the tin roof. They hurried out in consternation to help clerks and policemen hustle records and remnants of supplies to shelter.

It had taken two minutes short of half an hour. Out in the center of the compound, Chief Sitting Bull turned his wetted face to the sky and ended his song.

XVII

Beau's Wife

Grubsacks scantily filled, the Hunkpapa chief and his people went back to Grand River. Beau and Nora Crandall remained absent. Easterbrook worked up material he had gathered since Pine Ridge. An hour after he surrendered a mailing to federal care at the Agency postoffice, Bull Head came and summoned him to McLaughlin. The mailing lay slitted open on the agent's desk.

"Should have mentioned it before, Easterbrook," McLaughlin said. "Easier for all concerned if you'd clear these things with me, first."

"Afraid I'll have to protest your right to censorship, Major."

"Isn't a question of censorship or right, either one," the agent said. "What counts is that you've gotten the confidence of some of my troublemakers. With so much afoot, I have to take advantage of every source of information I can. If we can forget a bad beginning, I can do with your help."

"Might try asking me, next time," Chance suggested. He indicated the envelope. "As you've read there, nothing really is afoot. Some of them are excited over this messiah thing, but most of them aren't sure. They're waiting for the delegations from the other agencies to get back."

"They are back, Easterbrook. A note from Gallagher. Bands have started coming in. Rumors are flying. Gallagher, the damned fool, spooked. He had Kicking Bear and a couple of others tossed in the guardhouse. That did it just dandy. Bars will shut an Indian up quicker than a bullet. He couldn't get a word out of them, even when he let his police tie them up with wet rawhide and poke for the truth with sharp sticks."

"Little hard under those circumstances to tell which is the civilized nation isn't it, Major?"

"Hell with the means," the agent growled. "Ends justify the means out here. It's no debating society, but Gallagher's tactic was wrong. Left alone, those runaways would have told their story. Then the dependable progressives would have gone to work on it. Red Cloud, for instance. He's too jealous of his own position to let a heresy like this take hold. There are others with influence, too, ready to convince the rank and file there's nothing to this new religion or whatever you want to call it."

"You're sure there isn't anything to it?"

"Positive. Not a shred. Known that all along."

McLaughlin took a dog-eared envelope from a compartment in his desk. It bore a Walker Lake Agency postmark and was simply addressed to Sitting Bull at Fort Yates.

"Came late last August or early September. About the time you first showed up here. Apparently part of a broadside that Paiute sent out to all the tribes he knew of. Couple of other copies have been reported, at least. Naturally, I held this up, kept the news from our people. But that's how long I've known what was going on out there in Nevada. Take a look. You can see for yourself what it amounts to."

Chance drew the single sheet of paper from the envelope. It lacked heading, date, or signature. The message was traced in a schoolboy's painstakingly large, uncertain hand. Obscured by pidgin and spelling peculiarities, it was an attempt at a statement of Wovoka's preachments and vague instructions for the dance he urged all Indians to practice. A pitifully garbled, meaningless thing which Chance could not relate to the earnest, articulate Paiute to whom he had talked at Pine Grove. There was a good deal of malicious self-satisfaction in McLaughlin's smile as he put the letter down.

"Could have saved you a mighty long ride if you'd come to me before you and Beau Lane ducked out of Sitting Bull's camp on that wild goose chase of yours."

"Wild goose chase, Major?"

"Exactly. The Sioux aren't stupid. They won't take a thing like that seriously."

"I'm not too sure," Chance said. "They may when they get the dance. Some of the more superstitious and religious, anyway. And the dance will come here, that's certain. What do you intend to do, then?"

"That, Easterbrook, depends entirely upon your friend, Sitting Bull."

"Why him in particular?"

"Look, I won't admit this officially. It's against my policy and has been from the beginning to give him credit for anything he claims. But Sitting Bull was the high priest of them all in the old days and still is to a lot of them. They'll watch him. If he doesn't take this thing up—this dance—it will fall to the ground, as they say. It'll die of itself. No official action, no public notice will be necessary. And that's the way I want it. I want you to tell him when you get the chance. I want you to make him understand."

"What if he does take it up or allows others to?"

"I can't afford to let that happen, Easterbrook. And I won't. For one very good reason." He tapped the envelope between them. "You've got it here. Settlers. We're surrounded by them. The fact that our people here are quieter and better ordered than they have ever been doesn't mean a damned thing. Neither does the religious idea behind this whole affair.

"I tell you straight, Mister, if word ever gets around that the old Bull has got the Sioux dancing, the fat will be in the fire. It wouldn't make any difference if Jesus

Christ, Himself, was down there at Grand River. Public opinion would force the War Department to order in troops. And if troops ever come onto any of these reservations in force, that will be the end, right now. That's what I intend to keep from happening."

The agent brought a lockbox from a desk drawer.

"I noted you had some vouchers in your mail," he said. "Thought you might be getting short of cash. I keep a fairly good-sized emergency fund on hand these days."

There was ample currency in the box to cash the vouchers in Easterbrook's pocket but McLaughlin withheld two hundred dollars.

"Advanced it to Beau Lane," he said. "Both Beau and Miss Crandall thought you wouldn't mind under the circumstances."

"Long overdue," Chance agreed. "But where is Beau? No one seems to know."

"I don't believe it was meant to be any secret. They went down-river to Pierre to get married."

Three nights later Lane was waiting in after-supper darkness when Chance came down the steps of the Fort Yates mess-hall. He wore a white shirt and a new pair of pants.

"Suppose you heard," he said.

"Congratulations in order?"

Beau did not answer that.

"Nora wants to see you."

The Dakotan's voice was troubled but Chance knew him too well to force a question. They walked across in

155

silence to the lean-to quarters back of the school. Beau let them into a cramped kitchen. Chance followed him into a sort of sitting room. Nora Crandall was in a rocker. She looked up resentfully, her hands folded over the bloat of an advanced pregnancy.

"You can go, Beau," she said. "I want to talk to him alone."

Lane glanced apologetically at Chance and went back outside, closing the door behind him. There was a straight chair by the window but Nora did not ask Chance to take it so he remained standing.

"Beau is taking this hard," the teacher said in a carefully controlled voice. "He keeps insisting he owes an obligation to you, Mr. Easterbrook. To them. I promised I'd try to make you understand."

She nervously smoothed the front of her ill-fitting dress.

"I am a proper person. Have been all of my life. These have been hard months for me. Hard to talk about, even now. But you should know. It happened at Grand River. I tried to explain to you there but you wouldn't listen. The dark side of Beau's nature, pulling him away from himself, away from me. He goes back to them, back to the blanket. It always happens when he's around them.

"No matter what he's gone through, how hard he's tried to make something of himself, he gets into their quarrels, their petty complaining, and winds up taking their part, however wrong or illogical it may be. Before long he starts thinking like them—even acting as they do. Major Mac has had the patience of Job with him, but he won't forever. He can't.

"That isn't the man I fell in love with, Mr. Easterbrook. That isn't the man he really is, that he's got to be. But Beau can't do it alone. He needs help, all the help he can get. That night down there at Grand River I thought I could give him something else to work for, something to help him fight off the dark blood. So we lay in the grass because we didn't even have a bed.

"He loved me, then, he said. He meant it, then, too. But two or three days later he was Indian again and off to Nevada with you with not even a word. Well, I've paid for that, now. And this time I'm entitled to my way. He has made his choice. Pay him what you owe him and let us get out of here before it's too late."

"Believe me, Nora, I knew nothing of this," Chance said. "I know how you must feel. But aren't you making a mistake with Beau?"

"No. I've already made my mistake with Beau. I'm not going to make another."

Determination was a hard core in her voice. Chance realized that as the Sioux said, there were no more words. He turned to the door, but she stopped him and said: "One other thing, Mr. Easterbrook. What makes it hard for Beau is that he respects you. Well, I do not. I kept telling Beau that night that you'd be sure to know what was going on, sitting alone in that tipi. He just laughed, then, and said he didn't think so. Now I've made him tell me why. While we were lying out there in the grass, you had an Indian woman."

Chance said nothing. Nora's voice rose beyond her effort at control.

"An Indian! And don't think I don't know what you're

thinking. But at least Beau is half-white!"

The revulsion was startlingly violent. There was so much Chance could have said, but he said nothing. He pulled open the door and stumbled through the weeds of the yard. Lane was leaning against the schoolyard gate.

"I talk too much," he said.

"Forget it," Chance told him. "She'll get over it."

"I don't know. It's been a long wait for her. Got to blaming herself pretty hard, I think. Just thought it might make her feel a little better to know we weren't the only ones that night. If I go her way a while, will you stay, Chance?"

"Long as there's anything I can do. But I'm afraid it won't be much without you."

"I owe it, Chance. Something I've got to do."

"I know that," Easterbrook said shortly. "Come on over to the barracks and we'll settle up."

They crossed to the post in silence. Beau waited on the barracks stoop until Chance returned with the money. He was uncomfortable and ill at ease, and he wanted to settle for a round sum at his disadvantage instead of working out a proper accounting of time and suitable credit for the horses and outfit he had abandoned to the Paiutes in their extremity. When Easterbrook insisted, the Dakotan waited restlessly through the calculations. He signed a receipt but seemed to have no real interest in the substantial sum Chance handed over.

"One thing bothers me more than anything else," Lane said. "Marie keeps telling me a woman can get pretty unreasonable at a time like this—"

"Marie?"

"McLaughlin. She and Major Mac sort of saw to Nora while we were gone. When they heard we were on our way back, they made plans. A big wedding over to the Agency house on ration day, so there'd be plenty of people and a kind of celebration, Reverend Riggs to say the proper words, and the major even rigged up some Bureau business for me at Pine Ridge so's we could go down there at no cost. There's a good dispensary at Pine Ridge and a new young doctor that's just come in. He's got a name like yours. Eastman, I think the major said.

"But what happened? Nora wouldn't have an agency wedding. She wouldn't go to any agency doctor. Insisted we go down to the capitol at Pierre to do it. So we did."

"First law with a woman's to please her, Beau."

"Sure. But did you ever see that town, Chance— Pierre? The judge that married us was drunk and tried to pat her belly. The doctor they sent us to stank and charged me thirty dollars. Now she says she's going back there to wait out her time."

"Then do it."

"You don't see what I mean," the Dakotan persisted. "That new doctor at Pine Ridge is Indian. First we've gotten out here, far's I know. Marie McLaughlin's Indian, too, Chance. A Santee. The ration-day crowd that was supposed to come to the wedding would have been mostly Indian. And look how she's taken on about you and Shining Woman—"

Beau shook his head with a deep and puzzled sadness in his eyes.

"She's a good teacher, Chance. Best he's ever had out

here, Major Mac says. The kids like her, even the big ones. So do their people. Bring some of them in from as much as twenty miles out. She takes good care of them, cleans them up if they need it, teaches them games, and they really learn. She sews for them and washes for them, holds parties and feeds them and wipes their runny noses. How can she do all that and hate them so much?"

XVIII
Roll Call

Easterbrook did not see Lane again before the Dakotan and his wife flagged a down-river steamer. No word came from Grand River. Easterbrook remained at Fort Yates. He did not believe that without Beau's good offices he should try to impose further on Hunkpapa hospitality until so invited. He worked desultorily on a couple of further articles and was displeased that the air of suspended animation which had settled over Standing Rock seemed to have permeated his reports so that they were straw and cotton where he intended meat and sinew. However, McLaughlin passed them without comment and he sent them off.

In August Nora Lane was delivered of a son in Pierre. The child did not live long enough for the mother to see her flesh. As fall drew on, Beau brought her back to Standing Rock. There was, as he said, nowhere else for them to go. The curiously impersonal grief of her loss lingered with Nora but she also seemed to have lost much of her bitterness. She began preparing for resumption of the Agency school. Jim McLaughlin put Lane on Bureau payroll and set him at a series of odd jobs about the compound. Nora showed no hostility toward Easterbrook nor did she make an apparent effort to keep Beau apart from him. Still, when they encountered each other from time to time, the Dakotan seemed to have no words and Chance himself could find none.

Rumors came with every wind. They heard Kicking Bear was at last back and had been busy. The ghosts were dancing on the southern reservations. Each circle was larger and more ardent than the last. Agent Gallagher was replaced by a man named Royer. He made new laws and the dancers defied him. They moved their dance grounds to more secluded places.

At Grand River Sitting Bull waited for the dance. His people waited with him, secure in his wisdom. White Hair McLaughlin waited with equal patience at Standing Rock, recruiting more of the restless young men to the badge and uniform of his Metal Breasts.

Early in October they heard Kicking Bear had finally arrived at the Bull's camp. McLaughlin sent for Easterbrook at once.

"You'll be going down there, I suppose?" he asked.

Lane and Lieutenant Bull Head were putting up some shelving in the office. Chance looked at the Dakotan but his eyes were avoided.

"If they'll have me," he agreed. "It's what I've been waiting for."

"You remember my orders to the Bull? Well, they still stand. No dancing. I want you to see just how far I intend to go to enforce them, Easterbrook." The agent turned to Lieutenant Bull Head. "Round up all the boys that are in and bring them here."

Bull Head saluted and left Lane to continue with the shelves alone. McLaughlin leaned back in his chair. He looked tired but his leonine, white-crowned head and hard-cut jaw made a powerful silhouette against the brilliant external light. The summoned Metal Breasts began filing in. Sitting Bull's nephew One Bull, the post freighter, was among them. He wore the postal badge to which he was entitled because he also carried the mail. There were nearly two dozen in all.

"You all know that Minneconjou troublemaker, Kicking Bear," McLaughlin said to them. "You know the uproar he and some others have caused down at Pine Ridge and Cheyenne River with this dance they brought home. You also probably know he's now at Grand River with the same mischief.

"You know me as a fair man, too. I'm going to give Kicking Bear a fair warning. But if he doesn't have sense enough to take it, I want you to show Mr. Easterbrook how many men I have to run those Minneconjous off my reservation."

Every man raised his hand without hesitation. The agent smiled his satisfaction.

"Tell the old man, Easterbrook. If that doesn't convince him, maybe this will—"

He swung back to the Metal Breasts.

"You all know how it is with Sitting Bull and me, but he is one of my Indians and I have to protect him. If he keeps on stirring up trouble and bad blood, somebody is going to get tired of it and kill him. You all know that, too. If he keeps on disobeying orders and exciting the people, I'm going to have to bring him in here for his own good, where he can be watched and protected. If he forces me to that, how many of you men do I have to do it?"

This time the question hung heavily in the air. Finally One Bull, the freighter, spoke.

"Father, you need no men. When you wish my uncle here, send him word. He will come in his own wagon."

"You wouldn't go after him?"

"Father, he is chief."

McLaughlin looked hard at the Indian. "You're through, One Bull," he said. "Turn in your badge."

The Bull's nephew jerked his postal badge free with a rending of material, flung it down, and shouldered a passage to the door. McLaughlin repeated his question.

"How many men?"

A Metal Breast pushed resolutely up to the desk.

"White Hair, hear Standing Soldier," he said, "You have been here a long time now. You know us well. We cut our hair short for you. We wear these clothes and carry these guns. Because of us you do not need many soldiers here. We do many things. We are brave men. But no man can arrest Sitting Bull."

McLaughlin remained unruffled. "Turn it in," he ordered.

The Indian regretfully unpinned his badge and dropped it to the desk. Another man took his place. Chance saw that Beau Lane had given up any pretense of continuing with his chore and was watching the agent with open enjoyment.

"Now hear Grasping Eagle," the man at the desk said. "Why do you make this talk of arresting Sitting Bull? What has he done? He does not love you but he does no one harm. He is an old man. That place out there is his home. He was born on Grand River. He does not belong here."

The speaker looked appealingly at the agent but saw he would have no answer. Jaw hardening, he put down his badge and walked out.

"Any more?"

Another started forward. Bull Head moved to check him but an older man in captain's uniform dissuaded the lieutenant with a sharp look.

"Hear Big Mane, White Hair," the man said harshly as he reached the desk. "As my brothers have said, you know us well. It is true Sitting Bull has some enemies. Such things happen to a chief. But he also has friends. Many of us with badges are Yanktonais and Blackfeet, not Hunkpapas. You know those friends of Sitting Bull would not let us take a Hunkpapa chief out of his own camp."

Without waiting for reply, the Indian rang down his badge and left. Another who was not in uniform pulled his badge from his pocket and flung it on the desk.

"We are used to hearing foolish words from white men. But not from you. What crazy thing is this? Some of us have relations down there. Are we going to start a fight and spill blood in our own lodges? Some of us have families. Women and children to feed and care for, and some of us would be killed if we tried to do this foolish thing. Who would keep food in our lodges, then? The Government? It does not even do that when we are alive!"

The speaker wheeled and went out with a fine, long stride, slamming the door behind him. The man in the captain's uniform stepped forward. Astonishment showed on faces behind him. For the first time, McLaughlin stiffened.

"Don't be a fool, Captain!" he warned.

"Not Captain," the Indian said. "Not any more. I have heard a bad thing today. I take back my own name. Now I am Crazy Walking again, an Indian. I do not wish to be a Metal Breast and do harm to my own people."

McLaughlin would have protested but the Indian turned his back and left. The agent studied those who remained. There seemed to be no other disaffection. He swung around to face Chance.

"That last one hurt. The rest of you, dismissed! But six out of forty, Easterbrook—maybe two or three others when word gets around or some of their friends start working on them—mostly ones I've never been able to depend upon, anyway—that's the Bull's influence, measured exactly. That's his strength here—anywhere else on these reservations. That's exactly how much he represents, the Sioux nation, whatever you've seen fit to write on the subject."

"You'd actually arrest him?"

"Mr. Easterbrook, I'd hang him to the nearest tree before I'd let him stir my people up to the pitch they're at on the southern reservations right now," McLaughlin said harshly. "You tell him that and make him believe it!"

The agent rose and crossed to Lieutenant Bull Head, who had remained near the door.

"I don't know yet what has to be done, but I had to know they would do it," he continued. "Now I have some good words for them. Tell them we will not talk any more of Sitting Bull. Tell them I do not think there will be any need. I do not think there will be any trouble, any fighting. But if they worry about that, tell them that from today on the Government will pay a good pension to the family of any man who dies in that uniform they wear. That goes for new recruits, too, and we'll need some. Good ones, Bull Head. The best you can find."

Bull Head showed his teeth.

"I know the men."

McLaughlin returned to his desk. Chance scowled at him. The man's psychology was simple and flawless. His policemen would stick with him now, even against older loyalties. Promise of a pension insured that. Security for their families. For this they would cease to be men of honor if necessary. For this they would serve an alien race against their own. Chance rose with no liking for the man.

"Major," he said quietly, "you are a son of a bitch!"

"I can be," the agent agreed.

Lane moved to the desk.

"Turning in my badge, too," he said. "I'm going back with Chance."

"You'll catch hell from Nora," McLaughlin warned.

The Dakotan shrugged.

"Bound to, sooner or later."

He walked out into the sun with Easterbrook. They

crossed together to the quarters behind the school. Nora listened quietly while Beau told her of the coming of the ghosts to Grand River and McLaughlin's reaction to the news. To their surprise, she made no protest when Beau told her of his own decision.

"Trouble is coming—you're both sure?"

"If something isn't done," Beau agreed.

"And you think you can do it—just the two of you?"

"We can help. At least we can try. We have to, Nora."

"Yes, I suppose. I suppose you do, Beau. But you're not going alone and we're not staying with them in the camp. Jack Carignan will put us up at his school. He has plenty of room. How long shall I pack for?"

"A few weeks, to be on the safe side."

X I X

The Ghosts Dance

Grand River was in a foment of preparation and anticipation when Easterbrook and the Lanes rode in on One Bull's freight wagon. God had come to the Hunkpapas in the guise of Kicking Bear. A fierce God, a jealous God, an angry God. A *Yaweh* of the most ancient testaments, rolling back the sea, splitting the rock, fire by night and smoke by day, the Rod and the Staff upraised against the Philistines, invoking the firmaments with great thunders and a shaking of the earth.

Sitting Bull himself seemed gripped by the fervor of the Minneconjou apostle and the half-dozen assistants he had brought with him. The chief was in no mood to

accord McLaughlin's ultimatum the serious consideration both Easterbrook and Lane believed it deserved.

"White Hair likes to make big talk," he said. "That is
all this is. Tomorrow we make the dance here for the
first time. I think it is too bad he will not be here to see
it."

Beau and Nora rode with One Bull on down to
Carignan's school. Chance returned to the familiar
lodge. Even Shining Woman was under the Minneconjou spell. She would not sleep with him on the eve
of such a holy event as the coming of the ghosts.

In the morning, criers went through the camp at an
early hour. Everyone assembled but only about forty
actual participants had summoned courage to try this
new thing this first time. Kicking Bear and his assistants
were wearing muslin shirts similar to the one Wovoka
had given Easterbrook. However, the painted designs
were more intricate and imaginative.

They came out before the assemblage and faced west,
toward the *Wanekia*. Hands upraised, they began to
sing. It was a song no Hunkpapa had ever heard before,
with a thin, wailing melody of great sadness.

"The Father says so—*E'yayo!*
The Father says so—*E'yayo!*
You shall see your Grandfather—*E'yayo!*
You shall see your Grandfather—*E'yayo!*
The Father says so,
The Father says so.
You shall see your kindred—*E'yayo!*
You shall see your kindred—*E'yayo!*

The Father says so,
The Father says so."

Kicking Bear explained to all that this was the opening song and first prayer of the dance. Then he sang alone another song with different words and a stronger, happier melody.

"My son, let me grasp your hand,
My son, let me grasp your hand,
Says the Father, says the Father.
You shall live,
You shall live,
Says the Father, says the Father.
I bring you a pipe,
I bring you a pipe,
Says the Father, says the Father.
By means of it you shall live,
By means of it you shall live,
Says the Father, says the Father."

"You shall live"—good words! And the pipe—surely the ancient Sacred Pipe of the Sioux was meant. The Pipe given to the Dakotas that long ago time they were also given seeds of maize in colors of white and red and yellow and blue and the good green leaf of corn. Clearly it meant a sacred thing. This sacred thing. This dance. *"By means of it you shall live."* It was a good promise. It was a good song.

Kicking Bear stood rigidly, head back, eyes closed. Suddenly he fell to the ground like a man killed. His companions would let no one near him. After a time he stirred and rose again to his feet.

"I have been to see God," he thundered. "He is glad to see his children here. He gives me a sign. See this! My left hand is stronger than that of any man in the world."

At the urging of the other Minneconjous an unusually large and powerful Hunkpapa stepped forward and touched the smaller man's hand. At the moment of contact he leaped back in dismay. Those closest said he had felt fire and the force of a great blow. The priest bent and snatched something from the ground. He held it high above his head and convulsively compressed his fist. When he opened his fingers, shards fell at his feet. Some said he had crushed a stone with his bare hand. Others said it was but a lump of clay.

Kicking Bear called for those who believed. They went with him to where sweat lodges had been prepared, stones already heating in the fires and water at each door. They stripped and went within to sweat all evil from their bodies while they sang it from their hearts as they huddled over steaming rocks. They washed away the tainted residue by plunging into the river. They dried with sweet-grass and dressed and painted their faces, mostly red. That was the color of happiness and it was that for which they would pray.

The dance ground was smaller than that Easterbrook had seen in Nevada. A Tree of Life was planted in its center, a dead snag of cottonwood, for all its symbolism. The Minneconjous tied feather tufts in brilliant colors and other small gifts to it. As the Hunkpapas came to understand, the tithing grew. Moccasins for the long journey into the spirit world. The doll of a long-dead child a mother hoped to embrace again. The old-time bull-hide shield of a grandfather who had been a great warrior and might grant courage to an aging grandson who had lost all spirit for living.

A chill wind blew. The offerings on the sacred tree danced with mystic life. The Minneconjous chose a virgin. They gave her a bow and four arrows with heads removed so that they were messengers and not weapons. She shot these into the four directions. They were retrieved, tied into a bundle with the bow, and suspended with much reverence from the Tree of Life.

Another song began and the circle formed, hand in hand. Kicking Bear alone remained in the center, a curious wand in his hand. It was decorated with bands of brilliant color. At tip and butt long pony-tails of hair waved sinuously with any movement. A few inches below the tip a pair of polished buffalo-calf horns had been affixed transversely so the effect was of a cross with upward-curving arms formed by the horns.

Jerking this in contrapuntal syncopation to the rhythm of the song, Kicking Bear set the circle to dancing, circling to the left, hand in hand, left foot followed by right in a sidewise shuffle. And the plumed wand imperceptibly quickened the tempo. Kicking Bear danced within the circle, facing one dancer after another at the distance of a yard—eyes compelling, voice compelling, wand compelling as he urged in rhythmic monotony: "Believe! Believe! Believe!"

Out of chant and exhortation and intensity, Easterbrook became aware of a startling echo. The echo of litany and censer and chime and an older chant in another pagan tongue. Dust arose. Sweat came. Presently Sitting Bull approached the ring. Hands parted to accept him. Catch The Bear watched the chief begin to dance. His eyes gleamed.

"Now we will see," he said. "If God is there, Sitting Bull will find him."

The dancers shuffled on.

"A whole world is coming," they sang.

One of the Minneconjou dancers in the ring faltered and began to stagger. Kicking Bear was before him in an instant, the wand waving before his glazed eyes. The dancer broke away from those to right and left and unseeingly followed the priest back toward the center of the circle.

"We shall eat pemmican again," they sang.

A young Hunkpapa woman, breast heaving with near exhaustion, began to stumble. Kicking Bear bounded over to her. Companions freed her and she reeled toward him, eyes following the motion of his wand. She moaned, ran crazily in a little circle, and pitched onto her face, inert as the dead. Kicking Bear abandoned her at once, returning to the dancers.

A man began a convulsive leaping, uttering great, tortured cries. He followed the priest a little way toward the center of the circle and also fell dead. Kicking Bear signalled for the song to end and the dance to stop. Everyone waited to learn what came next. The Minneconjou who had first fallen regained his feet and stood by the Tree of Life.

"While I was dead I went a long way," he announced

to all. "My friends remember I saw my father die a long ago winter, flopping about in the snow with black blood coming out of his mouth like a lung-shot buffalo. That was in one of those hard fights with the soldiers. Well, just now I saw him in the place I just visited. He was in good health, like a young man, with a fine cowskin tipi, all new. He spoke to me. He took me in and gave me food. It was good buffalo meat. He said soon all those dead people would be coming. He gave me pemmican for my return journey. I have it here in my hand, now—"

Kicking Bear seized something from the Minneconjou and held it triumphantly high.

"Here!" he cried. "Taste and believe."

Several of the dancers rushed in and struggled for a morsel. Some were ecstatic. It was true. It was old-time pemmican of buffalo. Some were not sure. They did not remember that flavor. Some thought it was only ration beef.

The man who had cried out came alive. He had seen an eagle while he was dead but he did not understand the meaning of this. The young woman from Grand River who had been the first to die was the last to return.

"They are coming," was all she could say, over and over with great conviction.

Her family and friends led her away with reverent attention. Sitting Bull quit the circle, limping wearily. Kicking Bear sent criers about to announce the dance was finished for the day. Somehow disappointed, Easterbrook rose stiffly and looked about for Nora and Beau Lane, whom he had earlier seen across the dance ground. Reverend Riggs, passing, overheard his inquiry.

"They went back down to Carignan's a couple of hours ago," he said. "I'm afraid Miss Crandall—Mrs. Lane—did not care for what she saw here."

"How about you?" Chance said.

The minister watched the dissipating crowd thoughtfully.

"Forty years," he said slowly. "For forty years we've been trying to Christianize them. How many baptisms for me in all that time? Ones that really took. Fifty? Not over twice that. And here's a lifetime's work done in a single day!"

Chance was startled. Reverend Riggs smiled.

"That's what it's got to be, isn't it? Look at their faces. And you can't have a belief in the second coming of the Messiah without some kind of faith in the first. But I can't help wondering—will they have to have a Crucifixion, too?"

Someone called to him. Reverend Riggs moved on to a wagon loading with his students for the drive back to his mission.

McLaughlin had said that if his ban against the dance was broken he would act at once. And he did. About twenty Metal Breasts under a man Easterbrook did not know, arrived a little after noon the next day. The dance had already been in progress several hours and Easterbrook doubted the actual dancers were aware of the new arrivals. The policemen, obviously expecting to make some sort of entrance, pulled up uncertainly, baffled by the scene before them.

After some council among themselves, they dismounted. One by one, in personal curiosity, they vanished among their Grand River brethren. Somewhat later, Easterbrook saw that two, without hats, tunics, or arms, had been permitted or seduced into places in the ring of dancers.

"All men are brothers," they sang with the rest.

The number of dancers increased during the afternoon. More of them died. One, a man, fell outside the ring and quite close to where Easterbrook sat. Presently a vaguely wandering Metal Breast came over to look at him and sank to his haunches at Chance's knee. The policeman's eyes fascinated Chance. They were filmed, opaque, as though turned inward on some awesome thing. He was well wetted with sweat and breathing rapidly.

Sitting Bull approached and lowered himself to the ground nearby. Catch The Bear shuffled over and rumbled at protesting joints as he joined the chief. The Bull looked up and crooked a finger. Beau Lane, wandering alone along the edge of the crowd, also came over and sat down. They all watched the unconscious man on the ground. There was no apparent breathing or pulse. Kicking Bear came back and fixed his eyes on the inert man. His gaze held unwaveringly for about ninety seconds. The unconscious man shuddered, began to breathe rapidly, and opened his eyes. He came unsteadily to his feet, wet his lips, and pitched his voice oratorically.

"Some of you know I have but one living son, now a young man," he said. "Hear this. If I do not speak the truth, let the white man's pox strike him and his manhood rot in his clout."

It seemed a sufficiently binding oath. Even Sitting Bull nodded soberly.

"It is also known that for many years I have had bad luck," the man continued. "One wife gave me this living son and three other things dead when they were born. Now she is a long time dead herself. So is another woman who brought me two children and made my lodge happy for a few years until sickness came again and they also died.

"Well, they are not dead. Just now I have seen them all. Both those women share a lodge where there are many children of mine. One of those three dead when they were born is another son. He has my name and is very strong. I held them all in my arms. They were warm against my body. They follow the buffalo. Soon they will be here. I myself have been dead. Now I live again."

The testamentor moved away with marvelling friends. Kicking Bear looked challengingly at Sitting Bull.

"Father, that man lives?" he asked.

"He lives," the Bull agreed.

"But he was dead?"

"It seemed so."

The Minneconjou high priest smiled and fixed his eyes on the Metal Breast squatting at Easterbrook's knee. He made no sound, no movement, no diversion of any kind, but the man in uniform began to rock on his haunches. A soft moan escaped him and he pitched forward. Kicking Bear thrust a moccasin into his ribs and rolled him partially over.

"See, Father, now this man is dead," he proclaimed.

"It seems so," the Bull agreed again.

A hand touched Easterbrook's shoulder. It was Shining Woman. The chief's wife was with her. So was Nora Lane. Nora looked at the unconscious policeman with aversion and would have spoken but Beau silenced her with a quick frown. They sat down behind the men in a proper place for women.

A woman brought an iron pot of embers to Kicking Bear and produced a four-inch sacking-needle from her sash. The Minneconjou took this, jabbed it into his thumb, and squeezed out a drop of blood for all to see. Bending over the man on the ground, he thrust and straightened, lifting the prostrate Metal Breast's arm and hand by the needle stuck through the web between thumb and forefinger. He withdrew the steel, showing all there had been no tremor in the inert body and no blood flowed from the wound.

The Minneconjou opened the policeman's tunic and jerked the tail of his shirt up to his armpits. He took two sticks from the pot of embers, the end of each glowing red. Nora gasped and hunched forward, seizing Beau's arm. He broke the grip so sharply she was spilled aside. Kicking Bear thrust the glowing sticks against the tender flesh above each nipple of the policeman's torso at the place where older men wore the scarred chevrons of the Sun Dance. Smoke arose but the flesh did not quiver. Nora cried out and scrambled back to Beau.

"Good God, are you all savages?" she cried. "Stop him!"

"It is a man's affair," Lane said harshly.

Easterbrook did not think Lane realized that he had spoken in Sioux. His wife shook him violently.

"Beau, listen to me—!" she pleaded.

The Dakotan struck her dispassionately and flung her back among the other women as any Sioux present would have done. She crouched there in astonishment and outrage. Kicking Bear pulled down the tail of the unconscious Metal Breast's shirt and sent the woman away with the needle and the pot.

"As you see, Father," he said to Sitting Bull, "this man is also dead. But soon he will live again."

The Minneconjou moved off to rejoin the shuffling dancers in the background. Shortly the man on the ground stirred. He sat up, clumsily stuffed in the tail of his shirt, and buttoned his tunic. As far as Easterbrook could tell, he felt no pain or even awareness of injury. An awed companion helped him off. Other uniforms gathered as they learned what had happened. In a few minutes the whole detachment scrambled back to saddle and headed back toward Fort Yates as though the devil was on their heels. Sitting Bull smiled.

"Yesterday when I made the dance, it was in my heart to see some things," he said. "I have but lately lost my daughter, Standing Holy, very close to me in spirit. I wanted to talk to her and hear she was coming home, but I saw nothing. Maybe I have too many years to dream like that."

The chief shook his head, his smile broadening.

"But now I see these ghosts do have some kind of strong medicine, all right," he continued. "Those Metal

Breasts did not do what they came here for and look how they ride away. White Hair will not be happy when they get back up there. I think that is all right."

XX

White Hair's Promise

On the third day of the Grand River dance, an Agency wagon came up-river from Jack Carignan's school. Carignan and Beau Lane rode in the box with several down-river Indians. Two white women rode the spring seat beside the driver. One was Nora Lane, the other was Catherine Weldon. The older woman was windblown and powdered with the dust of a long and hurried drive.

Sitting Bull did not show surprise as he went out to greet his friend. He would have escorted Mrs. Weldon to his cabin for rest and freshening, as he understood hospitality, but she was on crusade, with no time for niceties. She pointed at once to the circling dancers.

"You must stop them at once!" she ordered.

"White Hair is a good general," the Bull said wryly. "I did not think of this."

"Naturally I came at once when he sent me word," the woman admitted. "This time Mr. McLaughlin is right. You must not let those Minneconjou renegades influence your people."

"They do no harm."

"They've made armed camps of the southern reservations. Do you want that here?"

"Do not bring me White Hair's words," the Bull protested. "Bring me your own."

"Don't you understand?" Mrs. Weldon cried. "You have enemies. Let Kicking Bear stir them up, mark my words: your own people will kill you!"

"You have heard the voices, too, my friend?" the chief asked quietly.

"Voices?"

"Lately I walked by the river. A meadowlark was singing there. That is what it told me: 'Your own people will kill you.'"

Mrs. Weldon looked again at the dancers.

"Let me talk to them. Let me show them they are making fools of themselves."

The chief shrugged and led the way to the dance ground. Lane walked behind with Chance. After a few paces he spoke quietly.

"Nora's quitting, Chance."

"Quitting—you?"

"That's what she says."

The Dakotan said no more, nor was there anything readable behind the uncommunicative eyes.

The Bull stopped at the ring of dancers. Chance and Beau came up behind the women. Catch The Bear and Middle, nearby, moved over to stand by their chief. Kicking Bear could not ignore such a group. He signalled. The dance and song stopped. In the sudden silence, Catherine Weldon's voice rang out clearly. She spoke in dialect with full and proper Sioux arrogance, disdainfully pointing at the Minneconjou priest.

"That man lies. This is all a lie."

"No woman speaks here!" Kicking Bear shouted angrily.

"I will. And you'll not stop me."

"Woman, the Father will silence you."

"You speak for God?" Mrs. Weldon demanded. "Then speak. Call the thunders. Call the lightning. Strike me dead."

She burst suddenly through the ring, ran to the Tree of Life, tore the bow and sacred arrows from it, and flung them to the ground.

"Liars and sons of liars!" she cried. "Lies and sons of lies!"

None but a sanctified maiden would touch such holy objects and these were words few men would dare to use to another, even in the heat of anger. But they had been said loudly. They had been heard by all. Even Sitting Bull was awed by the audacity. The woman sensed this and raised her voice even more theatrically.

"Ghosts, you say. Well, tell them to come. Tell them to bring the buffalo. Tell them to drive them over me until I am blood in the dust. Look about you. See all these Hunkpapas and their sons, these wise women and their daughters, acting like children. Look at these Sioux, these proud Dakotas, warming themselves like blind old women beside a cooking circle in which there is no fire!"

Chance felt a flash of admiration. It was the boldest demonstration of raw courage he believed he had ever seen. Nora Lane seemed to sense his reaction and turned on him, ignoring her husband.

"What kind of man are you?" she demanded. "She

can't do it alone. Help her. You know she's right."

"No, Nora, I don't," Chance said. "I think she's wrong."

It was Sitting Bull who went to Catherine Weldon's aid. He limped quickly into the ring and interposed himself between the furious Minneconjou apostle and the embattled white woman who was his friend. They stood so a moment in impasse, then the chief took Mrs. Weldon's arm and turned her gently away. Tears streaked the dust on her face as he brought her back out of the ring. Jack Carignan came up and she permitted him to lead her over to the Agency wagon. Easterbrook thought it was with relief that Sitting Bull watched her go.

Nora Lane started to follow the older woman. Beau seized her arm.

"Please, Nora—" he said softly.

She struck his hand away.

"Maybe I couldn't make a white man out of you, but you're not going to make an Indian out of me!"

She half-ran to the wagon. Carignan helped her up beside Mrs. Weldon. The driver shook out his reins. When Chance turned to speak to Beau, the Dakotan had disappeared. The wagon was still in sight down-river when he returned, wearing nothing but moccasins and a borrowed breechclout. He avoided Chance and took a place among the dancers. Kicking Bear commenced to sing and the dance began again.

It was nearly dark when Lane returned to the lodge for his clothes. Shining Woman slipped out and left them alone while he dressed.

"Well, Beau?" Chance asked.

"I saw my mother."

Chance waited but nothing more came. He shook his head. There was much he wanted to say but he could not.

"Who was she? I've often wondered."

"The Bull's favorite niece."

"And your father?"

Suddenly hatred showed, deep as the marrow of the bone.

"The United States Cavalry," Beau said savagely. "It was after the fight at Killdeer Mountain. The women were scattered and they rode right through the camp. Five of them came together up the ravine where she was hiding. Afterward, how could she know which—or care?"

Beau followed Nora back to Carignan's school, but she was not there. She had returned to Standing Rock with Catherine Weldon. On his return he refused an offered place in the lodge and found quarters elsewhere in the camp. Shining Woman was hurt at his refusal of her hospitality. He was a strange one, she said. She did not think the bloods had mixed well. Sometimes he suffered for that.

His mother had not actually been Sitting Bull's niece. It was just a tipi word when used like that. Her father had been the Bull's friend. Her name had been She Stands Straight. She had been very young at the time of the Killdeer Mountain fight. No more than fourteen years. Shining Woman thought there had been more than five pony soldiers, too. Some of the old women said she had been very bloody when she was found.

As usual in such cases of hostile ravishment, she was given comfort and certain brewed herbs to exorcise the evil within her. Apparently they failed, for she began to grow with child. There was no shame in this but She Stands Straight's father was a proud man. He took his family to the Grandmother Country—Canada—where he had relatives among some Santee stragglers. Beau was born there, near the Milk River.

Later a sickness swept the Santee camp. Left without a family, She Stands Straight took her baby and went to cook for a white man named Lane who worked for the Grandmother Government. After a while this man found a way to put the boy in a government school. Beau stayed at the school a long time while his mother kept the white man's blankets warm.

When Sitting Bull's band had to run away from Bear Coat Miles and take refuge in Canada, not long after the big Custer fight on the Greasy Grass, She Stands Straight became homesick for her own people. She joined the Hunkpapa camp with her son, already a tall boy more white than red. Some time in the hard days before they all came down and surrendered at Fort Buford, Beau's mother died. He came back to the Dakotas with Sitting Bull.

"Some people do not like him because of all of that white blood," Shining Woman said. "I think it is hard to be two people."

"You're taking a chance with the same thing," Chance warned.

She wormed closer to him and laughed softly.

"You are not five pony soldiers. You are a man. In all this darkness, can I see the color of your skin?"

Beau Lane was one of the first on the dance ground in the morning. Shining Woman was yet sleeping. Easterbrook found a place in the sun and sprawled lazily to watch the dancers. There was already a change in them. There was no more food, no more clothing in the camp than there had been at summer's end. They heard now that there were soldiers at Mandan and Rapid City. A new regiment had moved into Fort Robinson. More were in Minnesota. And there were so many now at Pine Ridge that a general with two stars had come to command them.

Winter was coming on fast and all men knew harder times were ahead. But in spite of all this, it seemed to Chance that the deadly apathy which had everywhere seemed so shocking had lifted here. Even flanks and bellies did not seem so gaunt. If hope was food, he thought Sitting Bull's people were beginning to feed well. They all talked of when the spring grass came. That was the time.

Easterbrook was still lazing in the sun when the Metal Breasts returned. A tough, seasoned lieutenant named Catka was in command. They avoided the Bull's cabin, broke through the dancers, and pulled up in a body facing Kicking Bear. The Bull and some of his old men hurried out. It looked like a bad time for a moment. Surprisingly, Kicking Bear was the peacemaker. This was not his reservation and if White Hair wished him to leave it, he and his friends would do so at once. They wanted a good feeling, here, not a bad one, and their work was finished anyway.

The Minneconjou sent his companions to bring their horses and gear. The Bull and his old men were more angry than Chance had ever seen them and Beau Lane stood among them, as angry as any. But in the face of Kicking Bear's compliance, there was little they could do about this outrage. They watched in silence as the Minneconjous returned with their horses and belongings. Kicking Bear mounted up among them. The Metal Breasts rode them across the river under humiliating escort. Catka held back for a moment and indicated the broken ring of dancers.

"What am I to tell White Hair about this thing?" he demanded.

"Pray for a long life, Catka," Sitting Bull said harshly. "Tell him what you see."

Beau Lane began the song, then. Hands linked and the dance resumed.

The next day, McLaughlin came in person to Grand River. He asked for Easterbrook and was directed to Shining Woman's lodge. He had another *Herald* voucher, recently arrived at Standing Rock.

"Still owe Beau some money?" he wanted to know.

"No," Chance said.

"I see. I advanced his wife a little more. She seemed entitled. Will you cover it?"

"Better take that up with Beau."

"I intend to."

The agent paused. The sound of a ghost-song came

clearly from the dance ground.

"You're a hell of a poor messenger, Easterbrook," he said.

"Ever hear of something, Major—one of the constitutional foundations of this land of the free? The right of any man to worship God in his own fashion. Any man, including those out there."

McLaughlin shrugged. "If you can't persuade the old man, maybe I can. Coming?"

Chance nodded. They left the lodge and started across toward the chief's cabin. Others immediately appeared. Half a dozen wary and truculent old men, moving in the same direction.

"Look at them," McLaughlin said with something that was almost admiration. "There's your real ghosts. Maybe only fifteen of them left, but holding the whole lot back. A good grippe epidemic right now would solve a lot of problems for all of us."

The Bull was in the dooryard of the lodge behind his cabin. Lane and more of the old Silent Eaters were his audience. He was clapping his hands in command to an unhaltered horse. Chance recognized the fat old animal the chief had ridden that stirring morning the men of Grand River had escorted Beau and himself up onto the *coteau* at the start of their journey to Nevada.

The old horse knew several tricks and performed willingly. The Bull was enjoying himself. When he saw McLaughlin he called the animal to him, nuzzled and was nuzzled in return, then came to meet his visitor.

"Not bad for two old men," he said, indicating the horse. "Pahuska gave him to me when I left his Wild

West Show. Now the little ones call him my Buffalo Bill pony. A good friend like that is remembered a long time."

He gestured toward the interior of the lodge. McLaughlin shook his head.

"No council, this time, Sitting Bull," the agent said. "This is straight talk—straight from the shoulder."

"Why do white men say that?" the Bull asked. He tapped a place over his heart. "Straight talk comes from here."

"I sent you word to stop that dance over there."

"I did not care for those words, White Hair. I did not care for Catka or those other Metal Breasts. Do not send them here when we do no harm."

"You know what I can do if you do not obey my orders."

"No, I do not know that," Sitting Bull answered. "I do not think you know, either. I think no man does. Maybe it is time we found out. Both of us."

The two men—so different, so powerfully opposed—looked levelly at each other.

"I'd like that," McLaughlin said crisply. "Nothing would please me more than to have this quarreling settled, once and for all. But now is not the time for that, not in the state of excitement they're in. If we're to avoid the kind of trouble that is brewing at Pine Ridge, we've got to work together. Don't you understand that?"

"I only understand what they do, White Hair—that I am still their chief. And I see no harm to them in this thing."

McLaughlin was angry but he could not break the chief's impassiveness.

"Well, see that you understand this," he said. "I won't come down here again. If we have more words, they will be at the Agency."

Sitting Bull shrugged.

"When you have good thoughts—good for us—send me word. I will come."

McLaughlin turned to Chance.

"Bring Beau," he ordered.

The agent recrossed the camp in swift, long-paced strides. Chance and Lane were hard put to keep up with him. Once within the lodge, he spoke sharply to Beau.

"Catka told me you've been dancing with them. You know better than that. You know that when we've got one of them as far along with us as you've been and then he backslides, it gives every diehard among them encouragement. Encouragement we can't afford at a time like this. That the way you repay what everybody's done for you?"

"Some of the things that have been done for me I'll never repay, Major," the Dakotan said quietly. "The price would be blood. This is my affair."

"Don't be a damned fool, Beau!" McLaughlin protested. "You've already lost your wife over it."

Lane's lips flattened.

"Oh, I tried to reason her out of it for you, but I couldn't do a thing," the agent continued. "She quit me cold at the school and you owe me five hundred dollars I had to give her. She said she thought that was fair. And she doesn't want you following her."

"Where has she gone?"

"Up across the Cannonball with the Weldon woman."

Lane looked at Easterbrook. Chance withdrew the voucher McLaughlin had brought down with him. He endorsed it and handed it to the agent.

"I'll draw the balance over what Beau owes you the next time at the Agency," he said.

McLaughlin pocketed the voucher. He frowned at his own thoughts.

"I can't talk to the Bull," he said. "Too much between us that might explode. But I'm no ogre and I'm no fool. Under the circumstances, you're probably right and so is he. I don't believe I can stop them dancing here without risking something that would be a damned sight worse. Not as stubborn as he's being about it. As long as he keeps the peace, I'm going to have to leave him be."

"That a promise, Major?" Easterbrook asked.

"As long as he keeps the peace," McLaughlin repeated.

XXI
General Brooke

McLaughlin's promise brought a wave of good feeling to Grand River. Several who had not so far participated appeared at the dance ground, secure in the belief they no longer risked their chief's safety. Several of the women began to make the ghost shirts such as Kicking Bear had worn and dresses of a similar style for themselves. The spirit of the camp continued to improve. However, Sitting Bull himself seemed to have lost all personal interest in the Ghost Dance. More important matters were on his mind. His chief concern seemed to be the news from the south. Much was rumor probably, but he still wanted to know the truth. He again chose Easterbrook and Beau Lane as emissaries.

"White men will talk to the white man," he said. "Indians will talk to the Indian. If we have any bad trouble, it will begin down there. Kicking Bear left here too easily. It was not like that Minneconjou to let those Metal Breasts drive him away. I think he has some plans down there and wanted to get back to them. I do not like that man too well. Tell them all that I do not want foolish things done down there. Tell the white men and the Indians the same thing. See how it is and bring me back their words."

Shining Woman was not pleased but she set about preparing their gear. Chance promised her an early return and they set out on the third of November, riding in sunny weather but with the ground already frozen underfoot.

On Cherry Creek, well above Cheyenne River, they began to encounter empty lodge-circles beside fields in which fall crops had been abandoned. Hump's camp at the mouth of the creek was swollen with twice its complement of Minneconjous. They were dancing enthusiastically and anxious to know if it went as well with their friends to the north. But their chief was uneasy.

"We older men have lately had a hard time and we complain about that," Hump said. "Sometimes there is a little spark left in the ashes and one of us makes some angry talk. I do not worry about this grumbling. It is all right if it makes us feel a little better.

"But it is different with the young men. They have never been in a hard fight with the white man. They do not know how that is. They only know that in the old days they would already have won many feathers. It is natural that they should have feelings about that. And it is easy to be brave about something you do not know. But if they become too excited, now, and think that all the nations are growing strong again and standing together, I do not know who is to control them. I hear Sitting Bull has the same thought."

"They are dancing at Grand River," Beau said, "but the Bull only watches. They have a good spirit there and I think that pleases the Bull. He worries most about what Kicking Bear may do."

"Yes," Hump agreed. "I do not see any harm if the dance gives a good feeling, but many more dance when Kicking Bear comes here. Then they remember he was a war chief. At first they took nothing of the white man into the circle. Now they hear soldiers are at Pine Ridge and Fort Benton and those other places and Kicking Bear allows them to dance with guns. Many are saying that maybe Kicking Bear does not know the true road to *Wakan Tanka*, but if there is to be trouble over it, it is good to have a war chief leading the way."

"You think there will be trouble?" Chance asked.

"My friend, I think trouble is like the wind. If the door-flap is well-laced beforehand, it will go away."

"I think that is also the Bull's feeling," Beau said.

The Indian smiled.

"Yes. It has long been said we are both wise men."

They left a gift from Sitting Bull and went up the river to Big Foot's camp near the mouth of the Belle Fourche. It was also crowded with dancers as the chief had embraced the Ghost Dance wholeheartedly. His principal concern was that with so many additions to the camp and supplies so short, many would not be able to last through to spring grass and the promised resurrection of plenty. He had asked his niece's husband about that. Kicking Bear had agreed it was a hard thing. Still, it would not be so bad for some to die since they would be coming back with the other ghosts in the spring, anyway.

"I see many ghost shirts here," Beau commented disapprovingly. "They are no good, Uncle. Throw them away. You have wounds in your own body which tell you cloth cannot stop a bullet."

"Kicking Bear is your nephew," Chance added. "The Bull wants you to get him to change his words about those shirts. He says if there is any kind of fighting, this time you are all thrown away."

"I am an old man, my friend," Big Foot said. "I have a bad trouble in my chest with all this cold weather, and many no longer listen to me. Kicking Bear is one of them. And lately there are more difficulties."

"What?" Beau asked sharply.

"While Kicking Bear was up there at Grand River, a man named Short Bull has made himself big among the Brule dancers and some others. He does not say he just brings the good word. He says he is the *Wanekia*, that this Christ now lives in his skin. It is widely believed. And he is very hot against the white man and the soldiers. I think this business of the guns comes from him.

"We hear the Brules are selling ponies to buy ammunition. He says that to dance in our own camps is not the way. He says it must be a private place where white men cannot know and many camps can gather to dance together. Already they have had two thousand on Black Pipe Creek. More than that lately danced at a place near Mousseau's store on Wounded Knee. And the Brules will not say how many, but the biggest circle yet was at a dance ground on Pass Creek."

"How does Kicking Bear take this Short Bull and his claims?" Chance asked.

"I thought there would be trouble but now I hear they are together, calling in more dancers every day. When I cannot feed the people here, how can they feed so many? It means beef must be stolen and many other necessary things. So many people leaving their own camps to gather in secret places will not please the soldier chiefs. They will bring in more of their guns. Tell Sitting Bull I also hear voices on the wind, but these are the things which frighten me. Not those painted shirts."

Leaving Big Foot's camp with an increasing feeling of urgency, Easterbrook and Beau Lane struck across the Badlands. They reached Beau's objective in late afternoon. The Stronghold was impressive at this hour of long shadow. It was a steep-sided pyramid of clay and stone attached to a larger, lower mesa by a narrow earthen bridge. Beyond, the flattened top of the Stronghold was a well-grassed triangle two or three miles in extent. From its rim a commanding view of the Badlands could be had in any direction.

Beau went directly to the springs. Moccasin tracks were clearly imprinted in the water-thawed earth about them. They built a supper fire upon the ashes of others which the wind had not yet scattered. Beau shook his head with concern.

"The Badlands—the *macoce sica*—not even a pony track out here in the old days. But they've sure been scouting it, now. If they have to run, this is where they'll go, Chance. And God help anybody who tries to come after them!"

Pine Ridge was vastly changed. There were several small temporary camps close in, uneasy Oglala friendlies, fugitive from the big ghost dance camps further out. The Agency, itself, had been converted into a military cantonment. Sentries were on all roads. They were ordered to report to the senior officer. This proved to be General Brooke, two stars, who had taken over the Agency residence.

They were told by a handsome, crisp lieutenant to await the general's pleasure on the porch. The lieutenant had a table just within the door. Lying upon it was a magnificently careless quick sketch of a fighting mad Dakota pony. It was not necessary to see the bold signature.

"Remington?"

The lieutenant seemed surprised at this recognition in a man of Easterbrook's appearance but he displayed the sketch with pride.

"From himself. Because I knew where to find him some gin in this godforsaken place."

"Frederic Remington, here?"

"No quarters," the lieutenant said. "Every billet jammed. He went on to Rapid City, where there's a decent hotel."

"Pershing!" an authoritative voice called within the house.

The lieutenant disappeared. He returned in a moment and signalled. Easterbrook and Lane followed him. Chance thought General Brooke would have looked more impressive in a business suit than he did in a uniform, but he had the sort of bristling impatience plains campaigning seemed to induce in military men. He eyed his caller's long hair, leather shirt, and moccasins with disdain. Chance felt uncomfortable.

"I've spent most of the last fifteen months in the Sioux camps, sir."

"Thank God you don't smell like it. This is Jack Pershing, my aide, Easterbrook. You want a statement, he'll brief you. I've got a war to fight."

"War, General?" Beau asked mildly. "I thought that's what you're here to prevent."

Brooke glanced at the Dakotan and turned cold eyes on Chance.

"Beau Lane, General—a friend of mine."

"Indian, isn't he? Get him out of here."

"I said he was my friend, sir."

Brooke rose and came around his desk.

"What the hell do you expect to get from me, anyhow? What can any military man say before a fact that won't make him look like a fool afterward? What the devil do you suppose Napoleon would have said the day before Waterloo? —All right, so I'm not facing Wellington. But there's God's own lot of Indians out there. You tell me what they're going to do."

"I believe we could," Beau said. "If you'll withdraw your troops."

"Withdraw?" the General exploded. "These aren't simple savages. They're first-class fighting men. And smart as they come. Quietly pulling the various bands off into bigger camps. Because they're afraid of us, they claim. Whoever saw a scared Sioux? Unless we can break it up, they'll be united in one command in a few more days. If that happens, they've got an army and we've got us a war."

Brooke crossed to a window, looked out, paced restlessly back.

"Naturally, we're trying every means at our command. We still have contact with a few head men who have remained friendly. One of the local missionaries has gone out with them to see if they can bring some of the fugitives in to a parley. If they have luck, we may win a few over. At worst we've won a little time to bring up more reinforcements."

"What are you offering them?"

"What I'd offer any seditious force before engaging it. Unconditional surrender. Complete disarmament. Hostages for good behavior. Military control till order is established."

Beau touched Easterbrook's arm.

"We're keeping the general from a mighty big job of

work, Chance," he said.

Outside, Beau resoundingly kicked a loose board on the porch steps.

" 'Whoever saw a scared Sioux?' he said! Know what? You're looking at one, right now!"

The friendly head men and the missionary were successful. They brought many in to General Brooke's parley. Two Strike was the most important chief. He rode in a buggy with Father Jutz. A phalanx of warriors surrounded it in escort. Big Bad Horse came and his friends rode with him. High Pine came next in line. Warriors rode with him, also. Then Bull Dog and Turning Bear and Big Turkey. Beau did not know all the names or bands.

They rode in the old way, on their best ponies, resplendent in paint and feathers. Brass-studded cartridge belts crisscrossed elaborate ghost shirts. A rifle rested upright on each man's thigh. They rode two and four abreast, a long line of horsemen with a white flag fluttering from a lance-head before them. They came in peace, not in surrender. The carriage of every man proclaimed this.

Troopers gathered to stare at the long, silent file. There was no talk among the uniforms. It was a calculated show of force. The troopers understood it as it was meant they should:

Now is the time to talk straight. Soon it will be too late.

It was also something else. Something which had ridden back out of history to momentarily reappear in all the panoply, with which it yet lingered in the posses-sive memories of old men. Children appeared, eyes rounded, all along the line of march. Watching them, Chance could see their awe and feel it. They did not look at soldiers like this. These days they spat at soldiers and ran to hide. Many of them bore evidence of reser-vation and mission schools in dress and shortened hair. These had learned from teachers and books of many wonders. But this was the greatest wonder of all. This was how they were in the beginning. This was what they had been. The Dakota. The people. This could well be the last great war parade of the Sioux. When it had passed, the children vanished with sadness on their faces.

Brooke and his staff were better negotiators than East-erbrook anticipated. The Indians were shown courtesy when they met on the parade ground. Brooke was more reasonable in his demands than he had indicated in his office. And he did not crowd his luck by demanding immediate decision. Instead, he issued generous rations from his own quartermaster's stores, a gesture unheard-of in recent memory.

However, there was some disaffection on the part of a few magnificently ghost-shirted dancers likely sent in for this purpose. One was an unusually large Indian with a great, braying voice. Beau said his Oglala name was Porcupine. Another was of very commanding appear-ance, his magnificent physique and fine head belying his name, which was Little.

This Little began to single out and shame those who wore no sacred shirts. They were fools, he said. Here was the true road to salvation. Not the endless, empty words and promises of the white man. In a few minutes, he had attracted considerable attention. Porcupine then took over. He strutted about, boasting of his shirted invulnerability. He taunted several men to shoot at him and give proof to his words. His manner was calculatedly infuriating and grew more so.

Suddenly, before there could be intervention, two of those whom he had been badgering lost patience and obliged him. He was struck in the leg by one bullet. That seemed a fair enough end to it, but with the blood running for all to see, both Porcupine and Little loudly proclaimed he was untouched until the wounded man fainted and fell. Even then, Little and other ghost dancers closed in and carried him away without allowing others to approach.

Most present recognized the folly of the demonstration and would have laughed at its result but for one thing. That was Sioux blood which had been spilled and another Sioux had spilled it. It was a bad omen. Some pulled their sacred shirts off and flung them to the ground before they rode away. But others stared darkly at the troopers and seemed to find the fault with them.

Because of this, much of what General Brooke and his staff had gained was lost.

XXII
Colonel Cody

R Red Cloud's flag was amiably flying at the peak of the pole before his house, but he refused to see Easterbrook. It was winter, his messenger said. The weather was cold. The chief had a pain in his chest. His nose was running like a creek. Also he had lately eaten a tin of some food given him by the agent and he thought it had been poisoned a little. He did not care to visit on a sick belly. Some time later, perhaps, when all of these soldiers had gone away.

"The old man wouldn't commit himself now anyway," Beau said. "He's got to keep favor with the Oglalas who are out. Their dance is as big a threat to his authority as it is to the Bureau or the Army. You'd be wasting your time with him."

They finally found blanket space on the parlor floor at the agency dispensary. Charlie Eastman, the young Santee doctor in charge, was hospitable. And his optimism was welcome. Even when the ghost-dancers sent in arrogant word that the friendly head men could do as they liked but the dancers would not come in until the last soldier had left the reservations, Dr. Eastman was not unduly concerned.

"If only for one reason," he said, "the weather. Even the wildest are too practical for that. They've never fought a winter war. They know Dakota storms. Too much against them this time of year. Spring is different, but their messiah is supposed to be here by then. When he doesn't show up, it will all be over with. If General Brooke will just be patient—"

"Maybe," Beau agreed. "But they can't be left out there to freeze and starve till then."

"There's a way around that, too," Dr. Eastman said. "The Governor is sending Valentine McGillicuddy—the one they call Little Beard—down to see if he can calm their fears and bring them back in."

Beau shook his head.

"I don't know. Chance and I saw enough sign at the Stronghold. If they hole up there, no white man could get anywhere near them. Not even Little Beard."

"You could," Dr. Eastman said. "You could get McGillicuddy to them."

"Maybe," Beau agreed. "But Doc would be taking an awful chance. It'll be up to him when he gets here."

But another man arrived ahead of the former agent at Pine Ridge. He was Bill McKeever, Associated Press, whom Easterbrook knew slightly. Out from Chicago, he had hired a rig at Rushville and rolled onto the reservation with whiskey in his belly and reserve bottles in his grip. His delight knew no bounds when he discovered Easterbrook in this godforsaken place. Supposing the enthusiasm to be mutual, Mrs. Eastman invited the man to join the household at supper.

McKeever celebrated reunion generously. By the time Chance managed to appropriate the balance of the man's whiskey for Dr. Eastman's dispensary, it was evident that to turn him loose to wander the Agency was an impossibility. Eastman located another pallet for the parlor floor. Once the lamps were blown, McKeever quieted docilely. Easterbrook's relief was short-lived. The man suddenly sat up with a last story. A beauty he'd picked up his last night in Chicago. Off the record, worse luck.

General Nelson A. Miles was preparing to transfer his headquarters to Rapid City, South Dakota, to take personal command of the Sioux campaign. In his baggage was an abstract of Indian Service reports and correspondence containing a carefully culled list of the sixty-four most troublesome Indian leaders yet left alive. At the repeated insistence of an agent named McLaughlin, the name of old Sitting Bull headed the list. And attached to it was blanket authority from the War Department to remove any or all of these Indians from any position of influence among their people by whatever means and for whatever disposition seemed most expeditious.

At a banquet staged by well-wishers and political aspirants on the eve of the general's departure, he was seated next to another public figure also largely dependent upon the Indian for fame and fortune. "Colonel" William F. Cody, the P. T. Barnum of the Wild West. In the course of the dinner, a private deal was made between the two. Cody left the table with a signed commission to go to Standing Rock and personally arrest his old friend and one-time employee, Chief Sitting Bull of the Hunkpapa Sioux.

"Damned old highbinders!" McKeever chuckled in gleeful admiration. "Between them they've made as much news as any two men in the country. But when this breaks they'll get more space than Grant won at Appomattox!"

The drunken newsman lay down again and went happily off to sleep. Chance and Lane slipped outside. Dr. Eastman followed. Both Lane and the doctor agreed it was imperative for the Dakotan to remain at Pine Ridge until Valentine McGillicuddy's arrival in case the former agent needed him. McKeever's story admittedly might have no basis in fact but there was no time for attempt at verification and any indignity inflicted on the Hunkpapa chief at this time might be the spark necessary to ignite the Dakotas. Chance seemed the best hope of heading Cody off at Standing Rock. If McLaughlin was difficult, the old showman, at least, would understand the power of a hostile press which Easterbrook could command and might be persuaded to change his mind.

Indian mementos were currently in high demand among the troopers at Pine Ridge. With some such bribe, Dr. Eastman arranged for Easterbrook to ride with an Army courier team carrying a routine official pouch to Pierre, on the Missouri. From there the river steamer was the quickest means to reach Fort Yates and the route bypassed the ghost camps on the fringe of the Badlands.

These arrangements were necessarily made without official knowledge and Chance joined his escorts well out from the Agency. As they rode northeastward, a blue column filed into Pine Ridge from the south. Martial music hung over the distant troops. The air was unmistakable and Easterbrook rode with a rising tide of urgency and anger.

He made a fortunate connection with the riverboat at

Pierre and had barely time for a few personal purchases before the paddles were turning, eating away the miles up the river. He watched the banks slide past with grim impatience. He judged that this time he was heading into a full collision with Jim McLaughlin and he relished the prospect. To his astonishment, however, the major welcomed him gratefully when he strode unannounced into the Agency office at Standing Rock.

"Good God, I'm glad you're here, Easterbrook! Know what's happened, now?"

"I know what you *hope* is going to happen. I know Bill Cody is on his way here to arrest Sitting Bull."

"On his way!" the agent said. "If he was, maybe I'd have time to stop him. He's already here with a wagonload of candy and presents and a private collection of newspapermen. We're stalling him the best we can."

"Stalling?"

McLaughlin nodded wearily.

"Colonel Drum put his officers on shifts last night and they've carried on through the day, entertaining Cody's party and keeping the old toss-pot occupied. But he's still going strong and some of Drum's best men are weakening. For God's sake, get over to the post and lend them a hand."

"Major, I know you could keep your boots clean in a manure pile, but don't try to tell me you didn't have anything to do with this. How much more do you think these poor devils can take? Know what came riding into Pine Ridge as I rode out? The Seventh Cavalry, tootling *Garry Owen* like it was *The Star Spangled Banner.* Now this."

"Hell, Easterbrook, I didn't order the Seventh into

Pine Ridge and I didn't sign that order in Cody's pocket," the agent protested. "And it's no cheap publicity stunt, either. Not on General Miles' part. If there's one man alive who could ride into the Bull's camp and bring him back here, it's Bill Cody. He's the Bull's friend and the old man trusts him.

"It's a shrewd idea and it'd work. And don't get the idea I don't want the Bull in here. I do. You ought to know that by now. I'd go after him myself, in spite of that promise I made you, if I was sure I could get away with it. It's just that I can't risk the military interfering in any way, the mood they're in right now. I've got telegraphic tracers out all over but General Miles is in transit someplace and I haven't been able to reach him for a countermand to Cody."

"Think you'll get it?"

"Or my own discharge, the way I worded those telegrams. But I can't delay Cody much longer. For Christ's sake, take me at my word for once and go see what you can do."

The plea was too earnest to mistrust. Chance crossed to the post clubroom. Colonel Drum, white and strained, repeated McLaughlin's relieved welcome. He made a vague round of introductions and almost immediately disappeared. A few Old Army veterans, highly resistant out of long exposure, remained on their feet and active in the field, but casualties were numerous.

"The old son of a bitch hasn't got a hollow leg," one graying officer confided to Chance. "He's got two. No, by hell, it's three! Yes, sir, all three of them are hollow!"

He laughed thickly at his own imagery and backed

himself into a chair like a stern-wheeler coming into a landing. The gentleman whose alcoholic capacity had been so praised—now as in earlier times the most handsome man Easterbrook had ever seen—sat at a deal table. He was smoking a large cigar and playing what seemed to be a very alert game of cards with three dishevelled civilians who were obviously incapable of giving a damn. Colonel Cody did not get the name when Chance introduced himself but he was courteous and genial.

"Do you play whist?"

"No, sir, I'm afraid I don't," Chance answered quickly and defensively.

"A pity. Very cultivated game." The colonel shrugged. "Be a sport, then. See if you can find me a whiskey."

Chance obliged and returned to the table as spectator and tap-boy. Cody's partners dropped off, one by one. Supper was served and relief forces under the personal command of Colonel Drum took over until midnight, when the shift changed again. Sometime after that, Buffalo Bill Cody, looking taller and more magnificent than life, put a weighty arm across Chance's shoulder.

"Easterbrook, I like you," he confided. "You're a good conversationalist."

Chance could not recall having spoken for some time. Cody winked at him with great solemnity.

"Didn't you just say, 'Let's go to bed'?"

They left the room together. Chance found someone's empty billet and rolled in as he was. He seemed to have drawn but one deep breath when he was turned out by a worried orderly who told him to hurry. By the time he had splashed himself awake, Bill Cody had finished an enormous breakfast, thanked his hosts for their splendid hospitality, and was bellowing good-humoredly that it was time to get this show on the road.

Drum murmured a message to Chance from Jim McLaughlin. No word yet from General Miles. As a correspondent, Cody would not suspect Easterbrook. For the love of God would he accompany the showman's party and invent any delaying tactic he could.

The members of Cody's personal press contingent were not as familiar with wagon travel over reservation roads as Chance was. He outscrambled them to a place on the well-sprung seat from which Cody himself drove. Inventiveness at a very low ebb, Chance did what he could as they jolted away from Standing Rock.

"Quite a few camps out this way, Colonel," he suggested. "And plenty of time. These people all think a lot of you. They'd like to visit."

"Known some of them since they were pups," Cody agreed with a pleased nod. "Always got along, except for a couple of affairs like that duel I had with Yellow Hand. Ever hear about that? Single-handed, it was, him and me. Knives—no tricks barred—"

Chance felt in no mood for a detailed account and he could not suppress a little malice.

"I thought Ned Buntline invented that yarn."

The colonel looked at him reproachfully.

"Son, I invented Ned Buntline."

They rode along in silence for half a mile or so. Cody smiled at something in recollection.

"You know, I probably know more Indians personally

than any man in the country. Had a hundred of them in my show at one time or another. Even took quite a passel of them to Europe with me. Wanted the old Bull to go but he wouldn't. One of them sure had himself a time.

"An Oglala from Pine Ridge. Black Elk. Lost him in England, somehow, just as we were leaving for home. There he was without any money and not a word to his name but Sioux. They argue an Indian can't pull his oar in our so-called civilization. Well, this one sure as hell could. He got over to France, somehow. Got himself a girl—a real looker, too—to take care of him and feed him, same as if he was home. There he was, all fat and sassy, when we came back over again next season, and joined up once more like there was nothing to it."

Chance chuckled appreciatively and the wagon jolted on. A few minutes later a hard-riding detachment from Fort Yates overtook them and handed Cody a lengthy telegram. It was signed by General Miles and rescinded the commission for the arrest of Sitting Bull. There had been a change in military planning and it was expected the colonel and his party would leave Standing Rock as quickly and quietly as possible.

XXIII
A Word on the Wind

Easterbrook found that Jim McLaughlin generously credited him everywhere for Bill Cody's disgruntled departure. Lines of strain vanished from the agent's face. He was confident and buoyant.

The situation at Pine Ridge notwithstanding, the battle was won. Recall of Cody's commission had been an act of faith on the part of the government that all Sioux would understand. It would now take only a little time for the whole Ghost Dance excitement to fade.

Since Beau was still in the south and there was no word from him, Chance knew a report on the camps as they had found them on the way to Pine Ridge was overdue to Sitting Bull. However, he had a debt to Beau as well and he proposed a ride up across the Cannonball for a talk with Nora Lane. Time had passed and it was possible her disillusionment with Beau had given way to warmer feeling.

"She's not there," Jim McLaughlin said. "It's for the best, Easterbrook, believe me, although I'm glad I'm not the one to tell Beau. The Weldon woman's finally given up. She's gone home. Back east somewhere. Nora's gone with her. Almost two weeks ago. She won't be back."

Chance measured this news and decided the major was right. However hard Beau might take it, it was for the best. He discovered McLaughlin had relented and reinstated the chief's nephew, One Bull, on the regular Agency freight and mail wagon. He threw his gear aboard and rolled south for Grand River.

It was well after dark, a late hour for winter, when they reached Sitting Bull's camp. Chance was disturbed to find a sentry posted well out on the *coteau,* a precaution never observed before. The man told him the chief had been expecting him and would wish to know that he was here.

Chance left One Bull to outspan his team and went directly to Sitting Bull's cabin. One of the women answered his muted toe-stubbing. The chief came to the door naked, for he had already turned in, but his welcome was warm.

"It is good to see you home, Brother," he said. "I have much to hear and some words for you. But they will wait. Now is the time for blankets and I think another expects you."

Chance gave his thanks in proper form and went through the camp to Shining Woman's lodge. It glowed with firelight, visible at a distance, because others were dark. When he coughed and lifted the flap, warmth flowed out to him in welcome. He sat and Shining Woman brought him fresh moccasins. She took his travel-dusted shirt and gave him a robe for his shoulders. She brought a bowl of water, first for drinking and then to wash. In proof she had known he was coming and had waited, she showed him the pot simmering beside the fire.

They said the birds spoke to them. Sometimes an animal or the wind. It was nothing supernatural, for they accepted it as commonplace. However it was, they often knew when it was impossible to know and Chance had come to believe that in which he could not believe.

Chance luxuriated in this homecoming. He wondered if some prehistoric memory did not leave implanted in some men an unknown, poignant longing for such primitive simplicity of fulfillment. He wanted it to be so. He could, then, believe himself one of these fortunates and come to some passable understanding of himself during some of the incredibilities of these past fifteen months.

One Bull came to the flap as arranged. He put down before Shining Woman a burlapped parcel. It contained purchases Chance had acquired in Pierre and the post store at Standing Rock. He had meant to have something from Pine Ridge, too, for that was considered a great distance away, but time had been lacking for trading there. Shining Woman unwrapped the parcel and One Bull dutifully marvelled over the gifts this woman's man had brought to her. He would presently carry news of them through the camp where she, in all modesty, could not.

There were four Hudson Bay blankets. They were so thickly woven sleepers did not need a robe between them and the ground. They were so soft they would not chafe the most tender parts of the body. There were four so that at times a woman and her man could lie apart in decency and comfort and on other occasions guests could be honored with the best in the lodge.

There was a woman's headband in cut porcupine quilling, boiled and dyed to brilliant colors, stitched in old-time sinew into ancient symbols of a woman's fortunate lot. It had been put up for pawn a long time ago at the post store and had certainly belonged to a princess, for it was a tiara. One Bull, who did not understand that word, solemnly agreed it was so.

There was a pair of moccasins, winter ankle-height, Atsina style, beautifully worked in quilting and dye with thick, waterproof elkhide soles very hard to come by in these days. They were very soft, like finest doeskin, and could be rolled inside a man's clenched fist.

When tried on they fitted Shining Woman like her own warm skin.

There was another gift, a whim which had struck Chance when he saw it in a Pierre shop window. A small, dark-faced doll with Indian dress and a soft rag body and raven hair. This was a private joke One Bull did not understand. Or some kind of a white man's mistake. It was a child's toy. When a man had a woman, he did not give her a thing like this. He gave her a real thing to hold at her breast and suckle her milk. But Shining Woman snatched it to her and held it close.

One Bull left and Shining Woman made a bed of two of the new blankets. She fed the fire for the night with heavier sticks, thrust deep into the embered ash. She set a backrest on its side between fire and bed to fend off sparks and keep the light from their eyes. When Chance joined her he discovered she held the doll close to her naked breast.

"I already feel this thing in my heart," she said.

There were no more words and in time they slept.

Chance ate a lazy breakfast and went out to the dance ground. There were not as many dancers as in the first days. Perhaps by half. Shave Bear, a gentle old man somewhat scorned by many, was the leader, now. He sang well and with a pitiful earnestness, but his exhortations were not electrifying, as Kicking Bear's had been. There could be little doubt that the ghosts were on the wane.

Catch The Bear came along in search of Chance and they started together toward the Bull's council lodge.

They stopped on the way to watch Lieutenant Bull Head cross the ford from his house and lope off toward Fort Yates.

"They say the God they talk about over there when they dance made the Indian," the old Bear said. "I do not know about that. But I know who made that one— White Hair."

The old man looked long at the receding policeman.

"My belly gets hard when I think of that man. One time he did a bad thing to me. Some day I am going to kill him. You have such an enemy, too?"

"No," Chance answered.

"Make one," the Bear counselled. "Keep him in your heart like you would a woman. It fills you with warm juices. That is a good thing when you are an old man."

They went on to the council lodge. It was not a formal meeting. Many of the younger ones were there. Crow-foot and Andrew Fox, a son-in-law to the Bull, who had some agency school education and had come in from some outlying place to serve his uncle with paper and pen after Catherine Weldon's departure from the camp.

"We had a visitor while you were gone," the Bull said. "A Metal Breast named Running Hawk. He talked to one person here and another there. He told some men one thing and others another. It was not good talk."

"What did he say?" Chance asked.

"Well, he could see there are not so many of them these days but he said the government is going to take their guns away from any people dancing down here. Take away their ponies, too. Take away their children. Put them in this school someplace where they will not be seen by their families again and cannot learn any more bad things. He said to my son-in-law here that it would be a good thing to take his family and move up there by the Agency. He said pretty soon this would not be a good place to be. Did you hear any bad feeling like that up there just now?"

"No," Chance answered. "I think Running Hawk was just making big talk. White Hair doesn't like the dance. We know that. He does not like to have you here among your own people. We know that. But you have given him no cause to do anything and now he has given this promise. He will keep it, I think. He is a fair man."

"Well, that may be so," the Bull said without conviction. "But I do not trust that man. If he wanted me to come up there to Fort Yates, why did he get a soldier's paper to turn Pahuska back when he was already on the way to get me? Pahuska is my friend. I would go with him. Or the soldiers. I surrendered a long time ago. Since that time I have always done what the soldiers said. So have my people, even when it was not easy. But White Hair must stop sending those Metal Breasts. I cannot go with them. I am their chief, even when they cut their hair. I cannot let them put their hands on me. It is wrong to ask me to do so."

"If he sends them, let him send Bull Head," Catch The Bear growled. "That is the man I want."

"I had good words with White Hair after Pahuska left," Chance said. "He means no one harm. He will do nothing more, I think. There is no trouble here. He would be a fool to make some."

"That is true," the Bull agreed. "I am glad he is

thinking straight again. Now I will tell you some news from Pine Ridge. Beau Lane and that white man we call Little Beard have gone out to the Badlands. They have had good talks with some people there."

"Are they going to come in?"

"Some. A few more each day, we hear. But some are even more afraid since they brought in those pony soldiers we fought a long time ago on the Greasy Grass. They do not trust those white men. I think now they trust only me. They have sent me word to come down there. They wish to hear what I have to say about these things. They think the time to the new world is very short, now. They want me to be with them when this thing happens. I do not know about that but they are in trouble and I must go."

"No!" Chance said earnestly. "That's the one thing you must not do. If you start south toward those hostiles, White Hair will think the worst. It will give him the chance he's always wanted."

"My friend, I am no fool," the Bull protested. "I will not go without a pass from White Hair. But those are my people down there. If this new world comes as Short Bull and Kicking Bear say, no harm will be done. White men and Indians will no longer be in the same place. But if it falls to the ground, I can give them good words. They will listen to me. They will all go home if I say it. Then this trouble will be over."

"I know that," Chance agreed. "So does Beau and probably McGillicuddy—Little Beard. But not McLaughlin."

"I will do it the right way," the Bull insisted stubbornly. "I will make him a letter so he can see my thoughts. I will tell him my thoughts, all true."

"He will think you are lying."

"It is decided, Brother."

Chance spread his hands helplessly.

"All right. At least let me write it for you—deliver it personally—try to talk to him. But I warn you, chief—"

"No," Sitting Bull said. "This time all Indian. I have many messengers and this son-in-law writes well, all good school words. I have told you these things only so you know how they are."

Three mornings later Easterbrook and Shining Woman were aroused by the stamping of a horse outside their lodge and a harsh voice at their door-flap.

"Wake up in there! Wake up!"

The flap was brushed aside and two men entered. Catch The Bear was first. When he saw the occupants of the bed had not had time for clothing, he thrust his companion back outside and knelt beside Chance, shaking him as he might a child to make sure he was fully roused.

"Now we have it," he said in grim fury. "Now we know how it is to be. They are coming to take Sitting Bull after all!"

The old man's words poured hotly atop one another. A man from Grand River had met his brother, who was a policeman at the Agency. The policeman, highly excited, had warned him away from Grand River. Dangerous doings. White Hair was about to send the Metal Breasts after the chief. The brother had brought the news back to camp as fast as his pony would carry him.

The Bear's anger was fiery but there was harsh relish in it, too. No more waiting, at least.

"When?" Chance asked as he dragged on his clothes.

"Monday. Or some soon day like that."

"Then there's time enough for me to get to the Agency."

"I brought a horse," the Bear said. "The fastest one I think you can ride. You go up there and tell White Hair we are not afraid of his short-haired Indians. We have been wanting to kill some of them for a long time."

"No more of that!" Chance said sharply. "No fighting. Tell the others. Make them believe it."

"If they touch Sitting Bull—"

"If they carry him off like a side of beef, still no fighting. Make him see that. Whoever comes, whatever they want, tell him to do it. Peaceably, understand? That way he won't be harmed. I'll do everything I can at Fort Yates, but if there is some slip-up, it will be up to you."

The Bear glowered disapproval.

"I will say your words but they are not mine."

He bent through the flap and went outside. Chance turned to Shining Woman, trembling with what she had heard.

"It will be all right," he said. "Some mistake. You heard my words to Catch The Bear. The chief's wife is your friend, say the same thing to her. If they come here before I get back, she must make him do whatever they ask without any quarrel."

Shining Woman nodded soberly. He kissed her with a twinge of misgiving. There was danger here. Still, she would be safe in any event. She was his, a fact as well known now at the Agency and Fort Yates as here. That knowledge, in trooper and policeman alike would protect her.

She followed him into the gray dooryard and expertly folded one of the new blankets about his waist and over his thighs for protection against the dawn cold as he rode.

"Go in safety and return with many feathers," she said.

The pony selected by Catch The Bear was indeed a fast one. Chance rode it hard. It was barely noon when he reached Standing Rock. Colonel Drum was in the Agency office with McLaughlin. They made no attempt to deny or minimize the rumor that had reached Grand River. In fact, Chance suspected it had deliberately been leaked in advance.

McLaughlin showed him two telegrams that had come in the day before. One to him was from the Commissioner of Indian Affairs subjecting his authority to that of the appropriate military commanders. The second, addressed to Colonel Drum by order of the Army Division Commander, directed Drum to make it his especial duty to secure the person of Sitting Bull and to call on the Indian Agent for any cooperation and assistance necessary to that end.

"There it is, Easterbrook," McLaughlin said bitterly. "The thing I've been fighting against from the beginning. The Army taking over. Doesn't the War Department have any idea how the Indians hate soldiers out here? Any mistake the Army makes, now—and God knows they could hardly make a bigger mistake than this—the Sioux will turn out to get every trooper in the Dakotas. They're fools at Division Headquarters if they think soldiers can take the Bull alive."

"You're the fool because of your own damned stubbornness," Chance said. "Bull would have come in with Cody, but you broke that up. He'd surrender to troopers, if it came to that. He's told me so repeatedly, and he's tried to tell you. Anything but the Metal Breasts. That he won't abide. And now the Sioux are convinced that's who you are going to send."

"I am, if I can get away with it. Drum and I have talked it over. If we have to take him—and headquarters is explicit enough about that—ten times better my policemen than Army uniforms. Better than Cody on Army orders. Don't you see?"

"You're God-damned right I do," Chance said angrily. "The ultimate humiliation. You're determined to break him if it's the last thing you do."

"I'm trying to prevent a full-scale outbreak, and to top it all off, look what that confounded Indian's done. He's written me a letter telling me he wants to go down and join the rest of the wild ones in the Badlands. To investigate the Ghost Dance, he says. Investigate, hell! You know what would happen if the Army ever got wind he was even thinking of going to Pine Ridge!"

The agent threw the Bull's letter back onto his desk and paced powerfully across the room and back.

"You may not like me, Easterbrook, and I can tell you it's mutual as hell, but you've been here long enough to know I'm right. You know I've been able to hold the people on my reservation down in spite of the old Bull. The dance craze is past. It'll be entirely gone in a few weeks. They've stayed in their own camps where they belong. We haven't had one sign of trouble. Damn it, then, why can't those bunglers in the Bureau and the War Department leave us be? Now, when it's all over but the shouting, they force my hand."

McLaughlin slammed heavily back down in his chair. He looked as if he had not slept since Chance had last seen him. He ran his hand through his sweat-curled white mane.

"Look, Easterbrook, try to be reasonable. If it means anything to you, Drum and I don't like what has to be done any better than you do. But the orders are out and that's the way it's got to be. It's the best we can do, believe me."

There was a hard grit of finality in McLaughlin's voice. Easterbrook recognized the futility of further protest. He went out into the air. Colonel Drum followed him. Captain Fechet and a squad of troopers were standing near the Catch The Bear's badly blown horse.

"One thing Jim forgot to mention, Easterbrook," the colonel said quietly, "I'm putting you under protective custody. A military necessity under the circumstances, the mood you're in."

Drum nodded to Fechet. The troopers moved in.

"Come with us," the captain said.

XXIV
Night

As light faded, Shining Woman sat alone. No other knew but it had been two full moons since she had last bled. Her breasts were swelling and ached for the reassurance of caresses. There were many voices in the silence of the lodge. Some were frightening, for they were of the spirit world. A sadness hurt her that her man was not here. It was not yet the proper time to speak to him of it, but life was at work within her belly. It was the season of waiting for a woman but it was not easily done in solitude.

She ate as a duty and sat rocking over the little supper fire until it fell to embers. Fires burned beyond the chief's corral and they danced there for the ghosts. For some time, now, since the nights had become colder, old Shave Bear had been ending the dance at sunset. Sitting Bull had ordered him to do so. The chief said it was not good for the dancers to go on a visit to the spirit world if they did not come back. That was what would happen if they stayed out in night wind and cold. They would catch a sickness and die for good. But now this bad word had come from Standing Rock, they were dancing late again. There was need for much prayer.

Shining Woman was frightened by this talk. She wanted to dance, but Seen By Her Nation, who had much of the chief's wisdom because she had slept with him so long, said Shining Woman should not do so when her man was not there. She had not asked him what his feeling was about the dance before he left. It might not please him, so she listened to the distant singing.

It was very hard praying, all right. Sometimes a woman's voice rose in the anguished tremolo of utter grief. It was a sound usually heard only over the dead body of a loved one. Shining Woman knew those women were gashing themselves to make the blood flow and scrubbing the dust of the earth into their hair. She thought it must give the chief a good feeling that those people were doing these things for him.

In lonely substitute for her own prayers, she murmured the white man's word she had carefully learned. It was not an easy word, even with much practice, nor even a good sound to her ear, but it was the name they called him and it pleased him whenever she used it. In her heart she kept another word for when she thought of him. A beautiful, strong word of many soft Sioux syllables which sang when spoken, even in silence.

Captain Fechet's squad put Easterbrook in the orderly room in a front corner of the post guardhouse. It was clean, with a good cot, a table, and some chairs, and could not be considered a cell. But the windows were barred and the door strongly secured outside. At sunset McLaughlin came by with a copy of the orders he had issued to his Agency Police.

"Thought you'd like to know," the agent said.

When he was gone, Easterbrook read the warrant.

United States Indian Service

Standing Rock Agency
December 14, 1890
4:30 PM

Lieut. Bull Head or
Shave Head, Grand River:
From report brought by scout Hawk Man I believe
the time has arrived for the arrest of Sitting Bull
and that it can be made by the Indian Police
without much risk. I therefore want you to make the
arrest before daylight tomorrow morning and try to
get back to the Sitting Bull Road crossing of Oak
Creek by daylight tomorrow morning or as soon
after as possible. The cavalry will leave here
tonight and will reach the Sitting Bull Road
crossing on Oak Creek before daylight tomorrow
(Monday) morning, where they will remain until
they hear from you.

Louis Primeau will go with the Cavalry Command
as guide and I want you to send a messenger to the
Cavalry Command as soon as you can after you
arrest him so they may be able to know how to act
in aiding you or preventing any attempt at his
rescue.

I have ordered all the police at Oak Creek to pro-

ceed to Carignan's school to await your orders, this
gives you a force of 42 policemen for to use in the
arrest.

> *Very respectfully,*
> *James McLaughlin*
> *U. S. Ind. Agt.*

P. S.
You must not let him escape under any circumstances.

They were still singing out there on the dance ground but an ominous silence everywhere else seemed to stifle the sound. Shining Woman shivered. Sometimes it was as quiet when her man was here, but then it was not frightening. Sometimes they did not speak much, sometimes he would talk a great deal. He would tell her some things of his own country.

Some, of course, she had heard before. In good weather and better times, Sitting Bull had often made an afternoon circle at which women and children were welcome. He remembered, then, for all who cared to listen, many happenings from the days when he had traveled with Pahuska and had seen the whole world. Exciting things. Wonders.

It was strange to think about all those white teachers who had been coming here a long time, now. They did not know this was how a school should be. If they had been wise enough to do as Sitting Bull had done, they would long ago have had all the children about them and many others who were grown men and women, all eager to hear and to learn.

But it was even more exciting to hear her man. Such things! Some things he told her to amuse her, just as a father might do to children to watch their eyes grow round. They were tales which made her laugh because such unnatural things just could not be. Insisting then, with such earnestness, that he had seen them himself, she had to make him stop until she caught her breath. Those were happy times.

Women who did not have such times in their own lodges said it was a bad thing to live with a white man. They said white men gave a woman a sickness which made her teeth fall out and her breath stink. They said white men beat a woman and took her at the wrong time and made more dead babies than alive ones. But that was their own ugliness. To have her white man was to have an Indian. There was no difference except that there was more to do for him.

There was only one bad thing. This was not his country, perhaps one day he would go home. They did not talk about this but she knew it was so. Because of that she had her own song when she danced with those others out there. She did not let it past her lips but she sang it very loud in her heart.

It was a special prayer to let the *Wanekia* shorten the time to the new world. Spring grass might be too late. He might already be gone from here by then. Her song prayed to let him be with her when the new world came. She did not know how this would be but somehow she would get him up onto it when the time came. Then he would not be buried with all those other white people. She did not wish to live with the ghosts if he was not there. She wished to live only with him.

From his window, Easterbrook watched the cavalry detachment ride out at midnight. Captain Fechet had drawn command. He remained at the barred opening until the last sound of departure died. He was still standing there when the lamps in the mess-hall and barracks were snuffed.

The ghost dancers sang their closing song and came into the camp, weary and cold. Shining Woman heard muted complaints among them as they passed her lodge. A little later someone stopped outside the door-flap as though listening for sound within. She called out softly. Seen By Her Nation entered. The chief's wife looked very tired in the emberglow.

"Younger sister, my husband says it is not good for you to sit here without sleep," Seen By Her Nation said. "We have some others at our house but he says to tell you there is room for your blankets. Come."

Shining Woman proudly selected one of the new blankets. She wrapped into it the doll her man had brought her. She poured water from a bowl until the last hot ash of the fire died in steam. They felt their way out of the warm inner darkness into the biting cold of the night. Shining Woman made the flap secure against dogs and followed her friend.

Strikes The Kettle stood in his blanket outside the chief's door. He had a rifle in his hands and barred Seen By Her Nation's way with its barrel.

"Somebody just came from across the river," he

growled. "He say there is still light in Gray Eagle's house. Woman, do you know why?"

"Gray Eagle is only my brother, old man," the chief's wife answered. "I do not sleep with him."

"They have hung blankets over Bull Head's windows so if there is light it does not show," Strikes The Kettle complained. "What is going on over there?"

"Maybe Gray Eagle has brought some holy water down for his friends," Seen By Her Nation suggested. "It is known White Hair sometimes allows him to do that. Now they have those uniforms, those Metal Breasts do not think they are Indian any more. White Hair thinks the same way."

"Their privates have shrivelled," Strikes The Kettle said scornfully. "It will take more than whiskey to give them back their manhood."

The old man stepped back and the two women entered the cabin. Sitting Bull sat on his bed. His rifle and pistol and the belt that held his knife were on a folded blanket at its head. His braids were down for sleeping and he had removed his moccasins. His other wife and two old women sat in the opposite corner. The stove was warm, the air heavy with much breathing.

John, the young son, huddled against the wall, watching the lips of others for words he could neither hear nor speak. Crowfoot, the older boy, was near him. Catch The Bear and Brave Thunder and Spotted Horn Bull, those fierce old men, were there with some of their women. Also a few others of name and importance. All were tired, for it had been a long day. Several wore ghost shirts and dresses and a few were smudged with dust for having lain dead on the cold earth in communion with God.

The chief smiled at Shining Woman and indicated a place against the wall beyond his bed.

"Daughter," he said, "it is a good thing you are a small woman. I do not believe you will be stepped upon there. The white man has gone to do a thing for me. I wish it said I kept you comfortable in my house while he was gone."

Shining Woman nodded gratefully and settled herself as inconspicuously as she could. What was afoot resumed as it was before the interruption of her arrival.

"Strikes The Kettle keeps watch," Catch The Bear said. "One of the young men who wishes that honor will take over from him. I will take the watch myself when it is near dawn. That is when young men are most likely to sleep. And when they come, it will be at that hour."

"Do not worry so much," Sitting Bull said. "Many of you who believe in this thing have been dancing since morning. You will wish to dance again tomorrow. I do not want you losing sleep on my account. I do not want old friends standing out there in the cold as Strikes The Kettle is now doing. I do not think they will come tomorrow."

"Because the white man went to see it does not happen?" Catch The Bear asked. He snorted. "If those people up there will send Sioux to take a Sioux chief, they will not listen to the white man. They will kill him if he is in their way. That is the kind of men they are."

Shining Woman heard these words with a new grip of fear and huddled over the sudden hurt. Sitting Bull spoke gently—for her, she knew.

"That is careless talk, Brother, and not true. Think of this. It is only five days until ration time. I will not go up there in these times but the rest of you must make that journey if you are not to starve your families. Well, tonight I have my friends about me. All my warriors that are left. All my old fighting men. All those White Hair and His Metal Breasts fear most. They are not stupid men. They will come on ration day when most of you are gone and few remain with me."

"Whatever the day, we will kill them," Brave Thunder said. "They are enemies."

"No," the Bull corrected. "They are only young men. They hope to win many feathers. They wish to do a brave thing. They wish to bring me in. Well, I am not so old that my blood does not run hot when I think of that, but the words the white man left behind for us are right. I do not know the day, but when they come, my friends, we must do nothing. Maybe the white man will stop this needless thing up there. But I will go with them if that is what they say. That is my road."

Catch The Bear started an angry protest. The Bull stopped him with an upraised hand.

"Go to your lodges. If we sit here there will be no sleep for anyone. We will see how it is tomorrow."

Seen By Her Nation opened the door and most of them filed out. Seen By Her Nation went with them. By some household agreement or necessity of nature, she would not keep the chief's blankets warm tonight. That honor would go to the other wife. In addition to Shining Woman, this wife and the two old women who had sat with her and the boy, Crowfoot, remained in the cabin. All began to undress. Out of modesty, Shining Woman remained clothed, merely wrapping her blanket warm about her. As the chief slid into bed without concern for his nudity, Crowfoot put a wooden bar across the door, securing it according to the custom of the white man.

For a long time after the lamp was snuffed, Shining Woman lay in this warm and hospitable dark, listening with a good feeling, all fears at rest, to the deep, regular breathing and untroubled snoring of the father of her nation.

While Chauncey Easterbrook stood at the guardhouse window, staring through the bars, a tight body of heavily armed Indians in short hair and uniform rode silently into Jack Carignan's school, three miles below the Hunkpapa camp on Grand River. Roll was softly called. The Metal Breasts from Oak Creek crossed the river and rode upstream on the far bank, warily keeping to sod and soft, muffled going.

While Captain Fechet and Troops F and G of the Eighth United States Cavalry, one Hotchkiss and one Gatling gun in escort, rode smartly across the dark *coteau,* a supply wagon from Standing Rock took a higher ford across Grand River and came cautiously down to Lieutenant Bull Head's house. There the team was untraced and led away.

While Shining Woman lay warm in Sitting Bull's house, a small doll hugged in comfort to her breast, Jack Carignan and a small body of policemen passed within an arrow's flight of where she lay. They saw the unlighted windows and darkened Hunkpapa lodges and so reported to the tense, white-mufflered men in uniform at Bull Head's house. Carignan took Bull Head's wife and children and slipped off down the safe side of the river toward the school again.

While Jim McLaughlin slept in his bed at the Agency with one strong arm in abiding love about the woman beside him—a woman who after all was only half so Indian as the wily old enemy whose power he was about to break at last—the mustered forces of the Agency Police huddled behind Bull Head's blanketed windows. Ammunition was carried in and issued. A hundred rounds to each man. Shave Head and Red Tomahawk helped in this. They were seconds in command.

It was hard to find pockets for all this ammunition. Each man already felt heavy. Now he was weighted down. Somebody said it was many bullets for one old man. Another said that with this man it might not be enough. Better they had brought a cannon. The pony soldiers had one with them. Perhaps if a messenger was sent now it could be got here in time.

Bull Head did not like this talk. He knew the danger. That was Sitting Bull over there. He sent Shave Head and Red Tomahawk out to the wagon for the whiskey. While General Nelson Miles slept well in his suite at the Harney Hotel in Rapid City, the Metal Breasts baptized their fears in the holy water of the white man. The three leaders drank sparingly.

"If it happens this thing has to be done, then I will do it," Red Tomahawk said. "Such a feather keeps color a long time."

Bull Head liked this talk no better than that about the bullets and the cannon. Neither did Shave Head.

"Brother," he said. "Gray Eagle's house is the closest place. He expects us. Come on. We will go there now."

While Doctor Charlie Eastman and Captain George Sword of the Pine Ridge Agency Police and the Reverend Charles Cook of the Episcopal Mission—each as proudly Sioux as the most frightened and truculent ghost dancer—met constantly with Beau Lane and friendly head men and General Brooke in search of a way to ease fears and bring more people in, great fires burned in the Badlands.

While Short Bull and Kicking Bear fanatically urged the doctrine of ghost-shirt infallibility and proclaimed the awesome vengeance of God upon the white man, wiser counsellors who were at the limits of their own wisdom and beliefs kept their eyes turned to the north.

The message had been sent for some time, now. There had been no answer but he should be coming any day. They did not know this new God to whom the ghost dancers prayed. But they knew Sitting Bull. They needed God, all right, but they needed Sitting Bull more. They kept the big fires fuelled night and day to guide him to the Stronghold.

And further north, in the Cheyenne River camps of Hump and Big Foot, with soldiers pressing steadily in from Fort Bennett on the east and Fort Meade on the west and the end of all things inexorably nearing, the Minneconjous saw the smoke by day and flame by night and also anxiously awaited the coming of the Bull and his people. With him—with all these Hunkpapa friends and relatives—it would be safe to move south to Pine Ridge and a new peace. With Sitting Bull they would live. That they knew. That they believed.

At Gray Eagle's house some of the Standing Rock police knelt before a crucifix in Bull Head's hand. Some sat silently and prayed in another fashion. Neither seemed to do much good. One spoke a thought which troubled them all. What good was all this ammunition if this thing was contrary to the wish of *Wakan Tanka*—to the will of God? What if those ghost shirts did indeed have the power to turn white men's bullets? What kind of bullets were these they had now? Certainly they were not Indian. That was their own chief they were going to take.

Bull Head put the crucifix away and brought in more whiskey. Red Tomahawk swaggered and told a tale of battle. Once there was mention of blood, it was not so hard to think about. Another related a more fearsome deed. Presently they were boasting so loud they had to be quieted for fear they would be heard across the river. Gray Eagle became very fierce. That was his sister over there in the Bull's household. He would go with them and see her to safety. Even more. He would stand with them for a good gun and some bullets.

It was good to have a volunteer like that from the chief's own family. It did not seem such a monstrous thing, then. If there was trouble it would likely be a small thing, quickly done after all. Only a few troublesome old men. This time they would not spit on the badges of the Metal Breasts.

Bull Head looked at his lieutenants. They needed no

clock to know this was the time. They led the way into the pre-dawn darkness and were the first to mount their horses.

XXV
Dawn

It was the hard-packed earth beneath her ear which first spoke to Shining Woman. When she lifted her head, the sound was gone. For a breath she believed she had been awakened by the pound of her own blood. Then it was in the air as well as the earth. The beat of many horses, hard-ridden. It swelled to bursting against the cabin door. Other sleepers awakened. The chief spoke thickly in the darkness.

"What is it?"

Rifle butts crashed against planking. The bar gave way. The door flew open. The room filled with the sounds of men. Shining Woman crouched low under her blanket, felt for her moccasins, and pulled them on. A match flared. The lamp was lighted. She saw it was Shave Head who had done that. He wore a white muffler. There were many others. They were crowding, pushing at themselves, coming in and out the door like men who did not know what was to be done. Many more were outside. Many more than Shining Woman would have thought would have the foolishness to come here like this. She smelled the whiskey. They were not foolish, then. They were crazy. Only crazy men would do a thing like this.

One found the chief's rifle and pistol and belt where he had put them near the head of his bed. He carried them off with as much triumph as if he had already won his feather. He seemed very glad to get back outside again. The chief sat up. The old wife clutched at him with eyes not yet cleared of sleep. One pushed her aside and seized the chief's naked arm. That was Weasel Bear. Eagle Bear seized him by the other arm as though he was about to do some violence. The chief was a heavy man. They strained hard to pull him to his feet, naked before them all. Bull Head put a hand on him, too.

"I am holding you," he said.

"Brother," Shave Head said, and it was an ugly word on a younger man's lips like that, "Brother, we have come for you."

Red Tomahawk crowded behind the chief, jostling him over a few steps to make room to do so. He gripped him tightly about the body.

"If you fight you will be killed," he said.

Sitting Bull did not seem angered in all this excitement. If they wanted to make him look old and sag-bellied and foolish, holding him like this without his clothes, it did not work. He was a man. He tried to retain his balance as these three tugged him about.

"All right," he told them.

The old wife got some clothes about her. She stood up. She was barefoot but she was awake, now. This was her house, her husband.

"What do you jealous men want?" she shouted angrily.

A policeman found a pair of blue cloth leggings.

Another pulled an issue shirt from a wall peg. They tried to put these on the chief while those other men held him. He began to grow angry and struggled for freedom.

"Why do you honor me so? I can dress myself."

Someone found a moccasin and held it to his feet. The old wife snatched it away.

"Fool! That is mine."

"My clothes," the chief said to her. "If I am to go, I want my good clothes from the other cabin. And someone saddle the gray horse."

The old woman went out the door. She pushed through those crowding, short-haired men as though they were not there. Shining Woman saw Middle and Brave Thunder coming up outside, so there were some friends out there, now. And more people were hurrying across from the lodges. She heard them shouting as they realized what was afoot. Bull Head heard them, too.

"Come on!" he urged impatiently. "It is taking too much time!"

"You could have waited until morning," the chief said angrily. "I would already have been dressed by then."

"Get his horse," Bull Head ordered White Bird. "Hurry it up."

Shining Woman saw that the two old women who had been sleeping there had somehow gotten out of the cabin. There was no sign of the boy, Crowfoot, either. She was alone with the chief and these men, an unnoticed blanket huddled against the wall where the shadows were deepest. Her fingers gripped the doll against her breast more tightly. Bull Head peered anxiously outside.

"Come on!" he repeated urgently.

He pushed the whole group toward the door. The Bull began to struggle more violently.

"Even when I go to relieve myself I am better covered than this!" he protested.

They held him hard as they reached the door. Red Tomahawk was punching him in the back with a pistol held in his free hand. The Bull spread his arms and legs wide. They could not force him through the opening until Eagle Man angrily kicked his feet from under him.

"Brother, you should not have done that," the chief said furiously.

Eagle Man ignored him. "Keep out of the way!" he shouted to those outside. "Keep back!"

"Let him go!" they shouted in answer. "Turn him loose!"

"Get around him," Shave Head said to his companions. "Make a circle."

"Get him to the horses, quickly," Bull Head ordered. His voice was suddenly pitching upward like a woman's.

They did not get much beyond the door. They were too close for Shining Woman to slip out past them, which she desperately wanted to do. Once outside she could run away from these terrible happenings.

The Metal Breasts made their ring about the chief but that was all they could do. More of the old men, more of the people from the camp were coming up, blocking their way. Talk was fast out there among all those angry shadows. Bull Head shouted at them.

"There is no harm here. What is all this anger? White

Hair only wants him to come to the Agency."

"It is a good thing for everyone," Shave Head said to them. "White Hair wants to build him a house up there where he will be close and can do good things for all of you."

But all the time Red Tomahawk kept punching his pistol into the thick muscles of the Bull's back and repeating one order.

"Keep moving! Keep moving!"

"Turn that man loose before we take him from you," Strikes The Kettle told the policemen.

Crawler's big voice boomed in the darkness. "Shoot down the old ones first and the young ones will run. They are not men, just because they wear those badges."

White Bird came around the house with the old gray horse which had long ago been Pahuska's gift to the Bull. He saw how matters were and left it ground-tied in the yard at a little distance.

Gray Eagle was there in the ring. He had a pistol in his hand. He spoke very loudly to the Bull so all could hear.

"Brother-in-law, they say you are a wise man. Go with these policemen."

"Get away!" the chief told him angrily. "Get away from me!"

"I have tried to save you," Gray Eagle said. "Now I am through."

He put his pistol in his belt and went toward the other cabin in which Shining Woman thought Seen By Her Nation was hiding.

"Get out of there and go to my house, sister," Gray Eagle shouted. "Your husband is wrong. Do not stand up for him."

A policeman whose face Shining Woman could not see came close and spoke quietly to the chief while they were holding him there.

"Do not let these people lead you into trouble, Father. We will get proper clothes. We will not let harm come to you."

Another said a similar thing. It seemed the anger was cooling a little. But in this moment everyone heard a familiar, rumbling growl. It was Catch The Bear, a warrior whom many of those men had feared since childhood. He was carrying a rifle in both hands. His body was rocking and his head swaying a little from side to side.

"Afraid Of Bear," he was calling, giving this scornful name to Bull Head, "where are you? I am looking for the brave Afraid Of Bear."

One of the policemen was the old man's relative. He caught his arm.

"Uncle, do not do that. Do not say that."

The Bear flung the restraining hand aside with a slash of the rifle butt and levered a shell into the chamber of the weapon. That sound made all else silent.

"Afraid Of Bear, come here!" the old warrior challenged.

Bull Head took a pistol in his hand.

"I am here," he said.

With this, Sitting Bull made up his mind.

"I am not going like this!" he cried out to them all. "Come on, take action! *Hopo!*"

With great relish, Catch The Bear flung up his rifle.

He fired at Bull Head. The crashing of shots tore Shining Woman's flesh, her heart, as well as her ears. Bull Head's leg was smashed from beneath him. As he fell, he fired upward into the body of Sitting Bull. At the same time, Red Tomahawk, his pistol so long hopefully in position, fired into the chief's back. The Bull dropped without a quiver.

Strikes The Kettle shot Shave Head. The crowd scattered like an explosion itself. The shooting spread everywhere, hard and fast. The Metal Breasts fell back toward the cabins. The Hunkpapas, many of whom had come unarmed from their beds, ran back to the camp for weapons. But the old men stood by their chief.

Catch The Bear died there in the dooryard. Blackbird, too. Spotted Horn Bull and Brave Thunder. Jumping Bull, who kept his oath and died with his adopted brother. They fought until their guns were empty. Then, a horror the eyes could not believe, they suddenly lay there dead. Those old men, all of those memories of the olden times, gone forever.

In the midst of this, in that graying light where the ground was red and the end of the world had surely come, Sitting Bull's old gray show horse heard again the rattle of ammunition under a circus tent in some other part of the world and recalled his tricks. He danced stiffly backward through that leaden hail, shifting his weight heavily from side to side as he had been taught so long ago. He sat back on his haunches, both forefeet lifted, letting them hang at the first joints in a silhouette of prayer. When no one came to commend him for all this he continued to sit there, swaying to the rhythm of a martial music now only he remembered.

Some of the Metal Breasts stared in awe at the old gray horse and risked their lives for that. Seeing that no bullets touched the animal, they looked at the bloody body of their chief. They wondered if his spirit had risen in spite of this thing they had done to him and mocked them now from the body of this animal. If so, his vengeance was surely at hand. They would have run away but Bull Head shouted at them from the ground where he lay. Shave Head called more weakly from another place.

Some who lay there in uniform made no sound. Hawk Man was dead. So was Little Eagle. Shining Woman could not see them all but there were not enough to please her. Soon, however, they would all be finished. Those were Hunkpapas taking shelter over there in the timber. Their chief was dead and these were the men who had killed him.

Red Tomahawk was in command, now. He sent off messengers, riding very fast, and ordered the rest to take shelter with their wounded in the Bull's cabin. They brought Bull Head in and put him on the chief's bed. They carried Shave Head in with strings of gut hanging from his belly. In making a place for him they found Crowfoot, wedged between a bed and the wall; Red Tomahawk dragged him to the lamp. He was a boy but he was brave, even for a man. He had a right to ask for his life and he claimed it.

"Uncle, you have killed my father," he said. "I want to live."

They looked at Bull Head, groaning very hard over there.

"They have killed me," he gasped when he could. "Kill him!"

Red Tomahawk swung the barrel of his pistol against the side of the boy's head. Bone crushed. The policeman thrust hard at the same time. Crowfoot reeled through the door. Some of them out there shot him as he stumbled toward them. He fell near his father.

They found Shining Woman a moment later. She was terrified but she was a woman and they had no time for her. They only flung her out there where all that shooting was still going on. She ran toward the other cabin, calling for Seen By Her Nation, but there was no answer in all that sound of guns.

She heard bullets all about her. Her blanket tripped her. She fell hard, hurting her knee so that her stomach came up in her throat and would not go back down. She gathered herself up and ran again. She ran down through the camp, where others were also running. When she came to the river she hid in brush, nursing her knee. The ugly bruise was a small hurt to show for all the horror she had seen.

The sun was just lifting above the horizon when the messengers returned with the pony soldiers. They had two cannon. In the excitement they shot these big guns at the Metal Breasts at the Bull's cabin until someone made them understand their mistake. When the soldiers came, men ran down along the river, gathering up their women and children.

They would not fight the soldiers, they said. But now

that they did not have their chief, where would they turn? That was what the soldiers were here for, they said. To make them fight so that they could be killed. That was what had been planned. But they were not dead yet. They had friends to the south. God was coming soon down there. A day like this could not last forever.

Shining Woman heard these things but she remained in hiding until she was sure her white man was not with the soldiers. He had gone up there where they came from but he had not come back with them. He had gone up there to stop this thing but he had not done so. Who could know what had happened up there? Perhaps they had killed him, too. Certainly this was a day of death.

For her, now, there was no choice. She must go where her people went. She limped rapidly off after those who had fled before her. Like Crowfoot, she, too, yet wished to live.

XXVI

Epitaph

"*Tatanka Iyotanke* is dead."
"His own people have killed him."
"Whiskey has killed him."
"The white men have killed him."
"Sitting Bull is dead."

That is the news which swept southward. They heard it in Hump's camp. Women wailed. Hump pointed the finger of reason at all who wore ghost shirts. Would they now persist in being fools? Were they vain enough to imagine God would protect them with a scrap of painted cloth when He could not protect the greatest of their chiefs? He ordered them to stop dancing and make their lodges ready for fugitives. There would be many of them.

Big Foot's camp also heard the news. Scouts reported soldiers steadily closing in from Fort Bennett and Fort Meade. Now this! Big Foot, that gaunt, gray peace-maker, sang an old man's song. His voice was much broken up by grief and a racking cough. He sang for a dead friend. It was a sorry world. The years were too many. There was no good in them any more.

They heard in the Badlands. The great signal fires died. Short Bull made a talk at the Stronghold, full of hatred and anger and fierce promises of vengeance. But most eyes turned to Kicking Bear. He went to his lodge alone and laced the flap tightly from within. He stayed there in solitude and silence a long time. When he reappeared he carried his scarred old war-saddle, shaped to his body by hard and long usage. He tied up the tail of his best pony and fastened feathers in his mane. They saw this and ran for their ghost shirts and guns.

They heard at Pine Ridge. Some who had but lately come in to surrender and make some kind of peace ran away again. Beau Lane and Dr. Eastman and Captain Sword and Reverend Cook went at once to General Brooke. They, too, were angry men and never more Sioux than at this moment of grief and bitterness, but they knew the dead could not rise. What was done could not be undone. But there still remained hope that the nation might be saved.

They asked General Brooke to allow Chief American Horse, a brave man whom they believed had the biggest voice yet remaining, to attempt to take a deputation directly to the Stronghold. If those aroused and frightened people out there could be persuaded from doing some reckless thing which also could not be undone, American Horse was the only man who might be able to do it. The general gave reluctant consent. Beau Lane was the first man American Horse named to ride with him.

They heard in Chicago and New York and Washington. The wire service dispatch read:

"Standing Rock Agency, S. D. Dec. 16, 1890
. . . It is stated today that there was a quiet under-standing between the officers of the Indian and military departments that it would be impossible to bring Sitting Bull to Standing Rock alive and that if brought in, nobody would know precisely what to do with him. He would, though under arrest, still be a source of great annoyance and his followers would continue their dance and threats against neighboring settlers. There was, therefore, cruel as it may seem, a complete understanding from the Commanding Officer to the Indian Police that the slightest attempt to rescue the old man should be a signal to send Sitting Bull to the happy hunting ground."

At Standing Rock, where alone it was expected and

awaited most anxiously, the news came by courier. In the confusion of the arrival of Captain Fechet's cavalry detachment at Grand River, some of the fleeing Hunkpapas, vengeful and in need of transportation for the weakest among them, ran off some of the police horses. Taking what he could find, the messenger rode the dead chief's old gray show horse to the door of the Agency office. Even then the message was garbled and no one was sure of the facts until the afternoon and the night and much of the next day was gone. Then Fechet's men escorted the police supply wagon up to the dead house at Fort Yates.

Sitting Bull was in the wagon, all right. The bodies of four dead policemen were heaped atop his. The bodies of Catch The Bear and Jumping Bull and those other old men were not there. The body of Crowfoot was not there with that of his father. But for its size, the body of the old chief could not be recognized. Unwashed, partly dressed, frozen in an awkward position, it bore the wounds of seven bullets. Some of these had not bled. They had been inflicted hours after death.

It was known that Bull Head and Red Tomahawk had killed him. There was some argument as to which had been first. The post surgeon said either of their shots would have been fatal. Now they were carrying Bull Head into the dispensary to die on a white man's bed and his family was wailing over him. Soon only Red Tomahawk would be left. The feather would be his.

The soldiers explained another thing. After the fight was over, a man who was a relative of one of the dead policemen came in from the *coteau*. When he learned his kinsman had been killed, he became very hot and brave. He found a club and beat the body of the dead chief about the head. When some soldiers put a stop to that after a while, all men had looked for the last time on the face of Sitting Bull. Nothing remained but bloody wreckage. That was the way they brought him in.

The bodies of the slain policemen were laid out in the dead house. Marie McLaughlin gave their families new uniforms to dress them in. Somebody drove to Mandan for coffins. The priest came down the hill from his church, for these were Christian Indians. Over in his shop the post carpenter was making a rough pine box two feet by two feet by six feet, four inches. Soldiers kept coming in so they could later boast of it and drove some of the nails holding the box together. One cut an uncaked lock from the chief's heavy braids and put it aside for Jim McLaughlin as he had been asked to do.

A garrison officer and some Agency people were sent as witnesses. Care was taken to avoid any public ceremony. The Bull's body, just as it had come in, was forced into the carpenter's cramped box. They loaded it on a mule-cart and took it to a hole prepared in a corner of the old military burying ground, as far as possible from the sanctified earth of the cemetery of the church on the hill. Here several gallons of chloride of lime and a suitable amount of muriatic acid were poured into the box and the lid nailed down. The quicklime fumed angrily as the box was put in the ground and the unmarked grave was tamped full.

A document was prepared, attesting that the body of the head chief of the Sioux nation, not mutilated or disfigured in any way, had been sewed up in canvas, placed in a suitable coffin, and buried at the northwest corner of the post cemetery in a grave eight feet deep. Colonel Drum, the post surgeon, and several others who, like them, had not been present in person, signed this official statement, closing forever a troublesome Bureau file.

The press was invited to the funeral of the policemen and useful photographs were taken. They showed a cortege which extended a whole mile from the dead house to the church and cemetery on the hill. These had been brave and heroic men. The Agency saw they got their due. And while psalms were being sung up there, an un-rated trooper released Chance Easterbrook from the Fort Yates guardhouse. The pony he had borrowed from Catch The Bear was saddled in the compound. He was free to go. Anywhere, so long as it was away. Agent McLaughlin did not wish to see him.

Easterbrook did not ask to see the grave. Nothing was beneath that mounded patch of winter clod but the shame of a needlessness and his own overpowering sense of personal failure.

XXVII

The Plunderers

The Sitting Bull Road to Grand River showed much sign of recent travel. More than could be accounted for by the two-way official travel incident to the attempted arrest of the old chief. Indian movement, if any, Chance had judged would be to the south. However, the first northbound party he encountered, some miles above the Oak Creek crossing, was Indian. Yanktonais, he thought. Four of them, driving a dozen loose horses. Anxious for news of the situation at the Bull's camp, he tried to intercept them. In spite of his signals, they deliberately avoided him and passed a mile or so to the west.

A wagon was pulled up at the Agency Police cabin on Oak Creek. Several Metal Breasts were working on its load, which they covered at Easterbrook's approach.

"You come from Grand River?" he asked them.

"From that direction," one answered.

"Do you know how things are in the camp?"

"No," the man said. Chance knew he was lying. He pointed to the laden wagon. "Who do you have there?"

"Ask White Hair," he was told. "The wagon is his."

The policemen knotted up hostilely and waited for Chance to move on. There seemed little choice and he kicked his pony onward. The *coteau* remained empty, but a few miles further down he found a wide, recent track branching off toward Carignan's school. Distance being about the same by either route, he followed this curiously.

In about half an hour he came upon two northbound white men. They had stopped on a patch of remnant grass to re-stow one of the large packs they carried across the cantles of their saddles. They were strangers to him, nondescriptly marked by sod and saddle. He supposed they had come down on some business from the ceded lands north of the Cannonball and were homeward bound. They took in his long hair, his Indian pony, his leather shirt and moccasins, and the blanket folded about his waist.

"How!" one said.

"*Hau, kola,*" Chance answered automatically.

"Heading for Grand River?"

Chance agreed and asked anxiously of the situation there.

"Pretty well picked over," the man said. He flipped back the blanket in which his pack was wrapped. "Not much stuff like this left, if that's what you mean."

Chance stared then dismounted and knelt beside the blanket. It was heaped with personal Indian belongings. He lifted one trophy, a muslin ghost shirt painted with uncommon care and artistry. A heavy stain stiffened it under one arm.

"Where did you get this?" he demanded.

"Down yonder. Just lying around."

"With a dead Indian in it," the man's companion chuckled. "May be some odds and ends left in some of the tipis. Didn't go through them all."

Chance stiffened involuntarily. This, then, was the word. There were more dead down there. And the rest were gone. The camp was deserted. If a single Hunkpapa had remained, these scavengers would not have dared to venture in. He thought grimly of Shining Woman, the old men, the friends. Rising slowly, he dropped the ghost shirt on the pile of other beaded and buckskin booty.

"You thieving sons of bitches!" he said.

The man beside the blanket stood up, also. He hit without warning, hard and low. Chance was driven back under the feet of his own horse. The startled pony danced aside. Chance could feel the gout of outraged muscle in his groin as he straightened. The hurt was welcome. There had to be some pain somewhere and it freed his anger. He let the man hit him again to bring him within reach. His hands closed on flesh. He turned, using his weight, and carried an arm back and up in a vicious swing which snapped bone. The man dropped to his knees, clutching the tortured joint, and Chance kicked him in the face, hard. He spread-eagled backward and lay motionless.

The other man, suddenly frightened, scrambled for the rifle under the skirt of his saddle. Chance tore the weapon from him as he spun about. He raised the butt high and drove through upflung, defensive arms to hammer him to the ground, bleeding profusely from a deep scalp wound. He flung the rifle as far as he could off into the brush and caught up his pony. When he had got his seat and looked back, the scavengers lay motionless beside their heap of booty.

Easterbrook rode hard the rest of the way. Carignan's school was deserted when he reached it. The buildings were securely closed by big U. S. I. S. padlocks and the stock corral was empty. Teacher and staff had gone to some less troubled place. Or they had turned their backs so they would not have to see.

The first Hunkpapa farm patch lay just beyond the government fence. It was also deserted. A dog lay near the road, shot where it had run defensively out in the owner's absence. The cabin door gaped wide. The stove within had been knocked from its legs. The pine dresser which had been the only other piece of furniture was shattered. Nothing usable remained.

It was the same the whole way up the river. Destruction everywhere was wanton and thorough. There was no one anywhere. It was the same at Grand River. Some of the lodges still stood as though people lived among them but many had been toppled and choice hides cut from the covers. The doors of the Bull's double cabin swung wide. Beyond it some men were filling in a pit. They were short-haired Christian Indians in the stout, somber dress some of the missions provided in lieu of shabby, misfit Bureau issue.

Reverend Riggs appeared as Easterbrook rode up. The minister was in shirt-sleeves and damp with sweat in spite of the winter cold. He saw the anger in Easterbrook's face and shook his head wearily.

"God's will be done," he said. "Covers every shocked and sulphurous thing a man can say, Mr. Easterbrook. I looked to the girl's lodge first thing. And asked about. Nothing disturbed there that I could see. But she's gone. Apparently with the rest of them when they headed south after the cavalry came."

Work at the re-filled pit was now done. One of the mission Indians moved toward them. Chance dismounted. The Indian came to the head of the pony and stood there, kneading the horse's head and neck as he might the arm and shoulder of an old friend he had not seen for a long time.

"I went over to Gray Eagle's house," Reverend Riggs continued to Chance. "He says he saw her about sunup. He says she was all right then."

"For what Gray Eagle's word is worth," Chance said. "No doubt he was in with them."

"The chief was wrong, he says. He could do nothing else. Some of the policemen had come back here when I got here this morning. They were loading what was left in the chief's cabins into a wagon."

"For Major McLaughlin. I met them at Oak Creek."

"That's where she was when it started, Mr. Easterbrook. In the Bull's cabin. They found her afterward and let her go. Before the cavalry came. She was not harmed, they said. No women or children were hurt. They made a point of that."

"We just finished burying Crowfoot over there," the Indian at the head of the pony said. "With all those old men. His face was kicked in."

"Six others," Reverend Riggs said.

"Crowfoot was not a man," the Indian continued. "He was one year younger than my brother and my brother is not yet eighteen."

"There were seven bodies, all told, Mr. Easterbrook," Reverend Riggs said, continuing to ignore the Indian. "Left as they fell. None of them my people. But we could hardly leave them lying here."

"They kicked his face in when he was dead," the Indian repeated. "Red Tomahawk did that."

"That's just talk, Paul!" Reverend Riggs said sharply. "You know how we feel about that. When you don't know. You didn't see it."

"No, Father," the Indian agreed. "I did not see it. I would have had to fight, then. Even then, when it was too late, I would have had to fight. Grown men do not kill boys."

He gave the pony's nose a little pat and walked away. The Reverend Riggs shook his head in bafflement.

"I don't know, Mr. Easterbrook. I don't know. We should have come earlier but I was warned away. For two days I could get no one to come with me. Everything had been carried away by then. Some white men among the lot, too."

"I know about that," Chance said. "But most of this has got to be Indian work. Why?"

"An evil with us all, I'm afraid," the minister said wearily. "History has enough of it. Some kind of a purge to make up for long belief in something that is no longer to be believed in. The fall of English and French Kings and the excesses of the bloody rebellions which followed. People turning against their own blood and traditions. It seems to be bred in violence. It is probably what freed Barabbas and flung many a stone along the way to Calvary, too—you don't think it sacrilegious that I find a sort of Calvary here, do you?"

"No."

"Well, the chief was a great man, Mr. Easterbrook. In his way he was a very great man. There can be no doubt he meant to save his people." The minister wiped his brow with an earth-stained kerchief. "You—what do you plan, now?"

"Follow them. Find them."

"A white man crossing that river wouldn't get twenty miles after this!"

"I have to find Shining Woman."

"She's in a panic like the rest," Riggs said. "Wait a

few days. McLaughlin has already sent some of their relatives after them. They'll turn back in a little time. They'll have to or starve. Don't risk your own skin. You'll only make more trouble for them."

"I have to find her."

"This time you won't be riding with Beau Lane."

"I know. Thank you, Reverend."

Easterbrook caught up Catch The Bear's pony and rose again to saddle.

XXVIII

The Fugitives

Shining Woman remembered a few bad times when she was a young girl. Sometimes she still awoke remembering pangs of hunger and exhaustion and fear. But never had there been the nightmares now before her. From this there was no awakening. And she knew it would grow worse. Who was there to make it better?

She had her blanket and a good pair of moccasins. She was young and strong and had no one to look after but herself. There was not yet time for real hunger to set in. All the same, she was as relieved as any when the hard-riding little company of Indians from Fort Yates overtook them.

Some of these Indians had friends and relatives among those fleeing from Grand River. They brought good words with them. They said White Hair had sent them out as soon as he had learned Sitting Bull's people had run away in fear that they would all be killed. White Hair had quarreled many times with their dead chief, they said, but his heart was heavy that there had been all that fighting at Grand River. They were his people and he did not want them to suffer.

If they would come back to Standing Rock, White Hair would see they had food and necessities. Soon they could return to their own homes in safety. He understood they thought to join Hump or Big Foot or even go on to Pine Ridge. He wished to save them that. Soldiers were already closing in on those camps. He did not wish them to have more hard times, to see more blood on the ground. They were his children. He would welcome them home.

Some did not care to believe these things. White Hair was known to be a great liar. Some remembered the messiah was coming. White Hair had killed Sitting Bull, but he could not do that to God. Only bad lay behind. If there was good anywhere, it lay ahead. They would not turn back.

But for one thing, Shining Woman had a strong feeling for this in her heart. She wished very hard to have a good life. She wanted to see this day that was coming. She was curious to know how this new earth was to be managed so that it was not too fearful and frightening when it came. She wished to live in that promised all-Indian world. But she knew she must turn back to Grand River, back even to Standing Rock as these people who had been sent after them urged.

That was where her white man had gone. If he lived, that was where he would be, looking for her. She had been foolish to run away. She must go back and now was her chance. He would find her then and all between them would be as it had been before. If he did not live— if he was dead—she must go to the place where he lay.

It took some time for them all to make up their minds. More than half—perhaps two hundred—resolved to return. During this, Shining Woman learned two of the Indians from the Agency were asking for the woman who had lived with a white man at Grand River. She found them and made herself known. They drew her aside. These were hard times and they did not like to say what they must. This frightened her anew. She wanted to put her hands over her ears. White Hair had told them to find her and tell her the truth.

Let her know first that the white man lived. He had not been harmed. He had come up there before the arrest and made loud talk against it. White Hair and the soldier chief were afraid he would go back to Grand River and make further trouble there when they sent for the chief. That was why they put him in the jail-house. He stayed there for three days. When all those dead men were brought in and buried, they set him free. They gave him his pony. It was supposed he would return at once to Grand River. It was supposed he would follow his woman's people and find her. After that it was sup- posed he would make a big trouble that the chief was dead and something would have to be done about that. But that would not be necessary, now.

When this white man came out of the jailhouse it seemed his bow was broken and his arrows all spent. He spoke to no one and rode his pony north toward the

Cannonball. That was the road to Mandan. From there it was not far to the railroad at Bismarck. It was also the road to his own country. It was believed at Fort Yates that he had gone there and would not return.

Their message delivered, the Agency Indians left her. Shining Woman watched them go without seeing. She had always feared this. Now it was here. She sat apart and watched those Hunkpapas who were returning to the Agency start north with their friends. When they were gone from sight she found some things to carry for others and took a woman's place among the hundred and fifty Hunkpapas who yet believed God could be found in the south.

An empty land closed around them. It began to turn brutally cold as shadows lengthened. The men resolved to travel by night and hide by day so that they could not again be found. They sang no songs, even to the ghosts. But the same prayer was in every heart: shorten the way and hasten the day.

Chief American Horse and his party were not permitted near the Stronghold. Nor were the ghost dancers at first disposed to meet with these emissaries from Pine Ridge on any grounds. However, when it was learned that American Horse had brought gifts, the party was allowed to move up to the base of one of the mesa walls, where ropes could be lowered from above.

The offerings were appraised and it was finally agreed that American Horse could send one man up to the Stronghold entrance to meet the leaders there. If he had words acceptable to their ears, they would hear him out.

However, after much further shouted harangue, Beau Lane was the only man the dancers would accept.

Beau began the climb with considerable care, knowing those were nervous men up there and every movement suspect. When he reached the narrow land bridge leading onto the citadel proper, the hostile crowd at the other end was dense and large. He knew the count. The hard core here had been swelled by the fifteen hundred or two thousand who had already come into Pine Ridge to give this thing up and had been stampeded back again by news of Sitting Bull's murder.

It was supposed Hump would bring his Minneconjous down as soon as he could elude the soldiers pinning him down on Cherry Creek. Sitting Bull's people were believed also to be fleeing south to join either Hump or Big Foot before coming on. When these arrived, the nation would be wholly reunited. They would never be stronger and they knew it. That was what made it hard. They had no food. Even the wildest could have no hope. But they still had their pride. If any man knew that, Beau Lane did. He still had his pride, too.

At first the crowd gave Beau no chance to speak. They hurled taunt and invective and angry challenge at him, gouging at him to burst the seams of anger. Twice mounted men burst through the press and charged across the narrow way as though to run him down. He stood unflinching and dirt rained on him as they pulled up at the last moment. Finally it was a man afoot as he was who gave him the opportunity for which he was hoping, for he knew it had to be done right if it was to be done at all.

The approaching man was a young, big-bodied Brule. He flourished a gleaming new Winchester with the initials of the United States Army burned into the otherwise unscarred butt. He swaggered up to within a yard. He rammed the muzzle of the rifle against Beau's belly, levered a shell into the chamber, and hooked a finger about the trigger with the hammer at full cock. The will to kill was in his eyes.

"Shoot!" they cried behind the Brule. "Send him back dead. That is a message they will understand down there!"

Beau pulled up the tail of his shirt so his belly was exposed for all to see. The muzzle of the rifle was hard and cold against his flesh.

"Big doings!" he said scornfully. "What am I? A white man? All right, then, how many white men have you killed with that new soldier gun? Do as they say over there. Shoot. Kill the white man. But you will have killed the Indian, too. Me, yes. And you. And all those Indians behind you."

Many understood him at once, at least in part. They were quick to point out his mixed blood made what he said true. Some also were impressed by his bravery and said he should be heard. But they were shouted down. Finally their ranks broke and Kicking Bear himself came, striding forward, dismissing the truculent Brule with a sharp gesture.

"Why do we waste all this time?" he demanded. "Sitting Bull is dead. Do you think we intend to be next?"

"Brother," Beau answered quietly, "Sitting Bull was my uncle. I grieve with all men here."

"As an Indian?"

"No. Today as a white man. That was a bad thing. It will shame them for a long time. But I have another thing to tell you."

There was a stir behind Kicking Bear. The high priest of the dancers turned his head. Several of the older and more important men were moving up. They wanted to hear. It was a good sign. For the first time, Beau eased a little.

"You are afraid of the white man," he said so all could hear. "That is all right. A man is a fool who is not afraid when he is in danger. You all know that, but you do not see that the white man is also afraid of you. That is what has made him do some foolish things. Are you going to be foolish, too? The white man knows that when there is even a little war with the Sioux, many soldiers die. That is a lesson you have taught him many times. Now is the time to teach him how to make a good peace."

"You may be Indian," Kicking Bear answered. "But those are white man's words."

There was an ugly clamor of assent, the dangerous sound of anger poorly held in leash. Beau held up his hands.

"American Horse and those others down there waiting for me are chiefs and head men. You may not like them for what they do these days, but they are Indian and you respect them for what they are and what they have been. Am I to go down there now and tell them you will not even hear me?"

There was another clamor but Kicking Bear silenced it with a single word.

"Speak!"

"I say it is not the white man the Sioux have to fear," Beau resumed, speaking strongly, now. "See how it is at Standing Rock. Sitting Bull, the greatest man in our nation, is dead. But that murder was not done by white men. Those were Indian guns. Those Metal Breasts did that because they believed it was the right road. Well, they have traveled that road, now, they have stood against other Indians. That is a wound which will not heal.

"If this war you talk about comes, what good will it be to kill the white man? There will be others to kill, too. The chiefs waiting down there for me, the other chiefs and head men who have kept their people in at the Agency, the policemen and hired men who work for the Government—they will have to fight you to protect their own women and children. I have tried to show you where my heart is, but I would have to fight you then, too."

The young Brule broke away from companions and came bounding out again, cocking his rifle. Kicking Bear jerked the weapon from the man's hands. He swung to face Beau and fired the commandeered weapon. Gravel stung Beau's shins as the bullet struck close to one moccasin.

"You will fight no one!" Kicking Bear said malevolently.

Beau ignored the shot as well as the unmasked threat.

"You say you must wait out here for the *Wanekia*. Do you think he cannot find you at the Agency? Do you imagine he will only come here and ignore those people down there who have been making his dance a long time, too? Do you think his heart will still be sweet toward you when he finds you have broken his law and made a war? Wait until he sees how you have painted the ground with Sioux blood!"

"No Sioux will kill another!" Kicking Bear shouted.

"Those are a brother's words," Beau retorted. "Now take action as a brother. Allow these people to go back to their homes before they starve out here. Do you know what the children are saying? They are hungry and there is little fuel. Remember that it has been a long time now since even a brave man could feed his family with a gun."

This time they remained silent. It was not a new thought. Many had had it before. All eyes turned to Kicking Bear. There was no compromise in the look the Minneconjou gave Beau, but he was no fool. He turned to face his people.

"Let every man hear this," he said. "I want no man here who wishes to be in another place."

Kicking Bear tossed the rifle back to the Brule, who caught it eagerly. Beau knew he was dismissed. He turned his back and started unhurriedly down the approach trail. Behind him he heard the slap of palm on steel and a concerted catch of breath. He knew the Brule had thrown his Winchester up, sighted at the center of his back. He held his pace and did not turn his head.

At three hundred yards the shot had not come and he knew they would come in. Not suddenly. The first in a few days, perhaps. Not all at once. There would be many councils, many personal decisions. Those who first broke would be stung by the scorn of those who remained. But in the end they would all return to their homes.

Beau felt a sudden warming of vanity. All men love feathers. He regretted Chance Easterbrook had not seen this.

Chance would have understood what it had taken to do this. It would have made good reading. Chance would have recorded who it was who had really accomplished this thing. Not those chiefs waiting down there at the foot of this trail, not the friendlies remaining at Pine Ridge or the Army or the Seventh Cavalry. One man, only—Beau Lane, a half-breed.

His word, his arguments, and all those angry men accepting them. All but Kicking Bear, who would accept nothing not of his own doing. But Kicking Bear had been the easiest from the first. He was a war chief, a tactician, a general, and this was winter. Winter was not the time to make war. Kicking Bear knew that. He would have to come over, too. So the bad time was now done.

When they reached Cheyenne River Shining Woman was further from home than she had been since she was nine years old. She was also more weary than she could remember. Her strong moccasins were wearing thin. Her knee was swollen and pained her when she walked. They had taken great care to leave no sign even a scout could follow. But it did not seem possible it could take so many plodding steps to cover so little country in the long, dark hours between sunset and dawn.

Shining Woman sometimes wondered if these night marches would go on until her time was used up and she had to stumble aside to spawn her child on the brittle grass to die. When she thought this, bitterness churned like an herb emetic. This was the white man's way. He gave his body and it seemed the good thing but it was only to plant a parasite which grew, sucking breath and blood, until it was an intolerable burden which distended the belly and bent the back and dulled the spirit, while he went away to some other place to be free of it all.

They came at last to Hump's camp and were welcomed. The men met with the Minneconjous. Hope and wisdom returned. Medicine men who knew weather said snow would come soon and this was no season to travel in. This was a good place with friends about. Presently a Hunkpapa delegation could go down to the Cheyenne River Agency. Hump said there was a good Government man there. They could explain they had come here because they had been driven from their homes. This was also Sioux land and the agent could make some arrangements for rations and other necessary things.

While these matters were being discussed, a soldier captain came. At one time he had been in charge of Hump and his people and they regarded him as a friend. He said he had recently been stationed many hundreds of miles away in the country of the Comanches. Bear Coat Miles had sent for him all that distance to come here and explain what Hump and his people must now do.

"Now that Sitting Bull is dead, General Miles believes you are the most dangerous man left in this country up here," he told Hump. "He has to do something about that. So this, my friend, is what I want you to do. Take your people downriver to Fort Bennett. Give them your guns down there and camp close by until all this trouble is over."

There was much outcry at this. The Minneconjous said their homes were here, and besides they were making no trouble. They had even given up the Ghost Dance because their chief said it was not the road to peace. And what of all these Hunkpapas, these friends, who were guests here? Helper, a young man and Hump's son, was very angry.

"I will stay here," he said. "I will defend my fire."

Hump shook his head at this. He had too many lives in his hands. Four hundred of his own people and a hundred and fifty of Sitting Bull's band who no longer had anyone to protect them. He did not like the road he saw but he would take it. He told the captain to go back to his nearby soldiers and lead the way. In the morning they would follow the soldiers into Fort Bennett.

Afterward, Shining Woman's people talked together. They agreed that they had not endured hard times getting to this place only to become Agency Indians. They knew how to move at night and decided to go then to another place. When the time came, Helper and about thirty of his father's Minneconjous were of the same spirit.

Speechless John, the boy who had become a man since the death of his father and his brother, stole a gun as they left the camp. He stayed with Shining Woman while traveling because she also was without family. The night passed in hope that this would be their last flight, but when they came straggling into Big Foot's camp, they discovered that trouble was there, also.

Some soldiers had crossed over from Fort Meade, to the west, a direction from which they were not expected. They were now quite close and sent word they were coming to put Big Foot and his band under arrest. They were going to take their guns and march them down to Fort Bennett. As for the Hunkpapas who had just now come straggling in, they were Sitting Bull's people, known troublemakers and fugitives from their own reservation. They also would be put under arrest. All must be ready to move when the soldiers arrived.

When the soldier messengers were gone they held a long council. Minneconjous and Hunkpapas alike. Their very lives were involved in this, now. Criers went through the camp and summoned everyone. Big Foot had a hard cough making it difficult to say much, but he spoke earnestly. Shining Woman listened with the others. She knew his words were wise, the only words to be had at such a time, but they weighted her heart even more.

"I do not wish to say it but I think the same as you all do," the sick chief said. "I think they mean to take us over there and get our guns and kill us. Even if that is not so, I do not wish to be a prisoner in my own country. You Hunkpapas now have no father and have come here because you wish me to protect you. Well, see how it is. I am an old man now and cannot even protect my own children."

These were true words but they were frightening. A good and once powerful chief was saying them. When the big men of a nation had such feeling, what were the people to do? Some of the young men did not like to see those old man's tears in the corners of their chief's eyes. They tried to make some big talk but Big Foot silenced it wearily.

"To make these foolish boasts does nothing for us. A long time ago I made the white man a promise I would not fight. That promise I will keep. I see only one thing for us. The Oglalas at Pine Ridge are our brothers. Red Cloud is old but he is still a very strong chief down there. He has much influence with the white men. Even with Bear Coat. And he is wiser than those other men out there in the Badlands. He waits for the *Wanekia*. But he waits in peace at the Agency.

"It is a hard time to travel. It is a long road. But if we can keep all these soldiers from finding us until we reach Red Cloud, his blanket will cover us all. Go, now. Load your wagons and drags. Take everything. We will not return to this place again."

XXIX
Bear Coat Miles

Easterbrook's search came to an end in a prairie-dog hole on the frozen *coteau* within sight of the bare lodge-circles of Big Foot's abandoned camp. He was following no trail for there was none.

There were no stragglers, no word. Only that she had fled south with the others to join Big Foot. And now he, too, was gone.

Since he carried no other weapon, Chance was forced to use his "brother" knife to relieve old Catch The Bear's pony from the agony of its broken leg. That unpleasant duty done, he started on afoot, knowing that somewhere ahead, Shining Woman must be doing the same. But in half an hour he was intercepted by an Army courier team enroute from Fort Bennett to Fort Meade. No explanation he could offer for his presence here without horse or gear would satisfy the conscientious troopers and his name meant nothing to them. They took him into custody and resumed toward their destination.

They arrived at Fort Meade on the afternoon of December 23. Here Chance learned General Nelson Miles had set up campaign headquarters in the Harney Hotel in nearby Rapid City. He requested an immediate interview with the general. Not altogether to his surprise, he was summoned at once, as soon as his identity was learned. He went to the headquarters suite as he was.

The commander-in-chief of the Army of the West was a genial, self-assured man. He dispensed cordiality and sympathetic consideration with the conscious generosity of most popular and important public figures, a trait Easterbrook disliked in them all. He chided Chance upon some of his attitudes, particularly toward the military posture in the Dakotas in recent months, but complimented him upon the research and skill evident in his published reports upon the Ghost Dance and the ensuing troubles it had brought on. He poured him a drink from his private bottle. But he refused a pass to go on to Pine Ridge.

No one there, including his half-breed friend Beau Lane, knew the whereabouts of Big Foot's fugitive band at this time. However, if the girl he was so concerned about was with those Indians, she was absolutely safe. Every detachment in his command was looking for Big Foot and his people. They were known to be without supplies and in serious straits. Orders were to locate them as soon as possible, place them in protective custody, and escort them into Pine Ridge before worsening weather added to their already considerable hardships. Common sense indicated that there was nothing further Easterbrook could do at this time and he looked in need of a furlough, himself.

"In addition," the general said, "although it is clarifying rapidly, that's still a very delicate situation over there at Pine Ridge. They're coming in peaceably, now, but they stampeded once. We can't risk having them do so again. That's why I set my headquarters up here instead of over there at the Agency. They know me. They've fought with Bear Coat Miles before. I didn't want to alarm them further by showing up on the reservation until they're all in and under control.

"It will only be a few more days at most, Easterbrook. Get yourself a room and a bath and a square meal. Christmas season, you know. Buy yourself a drink. Lot of your competitors downstairs. I've had to restrict them, too. You can all go over with us on the headquarters train when the word comes."

Considering all things wearily, Easterbrook supposed Miles was probably right. And he was in need of furlough. He bought some fresh clothing and took a room at the Harney. He washed his hair and sprawled in the incredible luxury of a hot tub. He shaved with care and dressed. The feel of clean cloth against his skin was an almost forgotten sensation, but he did not abandon the comfort of his moccasins.

He ate alone but afterward found himself restless still and wondered if there was a palliative in the company of his own kind.

The Harney Bar was a large, gregarious room, filled at this hour with a number of townsmen celebrating the approach of Christmas, a few officers from Miles' command, and some gentlemen of the press. Easterbrook knew several of the latter and certainly they had heard of his arrival. But the word was obviously out. They moved around him. They traded ribald jokes across his drink. They jostled his glass against his teeth when he raised it. They trod on his moccasins. But they pretended he just was not there. He did not exist.

It was a familiar enough treatment. He had participated before, but not on the receiving end. He was astonished at how infuriating it could be. He succeeded in ignoring it for a while, but sometime after his third drink, he began to think about retaliation. He remembered the soddy farmer up on the *coteau* beyond Grand River who had hit him in the groin. That had turned on a fine fury in him. He decided that was what he would like to do. He would like to hit one of these game-playing, bar-reporter bastards in the belly.

He had another drink. The idea became progressively more attractive. He concluded the cooperative offense justified a kick in the crotch as well. He turned his back against the bar and leaned there in search of a suitable victim. None of them seemed to have an inkling of his dark thoughts. Several of them were seated with a couple of Miles' officers at the nearest table. They presently commenced a snickering and behind-the-hand comment he judged concerned his moccasins and cut of hair. He put his glass on the bar behind him with the firm, decisive bang of a man of action.

The only other solitary drinker at the bar was a great, barrel-bodied man with equally massive legs but curiously small and delicate hands and feet. He apparently had been watching Chance. He smiled with what seemed to be encouragement.

Chance felt no particular animosity toward the victim he had chosen. Not on a personal level. It just seemed a soul-satisfying thing to do. The man lifted up out of his chair with surprising ease. Chance turned him to a suitable angle. The blow went in neatly, square to the belt. The big man behind Chance at the bar bellowed joyfully in badly accented Sioux dialect.

"Hoka hey!"

The man Chance had hit belched alarmingly. He sat slackly on the edge of the table and skidded backward across it on his butt. The kick Chance aimed was timed too slow and overturned the table instead. That left a cavalry officer standing there in some surprise. Chance remembered that the cavalry had locked him up at Fort

Yates when he could have gone back to Grand River that day and saved Chief Sitting Bull's life practically single-handed, so he hit the officer, too.

The military man looked a little more surprised but he continued to stand there. Enjoying the opportunity immensely, Chance hit him again. That did it. He tipped over the table top and disappeared. Some of the other uniforms did not like that and started toward Chance. The big man from the bar bounded over ahead of them. That was all right with Chance. He swung again. This time it did no good. The big man fended off the blow. He grabbed Chance by the slack of his shirt and hustled him toward the door.

"Hoka hey!" the big man shouted at the other uniforms, brandishing his free fist in their faces. *"Hoka hey!"*

They got into the foyer somehow. The uniforms fell back. The big man dragged Chance up a flight of steps and into a room. There was a bottle of gin and one glass on a dresser. Chance got the glass. His companion took the bottle. Chance did not particularly care for gin but he was thirsty, now. The big man took a great swallow from the bottle.

"Want to fight the whole damned Seventh Cavalry?" he demanded with some admiration. "That was Colonel Forsyth you pasted!"

"I pasted him twice," Chance said.

"Damned if you didn't," the big man agreed. He put out his hand. "You're Easterbrook, aren't you? I'm Fred Remington."

Chance winced at the grip but he guessed they were

all big men tonight. He did not think it at all incongruous this genial giant was the most gifted artist in the nation. This was the way God should build genius and so seldom did, he said. Stature to match talent. Writers, too, by hell. Even newspapermen.

Remington considered this a lovely thought. Sheer imagery. But a problem as far as he was concerned. He not only painted and sculpted and drew. He wrote some as well. Right now on assignment from *Harper's Weekly.* So that was two talents and he should be twice as big. But it wasn't practical. Hardly find a horse stout enough to carry him now.

"Horse," Chance said. "Yes. Met a friend of yours at Pine Ridge a while back. Army. A Lieutenant Something-or-other."

"Pershing," Remington agreed. "Black Jack Pershing, they call him. And he likes it. Makings of a real martinet but he's got a nice feeling for the finer things of life. Traded him a horse for a bottle of gin."

"A drawing," Chance corrected. "I saw it."

"Not bad, was it?" the artist asked. "And worth more on paper than on the hoof. Really getting my rate up there, these days. Miles got you in durance vile here, too?"

"For a few days, he says."

"Hell of a way to see a war," Remington snorted indignantly. "He doesn't assign me to a field outfit pretty quick I'm going to draw him at a latrine with his stars all showing."

Remington looked at the gin bottle.

"A raid on the commissary seems to be in order, Easterbrook. We're worse off for rations than a couple of bare-assed Sioux!"

They took the stairs abreast. The military saw them coming and prudently retired from the bar. The remaining trade was respectful and reasonably hospitable. The drinks were on them, Remington said. They agreed and paid.

A military train rolled into Rapid City on Christmas Eve. It brought Casey's famous Cheyenne scouts and their mounts down from Montana. Remington, a great admirer of the flamboyant Lieutenant Casey was overjoyed. Somehow he wangled assignment to them from Miles. Easterbrook had greater difficulty getting through to the general.

"Cheyennes have been allies of the Sioux since God knows when," he warned Miles. "Practically brothers. You send them onto the reservations now and there may be hell to pay. The Sioux will think you're turning their cousins against them. It could be Grand River all over again."

A messenger from the wire office interrupted them. Pursuit was closing up with Big Foot's fleeing band. There had been no contact yet but the fugitives' direction was plain. They were already deep into the Badlands and apparently heading for the Ghost Dance Stronghold.

Miles briskly issued orders. Pursuit was to continue pressing in from the rear. Casey's Cheyenne scouts and Colonel Forsyth's battalion of the Seventh Cavalry would leave at once to try and intercept Big Foot short of the dancers. General Brooke was ordered to start a detachment from Pine Ridge by way of Wounded Knee Creek to cut them off from the south. Entrapment was certain.

"Well, Easterbrook," Miles inquired when the orders were on their way, "disapprove of using those Cheyennes, now?"

"Merry Christmas, General," Chance said.

The next day Frederic Remington had a taste of the action for which he was so eager. Headquarters was advised that Casey and Forsyth had sustained attack by a strong Ghost Dance scouting party from the Stronghold and stopped in their tracks. Miles hastily ordered disengagement to avoid expansion of the skirmish. He directed Casey and Forsyth to proceed at once to Pine Ridge, and put themselves under General Brooke's command there. Brooke was instructed to send his force at Wounded Knee on out into the Badlands to locate Big Foot's people and take them into custody at once.

After an uneasy twenty-four hours, Brooke wired excitedly that although contact had not yet been made with Big Foot's band, the entire Ghost Dance force at the Stronghold had struck their big camp there and were on their way into the Agency with the Cheyenne scouts and other detachments easing cautiously along behind to pick up any stragglers.

So General Miles' tactics had been right, after all. With this news, the rebellion—the great Sioux Outbreak of 1890—was all over but the shouting.

XXX
Wounded Knee

The only man in Big Foot's party who knew anything about the dreaded *macoce sica* they were crossing was a visiting Oglala who had been among them when the soldiers came. He was a ghost shirt man and he feared the Agency at Pine Ridge. Too many soldiers were there. It was much closer to the ghost dancers' Stronghold, he said. Over there, west, only a little way. That was where God was coming. That was where he wanted to go.

Shining Woman thought she wanted the same thing. She had torn strips from her blanket to pad her moccasins. She had given bits to others who had no covering for their feet. Hunger was past gnawing now and left only weakness. She felt like a woman in her last month instead of her fourth. She wanted to be quickly where God was. Or was it only that she longed for a camp where there was meat in the pots and the lodges stood for more than one night? She did not care, really, if only the way was short.

Others said the same thing but Big Foot refused to hear their words. His eyes were bright with fever, now. His old wife, with her blanket about both of them on the seat of the wagon, held the reins and drove. The chief's breathing could be heard two wagon-lengths away. In two days, he kept saying. In two days they would be with Red Cloud. They could live that long.

Yellow Bird, the medicine man, looked into the cold steel blue of the sky and threw dust in the air. Better not three days, he said. In three days it would snow. They knew what that meant. If they had not reached food and shelter by then they would die. Children shivered and whimpered. Many faces were already black with frostbite. They left their blood on the ground where they walked.

When night came they halted again in the open. Not many lodges were put up because of the labor of striking them again in the morning. All who could found space to sleep within the wagons or beneath them. A strong north wind came. For the first time in many days the chief said they could have fires. The soldiers might be close behind and see the glow but they could not go on if they froze here, anyway. There was not much fuel, much heat. John Sitting Bull sat beside Shining Woman at one of the small fires. That was how she saw a wonder not all in the camp were privileged to see.

There was some moon, very bright. A frost haze was in the air. Hearts were heavy. There had been no talk for some time. Suddenly John began to shriek fearfully, pointing into the Western sky. There on the highest ground to be seen a figure stood against the skyglow, beckoning. Shining Woman recognized man and dress at once. John's mouthings roused the camp but only a few looked up in time to see.

"Sitting Bull!" they cried. "He lives!"

Then it was gone. There was great excitement for a time. In the morning much of it had died down. Only twenty men—perhaps sixty people if their women and children were counted—found the courage to strike out westward with their Oglala guide toward the Stronghold to which they had been beckoned. Shining Woman had been frightened by the vision and would not go. John Sitting Bull had tears in his eyes that he had seen his father again, but he also would not go. Big Foot led them south again, the wagon tires squeaking as they cut tracks in the frosty earth.

Scouts fell back a little more, apprehensively watching behind them, but when horsemen were sighted, they were ahead. There were four, three of them plainly Indian. Two of the Indians and the white man with them wheeled and rode back the way they had come. The remaining Indian rode toward them.

People asked Yellow Bird what this might mean. He put on a ghost shirt. It was very dirty for he was an old and untidy man. Some who saw him do this hastily found cloth of white color and waved it earnestly. The approaching Indian had long hair and sat an Oglala saddle. But he wore a ragged blue pony soldier uniform. Many thought that was a bad sign.

The Indian came up in friendly fashion. He was a scout from Pine Ridge, he said. There was no cause for alarm. And it was a good thing he had found them when he did. He could see they were nearly done in. But that was all right, now. It was not far to the Agency. Even with their worn-out moccasins and weary horses he thought it was possible they could set their lodges up in Red Cloud's camp tonight.

It was also a good thing they had listened to their chief and not turned off with those others toward the Stronghold. If they had done so they would have found an empty camp, no food and no shelter. The ghost dancers were on their way in. Even Short Bull and Kicking Bear and all those other desperate men. Already they were gathering on White Clay Creek, not five miles from the Agency. A thousand lodges were said to be there. This bad time was all over, everywhere. The Sioux were one people again.

Shining Woman was not sure of all these words.

"Father," she asked Yellow Bird, "if this is the time, is it true then that the white men are already put away?"

"I only know that tomorrow snow comes," the old medicine man answered.

Soldiers rode into view where those other men had disappeared. They were riding hard in full battle order.

"It is all right!" the Oglala shouted. "They come to help you."

He was not heard. Old fear does not die so quickly. Shining Woman felt it vault in her stomach. White cloth waved everywhere. Even Big Foot, blanket-wrapped, shook out a rag of flour sacking. The soldiers rattled to a halt at a little distance and took a cannon from the back of a mule. They pointed it at the wagons. Big Foot had himself driven out to meet the blue-coat chief. The blue-coat seemed angry and it was a very short talk.

The chief sent back word how it was to be. He had told the blue-coat the bad way they were in. He explained they only wanted to get to their cousins at Pine Ridge as quickly as possible. But that was not what the blue-coat wanted. They were under arrest and must surrender at once, right here. There was a soldier camp at a short distance on Wounded Knee Creek, still fifteen miles or so from the Agency. They would be taken there for the night to rest and be fed. In the morning they would go on as prisoners to Pine Ridge.

"This is not the way a Sioux wishes to come among his relatives," the chief said. "But it is the blue-coat's wish. Let no man say hard words over it."

They started on, then. Big Foot's wagon followed two troops of pony soldiers. The weary Hunkpapas and Minneconjous strung out behind it. Yellow Bird, riding on the tailgate of a wagon, sang some ghost songs. The words he used were not the teachings of the *Wanekia*. The people closed their ears. What he sang of now was death.

Shining Woman looked once behind her. Closely following the last stragglers were two more troops of pony soldiers with the cannon. They were also singing.

"Yellow Hair's song," an old woman said. "Yellow Hair's men. It is not the day of God. It is their day. They still remember the Greasy Grass. Now we are dead."

After a long time they came to some abandoned cabins where people had lived but were now gone away. There was also a small store which the Oglala scout said belonged to a mixed-blood named Mousseau. It was also abandoned. Not much further on was the soldier camp. It seemed they had sent word in to Pine Ridge and they had sent out more soldiers with an important officer to take command of everything.

So many soldiers made many tents in straight and unfriendly rows. These were on flat ground back of Mousseau's place and near the creek. There was more flat ground right up to the edge of a ravine which ran off into some low hills in the direction of Pine Ridge. They were told to set up their lodges there. And they were to be prisoners, all right.

Soldiers and Indian scouts were across the ravine, blocking the way to the Agency. They put troops to watching on all other sides. There was a steep little hill at the end of the flat ground between the ravine and the soldier tents. They took some cannons up there and pointed them down at the camp. Some men stayed there as if they were waiting for something. It was a frightening thing to see that. Big Foot sent for Yellow Bird.

"I am too sick to do much," the chief told the old medicine man. "Tell them not to be afraid. The blue-coats mean us no harm. It is just their way of doing these things. Tomorrow we will be with Red Cloud."

Presently, starting to the creek for water, Shining Woman heard Yellow Bird speaking to a family of Minneconjous as the women stretched their ragged lodge cover.

"Do not be afraid," the old man was saying. "Already some of us have seen Sitting Bull. Other great things will soon happen. We will not be prisoners long. If these soldiers shoot at us, their bullets can do nothing."

These were not the chief's words. Shining Woman found no comfort in them.

She went on toward the creek. A soldier stopped her. She showed him the kettle. He took it from her and dropped it to the ground. He put his hands on her at soft places, feeling through her dress. She knew better than to cry out. They were many. More might come. So she fought in frightened silence. The soldier was strong and would soon have had her on the ground but a sharp voice spoke and she was free. An Indian scout was there and a lesser head man among the blue-coats. He cuffed the soldier off ahead of him.

"It is not permitted to go to the creek, sister," the Indian scout said. "It is dangerous, as you can see. Many of these blue-coats still have holy water in their tents since it was a big holiday only a few days ago. Make do until morning. Tell your friends to do the same. This is no time to have a bad feeling over a woman."

"Thank you, cousin," Shining Woman told him. "I will say your words."

She returned to Big Foot's lodge. John Sitting Bull was there. He was very excited. He took her out before the lodges. They had put up a soldier's tent there, staked around the bottom against the cold. It was a place for Big Foot. The sick man and his family were already there with a stove to make the air warm. And the soldier's doctor was bending over the chief, making a good medicine. It made a good feeling for all who came to see.

A big wagon with six mules, driven by an Agency Indian, drew up before the tent and inquired for someone to issue rations. A man was named and climbed up to pass out food. He gave Shining Woman enough for six people when she said some here had no one to cook for them and that she would feed that many. Big Foot's wife heard that and allowed her to use the chief's lodge since they now had this warm tent.

She cooked for John, two grown men who now lacked

families, and three ravenous old women who did not wish to take food from the mouths of their grandchildren in their own lodges. It was not a hunter's feast but it filled bellies as they had not been filled for many days. The long way was behind. Tomorrow they would be with their cousins.

Lights burned in the soldier tents across the flats a long time. They had stoves over there and they were singing. That was all right. A good feeling should belong to everyone. Eleven came to sleep in Big Foot's lodge. Reassured by the deep, close at hand breathing of others, Shining Woman lay hard against the doll clutched beneath her chin and slept heavily, without dreaming, for the first time since terror had ended that last peaceful night at Grand River.

The soldiers greeted the sun with blaring bugles. The Hunkpapas and Minneconjous who had been waiting, long awake, ventured uneasily outside then. More soldiers had come in the night. They were everywhere on all sides, now. But it was a good morning, a bright morning, with no wind. Another wagon came. It contained soldier hard-bread for them all. An interpreter announced that it was not much but it would keep back hunger until they reached the Agency.

After this he said the soldier chief, Forsyth, wished all men to come out before Big Foot's tent for a council. With all the trouble past, that seemed all right, so the men filed out. Yellow Bird watched them and sent back any who owned ghost shirts and did not wear them to put them on. Women, already packing and preparing to strike lodges, saw this and took time to put on their ghost dresses, also.

Shining Woman was dismantling Big Foot's lodge for his wife. John Sitting Bull came there for his blanket. He put it about his shoulders and slid beneath it the good rifle he had stolen when they left Hump's camp. Shining Woman signalled it was not good to take a gun to council but the Bull's mute son ignored her. She saw others were doing the same thing and did nothing more. Still, she was apprehensive as she resumed her duties.

The men sat in a semicircle before Big Foot's soldier tent. The flap was open and the sick chief lay on a bed within. Chief Forsyth of the soldiers came. He had a Black Robe with him. An interpreter made his words understandable to all. He wanted them to see this holy man so they would know they were safe at his hands. But they had escaped from their own reservations and the Government had much trouble finding them again. He wanted them to know there was not going to be any more of that kind of foolishness. That was why he had all these soldiers and those cannon up there. However, if they did as they were told, everyone would be kind to them.

Some were still not so sure of this. A very brave ghost-dancer stood up. He had talked during the night to a relative who was a scout, he said. He had heard the reason they had stopped here was that they were not going to be taken to Pine Ridge at all. He had heard they were going to be taken straight through to a town on the railroad, down there in Nebraska. A train of cars was already waiting and they were going to be taken so far away even the strongest could not find his way home.

Some of the men, very angry, stood up to walk away from the council when they heard this. Big Foot called weakly from the tent for them to hear the soldier chief out and they sat back down with little pleasure.

Chief Forsyth said these were lies. He signalled some of his men and they took the ghost-dancer away. He showed them what had already been done for them. They had been fed twice. Their hearts must be bad if they wanted to believe such things. They must still want to make trouble. If that was so, here was a good place to make it.

Only fools did foolish things he said, and he was no fool. He was not going to bring a whole camp of armed prisoners in there to Pine Ridge. He said for the men to go back to their lodges and bring all their guns and pile them up there on the ground. When the guns were there—all of them—they would make ready and start for the Agency.

A few more than a hundred men were sitting there before the white flag flying from the top of Big Foot's tent. All of the men and grown boys in the camp. Twenty or thirty of them who had the wisest heads got up and went to the lodges. The soldier chief was still angry. He said he did not have all day. And he could not hear what that old man in the tent was saying. He wanted him moved outside where he could be heard and watched the same as the others. So some soldiers carried the chief's bed out into the sun.

When the men returned from the lodges they put only two guns on the ground, both of them old and of no use.

This made Chief Forsyth even more angry. He sent soldiers to the lodges. They cut bindings and threw bundles to the ground where the women were packing. They took axes and knives and even awls. They put hands on the younger women, all over, pretending they were looking for weapons. They brought back all the iron and steel in the packs but they did not find many more guns. No more than ten or twelve, not much better than the first two which had been surrendered.

Mute John was not sitting in the circle. He was standing over there a little to one side. Shining Woman knew he still had his treasured stolen gun beneath his blanket. She knew there were a few others beneath blankets in the circle. Not many. With all these soldiers she could not see why Chief Forsyth thought there was any harm in it. But she did not like it when old Yellow Bird began to move slowly around the council ring, singing softly.

Some of the younger men listened, eyes gleaming. Wiser men put the words from them. One rose and flung back his blanket, holding the rifle hidden beneath it up for all to see.

"In my country a man who has no gun does not feed his family," he said. "It is for that reason I kept this. But if it is thought I keep it to kill someone, then I throw it away."

Treating the weapon well, as one did a prized possession, the man put it down before the soldier chief. Another man stood up, revealing another good rifle.

"Once I had many ponies," he said. "I gave six of the best of them for this. In all the time since I have not used it against the white man. It is now all I have. But if that is what it takes to show you what is in my heart this morning, I give it to you."

Yellow Bird kept circling, singing more loudly, now. One of the Oglala scouts standing among the soldiers in his blue uniform, stepped forward.

"You all see this uniform but inside I am Indian," he said. "If these people are not to be trusted, then take away my gun, too. If their hearts are bad, then mine is bad with them!"

Watching all this time from within his silent world, John Sitting Bull at last understood what was expected here. He started for the little heap of guns, no longer careful that the shape of his prized weapon did not show beneath his blanket. A lesser soldier head man said some alarmed thing, pointing at this boy who was not yet a man. Two soldiers came quickly at him from behind on either side, so that he neither saw nor heard. They seized him, grasping through his blanket for the rifle. He struggled instinctively.

It was a moment in which nothing lived but these three, filling the world. The gun fired. One of the soldiers fell away, the rifle clutched in his hand and blood came from his mouth. Shining Woman could find neither air to breathe nor means to cry out. Then the scream came, tearing her throat, and the earth exploded.

The sound was like the slow, steady ripping of an endless sheet of canvas, magnified to awesome thunder. A blue-coat on a horse, only trotting a little, rode right through the council ring where some of the men were falling over where they sat, before they could even get to their feet. The blue-coat did not seem excited at all.

When he was close enough to Big Foot's bed to have touched him by leaning only a little in his saddle, the blue-coat shot the sick man in the forehead. The chief's old wife scuttled into the soldier tent, yelping like a kicked dog. The blue-coat shot at her several times through the canvas before he rode off some other place.

Yellow Bird was there when the chief was shot. He ran for the nearest lodge, clutching a rifle he, also, had been concealing. A soldier started in that direction and Yellow Bird shot him.

John Sitting Bull sat dazed where he had been flung when they took his rifle. For some time he did not seem to understand what was happening. Then he leaped up and ran untouched through the nearest line of soldiers, disappearing beyond the smoke of their guns. The soldier chief and his head men stood there in the midst of all this and they did not seem to be doing much of anything.

Some men tried to get away from the council ring where all those dead and hurt Indians were piling up. One of them only had an old-time stone-headed war club. He swung it at the soldier chief but a trooper hit him in the chest with the butt of his gun and knocked him down. He shot him while he was lying there.

Another man crashed into the Black Robe who had been with Chief Forsyth. The Black Robe's back was to him and the Indian struck into it with a knife, very deep and high. The Black Robe fell down, badly hurt, but he got up again and went to another Indian who was standing there, looking at white bone and sinew jutting from yet bloodless forearm flesh where a wrist and hand had been. That was the work of those fast-firing cannons up on the hill.

More exploding cannon bullets hit everywhere. One cut down the white flag on Big Foot's tent. It fell on the dead chief's bed. Others fired some lodges and they began to burn very hard. A man whose face was so bloody she did not know him ran past Shining Woman and jerked at her.

"Come on!" he shouted. "This way—"

She ran after him. They shot him and she stumbled over his body as he fell. He tried to sit up but they shot him again and his head fell back to the ground. She scrambled up and ran past the lodge where old Yellow Bird was. It was afire all over but he was still shooting in there. Then the poles collapsed and fell in on him.

A woman ahead had a baby on her back and three other small children running with her. Blood was coming from the baby all over her but she did not seem to know that. She was trying to reach the cutbank of the ravine. Soldiers on the other side were shooting, too, but there was no help for that.

There was no other place to go. The woman did not have enough hands for all the children. Shining Woman caught the hand of one, a little boy scarcely old enough to talk.

They reached the ravine and fell into it. Already there were many dead people and a few wounded choking the bottom. The cannons had now been turned in this direction. To stop was to die. Soldiers were shouting nearby, running closer. Others were riding their horses in, shooting at anything that moved. Shining Woman ran very fast with the little boy, stronger than she knew as she fought her way through those ahead.

She saw many bullet-torn ghost shirts and dresses wrapping the dead. This was the day, all right. This was the day for which they had waited so long. Nothing remained, now. Even God was dying. He was being killed here.

When some fierce blow tore the little boy's hand from her grasp, Shining Woman kept on running and did not look back.

XXXI

Going Home

Beau Lane was breakfasting with Dr. Charley Eastman. It was a relaxed and self-congratulatory meal. They knew the claims the Bureau and the military would make and did not begrudge them as the price of peace. It was enough to know that they— together with George Sword and Reverend Cook—four mixed-bloods without authority—had won. Even the wildest of the incorrigibles were in the huge camp now strung out along White Clay Creek near Drexel Mission.

When Colonel Forsyth's cavalry escorted ailing old Big Foot and his destitute band in from Wounded Knee this morning, the circle would be fully restored. More Sioux than had ever been gathered in one place before, safe at last from official mistake and their own fears.

That knowledge was its own reward.

And Lane had another pleasant feeling. General Brooke had just notified him that Chance Easterbrook was in the press contingent General Miles was holding at his headquarters in Rapid City. They would all be coming over with Miles when he transferred his staff. In two or three days, probably. Beau was eager to see his friend. There was much to learn, much to hear.

He crossed to the stove with his coffee cup. As he lifted the pot the window at his elbow rattled gently with the unmistakable shudder of distant gunfire, sudden and heavy. Dr. Eastman looked up in alarm. Beau dropped the cup and ran out the door, forgetting even to take up his gun. He out-shouted a startled corporal on picket duty and caught up the first horse he could lay hands on in the government corral. He jumped it out over the gate poles without saddle or bridle.

Taking an Indian's mercilessly direct route without regard to trail or terrain, he rode the good, grain-bottomed government horse to the limit of its stride. Even then fifteen miles was a long way and others were before him. They were milling on the crest of a low ridge. A few men and some older boys. He took his stumbling horse up among them, risking a bullet for his white man's attire, and looked down onto the flats near Mousseau's store on Wounded Knee.

It was not yet an hour since he had bolted from Charley Eastman's kitchen but the havoc below was of an extended, day-long battle. Half of the lodges in what had been Big Foot's camp were down or burned out. Bodies lay everywhere and the Hotchkiss guns on a knoll commanding the flats still barked at any target which moved.

Out a few yards from the wrecked lodges was a staggering heap of dead, Indian and trooper alike, where a council seemed to have been in progress. There was some organized activity at this point. A few squads were engaged in retrieving their own casualties from this windrow. The balance of the command, in some madness, was ranging in complete and undisciplined disorder. Most were running down fugitives flushed into the open and trying to flush others from such scanty cover as was available. Nowhere in a vast area of nearly two square miles was there any evidence of official countermand or recall.

Beau could see what appeared to be Colonel Forsyth and some of his junior officers near their own tents, viewing the field with the motionlessness of suspended animation. For an instant he was urged to a frantic ride down in appeal to some common human decency but a surer instinct told him there was no humanity in uniform down there.

One of the Oglalas reined close and pointed to half a dozen troopers jogging along the cutbank of a ravine which appeared to be the only possible escape route. From the number of bodies choking this at all exposed places it seemed all in there must be dead but the troopers halted and one called out in clumsy Army Sioux.

"Listen in there. The fighting is over. Come out and surrender."

Other smaller soldier groups nearby gave up their

own hunting to watch. After a moment a group of children, mostly boys, diffidently appeared, companions helping one who was wounded or hurt. When they were well clear of their hiding place a trooper shouted and every rifle within range opened up. Even the fleetest of the youngsters ran only a few steps back toward the ravine.

"That is a way to make war!" an Oglala cried bitterly.

"There is a better way!" Beau said savagely.

In one fierce jerk, without regard to buttons, he tore open coat, shirt, and flannel undershirt, peeling them as one layer from his body. Leaping to the ground, he snaked off his belt and refastened it and the "brother" knife it supported about his naked belly, then stepped moccasin-footed from his pants and underdrawers.

The Oglala, eyes gleaming approbation, ripped a foot-wide strip from his own blanket and tossed it to Beau. Lane passed this between his legs and pulled the ends up through his belt, allowing the excess to hang free, front and back, in the old-time way.

Kneeling on the raw earth he scooped up dirt, sand, pebbles, and scrubbed himself with them. Not only for purification. He needed the strength of that Mother Earth from which all other things had sprung. The scouring brought an ecstatic bite of pain and freed the grief of blood. That was his paint. That was his sacred shirt.

Leaping onto the back of the wind-broken government horse, he kicked it into a shambling downhill run. He knew he was asking too much but kicked harder. The horse gallantly lifted to an erratic, spring-legged gallop and Beau sent ahead of him the eerie, ululating spirit song of long-dead Sioux fighting men. They knew the war-cry and swung eagerly toward him. Distance narrowed. One trooper fired his pistol. The others held on for a point-blank range more in keeping with the sport of the day. Other troopers were watching from a distance but they made no move to close in and spoil the game.

Suddenly, at fifteen or twenty yards, just as Beau was lifting one knee to fling himself off, his horse went down. He took a rolling fall on one shoulder and landed on his feet. Two of the cavalrymen veered past him to avoid the spill. The third was too close and Beau dodged aside. The fourth, starting to turn, swung around at an almost perfect angle.

Beau leaped in, hooking the fingers of one hand under the stiff forward edge of the man's saddle skirt. He allowed himself to be yanked along for one stride and swung up with the second to the cantle, tight behind the rider. Locking one arm beneath the man's chin and pulling his head around and back as far as possible, he slashed his knife across the straining belly, spilling life in a single gout of blood and gut.

He caught the rifle as it fell from nerveless fingers and pulled the horse to an abrupt halt. Holding the dead man upright before him, he fired twice at the last two troopers as they helplessly overrode him. One fell. The other stayed up but sagged over his pommel. Spinning the doubly-laden horse, Beau took it back up the slope.

The Oglalas were waiting in admiration at the summit. He spilled the dead trooper at the feet of their ponies. So savage had been the stroke of his knife that the body folded back unnaturally upon itself and broke nearly in two as it struck the ground. The Oglalas liked the color of this blood after all that other down there.

There was no pursuit. One trooper remained mounted, supporting his wounded comrade. The others stepped down to tend to the one who had been shot from his saddle. Others who had watched from a distance came up. They looked at the ridge but advanced no further. Beau signalled the Oglalas and they willingly joined in a charge. The troopers fell back hastily until enough other small, disorganized groups closed in with them to make a stand.

When it was folly to ride closer into their gun-muzzles, Beau swept around their flank with the Oglalas and rode toward the ravine in a hunt for other uniforms too scattered to defend themselves. They were Seventh Cavalrymen, all right, and there were a lot of them, but they were not singing *Garry Owen* now.

The snow came as had long been promised. Thin, dry, gritty stuff, riding a mercilessly freezing gale out of the north. Colonel Forsyth's disorganized command started regrouping as the rising threat of the storm began to return them to sanity. Beau Lane and the Oglalas continued to strike in swift, slashing forays and their number was seen to be growing. It seemed possible that warriors from the great ghost encampment supposedly moving in from the Badlands had been diverted by news of the fighting here and were now beginning to arrive in force. The worsening weather was distinctly to the Indians' advantage.

Supply wagons were impressed as ambulances and military casualties, living and dead, were hastily loaded as they rolled out for Pine Ridge. More Indian stragglers were, in fact, coming out of the hills. Sick and benumbed men who scarcely had belly for any more death. But they found Beau and joined him. Two or three score at most. Vengeful wraiths riding the blizzard.

Forsyth continued his hurried withdrawal, forcing his men back into some semblance of discipline as they moved. But they would have died to a man as had those other pony soldiers on the Greasy Grass so long ago had not General Brooke, belatedly learning the gravity of events at Wounded Knee, sent a strong column out from Pine Ridge in relief and escort. They were under constant harassment from Beau Lane's group the whole way in as the battlefield was abandoned to the storm.

General Miles' headquarters contingent from Rapid City, slowed by the weather and problems of transportation, arrived at Pine Ridge on the third day. The wind had blown itself out and the snow with it, but temperatures continued bitterly cold under a leaden sky. Bureau personnel, the military, whites from as far north as the boundaries of the *macoce sica,* and such friendlies as had already committed themselves and so had no other choice, were pulled into a tight perimeter about the Agency buildings. Pickets were posted at brief intervals and Brooke's entire force was held at full ready. Lane was generally supposed to be in complete command of the hostiles, but their whereabouts and disposition were not known and scouts were repeatedly driven back before any reliable information could be obtained.

Churning with impatience and a griping fear, Easterbrook sought out Charley Eastman and the Reverend Cook and George Sword of the Pine Ridge police, but they could tell him nothing. No survivors had been brought in. There had been no contact with those who might have escaped. They were his friends. They understood his anxiety. But they were bitter men. So were the head men of the friendlies.

What had been done out there could not be undone. Worse was to come. Indian casualties still lay where they had fallen. Friends and relatives beneath the snow with no attention for all of this time. Who could know where Shining Woman was or how she had fared—even if she had still been with Big Foot when he and his people camped at Wounded Knee? Who knew where Beau Lane was or what he might do next? He had been their friend a little while ago, but he was Indian, now. And the military would not attempt even a burial detail for fear of inviting attack. No soldier, no white man, was safe beyond the picket lines here.

"All right, no soldiers, then," Chance pleaded earnestly. "Civilians. Some of your Metal Breasts, George. The suttler, the blacksmith. Anybody with the decency to do something. I'll speak to General Miles. I doubt he has the authority to stop us. The dancers are bound to let us through when they see what we're trying to do. If Beau's with them as they say, he'll make them do that much. I know him too well."

"Maybe," Reverend Cook said wearily. "But you don't know his father and his grandfather—how many generations of Sioux back? That's what's out there, now. Not anyone you ever saw before. You'd better remember that, Mr. Easterbrook. For your own good."

"It's worth a try," Chance insisted.

"Anything is," George Sword agreed.

They separated and canvassed from door to door, quarters to quarters, man to man. Not many had lost anything out there. Not many were even sure just what had happened. Every trooper's mess at Pine Ridge had a different version. Not that it made any real difference after three days and nights of storm. They were dead. That much was sure. And they'd keep a long time in this weather, so there was no hurry.

But in the end there were enough who volunteered. Enough shovels and mattocks and a pair of wagons. General Miles faced a decision and reluctantly made it when he saw them all drawn up. He detailed two columns of troopers, freshly arrived, who had not been with Col. Forsyth's command, and ordered them out in escort with wagons and tools of their own.

"A decent burial," he ordered. "First aid for survivors, if you find any, and get them in here as fast as you can. But fall back if you're attacked. Avoid engagement at all costs. I've got enough heroes on my hands as it is."

They moved out of the compound. Wagon tires creaked on dry snow already grimed with drift-soil from patches blown bare by the wind. Shod hoofs struck unnaturally loud sound from hidden stone. It seemed to carry a great distance in the silence. Men watched the hills apprehensively and rode in funeral quiet.

Beyond range of the Hotchkiss batteries mounted behind the picket lines at the Agency, ghost dancers began to appear in small parties on distant high ground, warily watching. They formed a grim gauntlet along the entire fifteen-mile trip. But they made no overt move and Easterbrook believed Beau Lane was responsible for that. There was exaggeration at Pine Ridge—the usual aftermath of battle. Beau had not reverted to savagery as they claimed at the Agency. He had gone over to the Sioux, yes. That would be Beau's way. To counsel and calm them. To bring order and reason out of their fear and hysteria. He was a reasonable man. These were his people. He would not lead them in any other direction. He could not.

They found the first body a good two and a half miles from Mousseau's store at Wounded Knee. Easterbrook saw a woman's skirt and hurried forward. Dr. Charley Eastman, kneeling above the grave-like mound of snow, looked up and shook his head at him. It covered a nameless Hunkpapa mother, frozen in protective encirclement of a shawl-wrapped infant.

Dr. Eastman called sharply for a blanket. Miraculously, the child was yet alive. A round, frost-blackened little face peered out with stoic eyes from beneath a soft buckskin baby cap upon which the United States flag had been embroidered in brilliant beading. The mother's blood had stained the cap on one side but the infant bore no wound.

"Good God!" Chance breathed. "How many more of

them do you suppose there are?"

"Alive?" Eastman shook his head grimly. "Not many. But we'll have to get to them as fast as we can."

He handed the child, wrapped heavily in the blanket, to a man riding a wagon seat and the rigid body of the mother was lifted into the box behind. Humps beneath the snow became more frequent. Mostly women and children lay beneath them. There were a few men, mostly old, beyond fighting age. Some of the women were partially disrobed.

"Not what you think," George Sword said. "Ghost dresses. Wanted them for souvenirs—trophies. And shirts—from the men. You'll see. There's some hanging in every Seventh Cavalry bivouac at Pine Ridge right now."

The officer in charge of the escorting troops did not like working on the open flats like this or perhaps he understood the logistics of the problem facing them better than the volunteers did. He took his men to a small knoll beyond the burned lodges of the Indian camp and set them to work with their spades there. The first volunteer wagon filled with bodies and they sent it on to join the troopers. Two more very young children were found, barely clinging to life beside the frozen bodies of the dead.

Chance stumbled upon an old man who sat up in a frightening resurrection from the snow. His leg was shattered at the knee. His eyes were vague with suffering and in a sickening way he, too, looked like a child. He held up frost-clubbed hands and asked in a whisper for a pipe. Chance called for Charley Eastman but there was nothing the Indian doctor could do. He stood there helplessly while Chance clumsily loaded his own battered old briar and lit it.

The old man treated it as the finest ceremonial red pipestone. With painful effort he raised it as best he could to earth, sky, and the four winds. No strength remained to bring it to his lips, but he had made his peace with the gods. The Reverend Cook had come up beside Dr. Eastman. Chance saw tears in their eyes as the old man breathed heavily once and slumped over lifeless. They picked him up gently and carried him to a wagon now also nearly loaded to capacity with the dead.

Reverend Cook found Chance digging down to frozen flesh in another hummock. He bent and helped and they carried this, too, to a wagon.

"I've asked any who might know her to watch," he said. "The Indians, the scouts. But she isn't of Pine Ridge and there are so many—"

The minister trailed off with a shrug. What was there to say? They found no sign of Shining Woman. A few wounded incredibly yet lived, but all so close to death none could speak to tell them of Shining Woman, even if they knew.

After an interval they came upon a large group of Indian men and boys. One had been scalped. A messy, terrible butchery of a job of it.

"We know the man who did that," George Sword said. "Some of the scouts saw it and said his name."

"Said his name!" Chance exploded. "A trooper? He ought to be hanged!"

"I do not think he will live," the captain of the police said softly.

Some of the Indians had obviously been wearing ghost shirts for they lay stripped where they had fallen. They formed a terrible windrow of torn flesh where the council circle in front of the chief's tent had been. Troopers of the escort columns were removing the corpses like wagon-loads of freight. Big Foot's body was among those already carted off. Chance was grateful he was not obliged to see the old man in death. Someone had made a count when they first came up. Eighty in this one place, they said. Blown to hell before they could even get off their butts.

"A battle, they were calling it at Pine Ridge!" Chance said. "I heard them. The Battle of Wounded Knee."

"It'll read that way in the books," Charley Eastman agreed.

"The hell it will!" Chance growled.

"You can't do anything about it, Mr. Easterbrook," the doctor said. "None of us can. We don't write the reports. Wouldn't make any difference if we did. Not to these poor people."

They helped load the remaining bodies in silence. A messenger came down from the knoll where the troopers were at work and urged them to hurry. A large party of hostiles was assembling upstream and the escort officers feared trouble. The volunteers finished what had to be done and climbed the hill behind the last wagon.

Chance was aghast at what had been done up there. A final barbarism for all its practicality under the circumstances of threat, time, and weather. A six-foot trench, about as wide as it was deep and fifty or sixty feet long, had been dug in the iron-hard ground. The bodies were going into it like frozen cordwood and the earth piled in atop as swiftly as it was filled. There were Indians there, scouts for the troopers, who knew many of the dead and could have recorded names, but they did not. They stood woodenly, watching, or swung their eyes across the flats to the Indians gathering on the banks of the creek.

Chance turned his eyes in this direction, also. One of the hostiles, naked and painted in the chilling wind, rode a nervously stepping pony back and forth before the others, haranguing them or holding them in check. It was not possible to know which. But at twice the distance Chance would have known the man by the way he rode.

The last body and the last of the dirt went into the trench on the knoll. Uneasily watching the distant Indians, the officer commanding the escort issued brisk, impatient orders. The volunteer party moved out for Pine Ridge with the troopers in close order on either flank. Every man felt the urgency. Many knew as Chance did that that was Beau Lane down there. They had stretched their luck. The escort officer was right. Now was the time to ride.

Chance looked back once to where the hole had been dug. Beau and his Indians came up the back side of the knoll and appeared suddenly there beside the mass grave. Chance heard the lament. It was crying out in his own soul. But it was for no individual. It could not be.

No one would now ever know who was buried there nor exactly how many. He would himself never know. He had not seen all the bodies. That had been impossible. They had been scattered so widely and the work necessarily done so hastily by so many hands. But at least it was done.

Beau and the dancers came down presently and followed. They pressed, harassed, finally drove the Agency party as arrogantly as they might have hazed sheep. But they expended little ammunition and seemed satisfied to intimidate rather than attack. Only an escort trooper and one horse were wounded by random shots. The Sioux vanished when they came in sight of the friendly camps and military bivouacs surrounding Pine Ridge. Beau had succeeded in holding them in check as Chance had promised he would.

Early in the next morning Chance was summoned to General Brooke's headquarters where General Nelson Miles had personally taken over the combined command. Reverend Cook and Captain George Sword were also present by request. Dr. Eastman had been asked to attend, but refused. He had survivors from Wounded Knee in makeshift quarters at his dispensary and the Episcopal church and would not leave them.

Miles called Jack Pershing in with a file of preliminary field reports for Chance to read. He gagged at the first paragraph in which the Seventh Cavalrymen under Colonel Forsyth were referred to as skirmishers.

"What in Christ's name were they skirmishing?" Chance demanded. "An enemy—all those defenseless women and children, all those disarmed men and boys? God-damned murderers, General. I like my words plain."

Reverend Cook, standing behind the stove and chafing his weather-reddened hands as though to dispel a chill which seeped outward from the bone, spoke quietly.

"I am afraid the Army does not, Mr. Easterbrook. Quite possibly the only thing we brothers of the cloth and the carbine have in common. General Miles, if you will excuse me, my church is quite crowded today. We have forty wounded over there and Dr. Eastman needs my help."

"I need it here. The doctor's, too," Miles said.

"Later, if necessary. Let Mr. Easterbrook read the reports first. You can send for us."

"If you must," Miles agreed reluctantly. "But let Lieutenant Pershing detail you a squad in escort. That confounded Lane has a sniper behind every cover out there."

"We Indians have a saying we all have been using a lot these days: 'We want to live.' Moving around with a squad of soldiers is hardly the wisest way to do that. I'll do better alone."

Reverend Cook went out. Easterbrook dispiritedly lifted the sheaf of reports.

"Why subject me to this?" he protested. "Hell, I was out there, yesterday. I don't give a damn what you've got written down. There can never be justice now but, my God, can't we at least have the truth?"

"Look, none of us are dancing in the streets," Miles said angrily. "But somebody has to pick up the loose ends and bring it all to an end."

"Sure. The old Army whitewash. I know. You've relieved Forsyth of his command and are recommending court martial. But actually for what dereliction of duty? The stupidity of stationing his troops on all sides of a hollow square so their own crossfire and Hotchkiss shrapnel caused virtually every casualty they sustained? Or the brutal, senseless massacre of three hundred men, women, and children?"

"The measure of civilized man is his ability to recognize his mistakes, Easterbrook."

"Mistakes!" Chance swung on the captain of the Agency police. "Tell the general about that Hunkpapa we found scalped out there, George. Scalped by one of his civilized troopers. Tell him what his own scouts already know—his name and outfit."

"I know, too," Miles said. "He would have been in irons the minute I heard, but he disappeared during the withdrawal from Wounded Knee. Your friend Lane picked him off and sent him back to us in a wagon just after daybreak this morning. Tell Mr. Easterbrook about that, Captain."

"It was the same man, all right," George Sword said. "He was dead but he had been quite a long time dying. All of the time Beau had him, I think. Three days— maybe four. It was done very old-time. The scalp, first, to make up for that other he had taken. Then the eyebrows, mustache, hair of the chest and belly. Very careful knife work. Not every man could do it and keep them still alive, even in the old time.

"Later, while he could still feel that, too, they cut

through legs and arms at the joints so only the sinews held them on. The muscles cannot be stopped from trying to move and it is a very bad torture. When it is time, the man who has done all this fine cutting puts his knife into the heart and it is finished. That was Beau's answer for that Hunkpapa scalp."

"Beau's answer!" Chance protested, shocked. He turned to General Miles. "Why lay it to him? Sure, he's gone over to the Sioux. What else could he in all decency do? He's bound to feel he helped bring them in to be killed and he's trying to make up for that as best he can. I've been with him too long and too close not to understand that. But I can guarantee he wouldn't have anything to do with this kind of butchery."

Miles nodded to the policeman. George Sword pulled back his tunic, took a knife from his belt, and put it into Chance's hand.

"It was still in the trooper's heart when the wagon came in."

Chance slowly put the knife down. It was the Hunkpapa brother of the blade at his own side. Miles picked the weapon up and balanced it across his fingers. A deeply troubled look was in his eyes.

"I understand how you feel about these people, Easterbrook," he said carefully. "We may not be so far apart in our sentiments as you imagine. But there has to be an end to this and I am charged with winding it up as soon as possible at the least possible cost. I need your help. But I can get along without it if I have to. Lane may believe he has us pinned down here but I can assure you it is only because General Brooke and I are reluctant to apply further force."

"You want Beau."

"I do—for the simple reason that I believe him to be the only Sioux left in the Dakotas who is still a dangerous man." General Brooke spoke for the first time.

"We appreciate your position, Easterbrook. I personally came to like Beau Lane myself. No one tried harder here than he did before he went over. But he's done a lot more than just go back to the blanket, Easterbrook. He's gone back God knows how many wild generations."

"He has gone home," George Sword said. "That is how we say it."

"Half-breeds almost always run rogue when they turn coat," Miles continued. "We'll get nowhere with the rest of them while he's out there. He's got to be brought to his senses. But I don't want to go after him. Not with troops if I can help it."

It was Jim McLaughlin's infuriating old argument. Chance saw the validity, now.

"No," he agreed. "They wouldn't give him up. It would be the arrest of Sitting Bull all over again with hundreds instead of a few dozen. But I don't know—" He turned to the captain of police. "—Would he come in, George? Would he come in to talk?"

George Sword shrugged.

"For you, maybe. Nobody else."

Chance nodded. His eyes went to Miles.

"This is why you have George here, isn't it? This is why you wanted Reverend Cook and Charley Eastman. Persuasion."

"Do I need them?"

"No, I guess not. But I'll tell you why. It's what Beau would tell me to do. The old Beau. For them."

"I'll detail an escort but there'll be some risk."

"You frighten me, General."

"Understand, Easterbrook, he must agree to bring them all back—voluntary surrender of arms and ammunition, suitable hostages for good behavior, that sort of thing—or he doesn't go back himself."

"Even under a flag of truce?"

"My flag, my friend, is the Stars and Stripes. Your escort will be the best marksmen in the command. They will have their orders if he leaves without an agreed signal—say without shaking your hand."

Chance sat in irresolution for a long moment until he realized that under a different penalty, he also was being afforded no choice.

"Get the message to him, George," he said to Captain Sword. "I want him to come. I want him to at least listen. Understand?"

The Indian policeman nodded solemnly.

"I understand."

Chance realized he did, fully.

XXXII

Thrown Away

George Sword rode out from Pine Ridge. A few hours later the Ghost Dance snipers who had continually harassed all government installations and movement since the retreat from Wounded

Knee were suddenly withdrawn. An air of suspended animation settled over the whole cantonment at Pine Ridge and the friendly camps as well—if any living Sioux could now be considered friendly. Everyone, red and white, knew the importance of Easterbrook's mission. He doubted, however, if any had real hope of success. He had none, himself. Desire, yes—deep to the core—but as the Indians had been saying for so long, there was no hope.

The escort Miles and Brooke provided was six troopers of the Seventh Cavalry and two of the Ninth. Men, mounts, and equipment were in parade dress. Chance had put away his Rapid City purchases in favor of his old outfit. He thought Beau would understand the gesture, but he felt shabby and unkempt in contrast to the natty troopers.

George Sword had arranged the meeting at the Cheyenne Creek crossing of the Drexel Mission road, far enough out to afford Lane and any with him a feeling of security. However, out of audacity or arrogance, the Dakotan was waiting half a mile closer in. He seemed alone. No support was in evidence. But his person and pony were painted for war.

No man could now mistake Beau for anything other than what he was. If he had ridden half across the continent as a white man to hold a winter's talk with God in a brown Nevada valley, it had been in other times now far distant. This solitary horseman against the dirty grays of winter growth and the thin, stained, patching snow was a fitting subject for the pen and brush of Frederic Remington.

The lamentable thing was that the artist had left Pine Ridge more than a week before—three days before Wounded Knee—believing the campaign was over. Business, he had told General Brooke. But everyone at Rapid City and Pine Ridge had believed it was over, then. So the tragedy and terror that was never to be forgotten, the stark and pathetic beauty beneath the hummocked snow, had been lost to the fine, artistic talents of that drinking man with the belly and soul of a titan. The last tragic portrait of the American Indian. But perhaps this picture of one man, riding in to treat a last time with his enemies, was the more memorable.

Chance spoke to the sergeant in charge of his escort. The squad pulled up. Chance rode on alone. Beau jogged out to meet him in middle ground. There the Dakotan reined aside, dismounted, and stepped back into the middle of the roadway. Chance did likewise and moved forward to meet his friend.

At this range, recollections surged powerfully. Many places. Many times. The good feeling of pleasant things, well remembered. Yet there had been only seventeen months in all.

As he came up, Beau looked past Chance to the escorting troopers, now dismounted beyond earshot and at ease, but with their rifles casually at hand.

"See the difference in blood?" the Dakotan asked in the dialect. "I come alone but even now you do not trust me."

Chance was not pleased that they should begin this way. Beau smiled a little as though forgiving and put his hands to Easterbrook's upper arms, gripping flesh and bone through Shining Woman's shirt in a searching, kneading fashion, travelling upward to the ridge of muscle over the collarbone and ending there. A wordless substitute for inane habitual greetings whose meaning had long been lost in custom: "How are you?" and "How have you been?" The answers were reassuringly there, in health and tone of body, under those gently inquiring Indian fingers.

The hands dropped. Beau sat easily on his hunkers in that squatting position so paralyzing to the uninitiate and so effortless to the familiar. Chance settled in the same posture, facing his friend.

"A long time, Brother," Beau said.

"Many doings," Chance agreed, pleased and finding it fitting that they continued in Sioux.

"Yes. We have both lately had some," Beau said, his features flattening a little. "At this time, my friend, I think I wish to say a few words about my uncle, Sitting Bull."

"I listen," Chance assented gravely.

"Well, I loved that old man. That is not too strong a word for you?"

"No. Not for him."

"It is good you understand, for that is the first time I felt like going home. My heart was hot when they killed him. I wanted to be in that fight. I would have killed some more of those men up there."

"My heart was hot, too," Chance said. "I think White Hair was afraid I might do the same. I think that is why he put me in his jailhouse while all that bad business was being done."

"We heard how that was. We also heard that White Hair had it said that you had gone back to your own country afterward. I knew that could not be so but many believed it. That is why you did not find Shining Woman waiting when you came back to Grand River. That is why she ran away with all those other people. Is it true you would have killed some of those Metal Breasts if you had been at the chief's camp in time?"

Anger shook Chance at the lie Jim McLaughlin had sent south. All of those frightened miles for her. All of those bloody footprints. And the horror of Wounded Knee. A few had escaped. They knew that, now. Beau would know if she had been among them. He had only to ask. But not now, he knew. There was much to be said between them before they spoke of themselves. He could not ask until the question could be regarded as proper. The anxiety was hard to contain. He shook his head in answer to Beau's query.

"I think so. But I do not know. I have never killed a man."

"Still you know the feeling?"

"I know the feeling," Chance agreed grimly.

"Good," Beau said. "You have my ears and now it seems I have yours. I did not know you had finally come here to Pine Ridge or I would have been first to send a message. I am told you have some things to say."

Now was the time, Chance knew, and for all his vanity in acquisition of this alien tongue, he had sudden warning of his inadequacy in its use. What he had to say was of the utmost importance but his long hair did not make him any more fluent. Neither did a leather shirt and moccasins and an ability to squat interminably on his heels in the frost-hardened mud of a reservation roadway. Conviction did not make him articulate nor did empathy, however agonizing.

"You know exactly why I'm here, Beau," he said in English.

The Dakotan looked at him in an intensity of expectation, as though he had not spoken. He saw he was to be denied the refuge to which he had turned. He shrugged helplessly.

"All right," he said. And in the language of the Dakotas, "You know what is in my heart."

"Yes. Many things. Foolish things. I have heard them all. Great things for the Sioux. Good things for the Sioux. Done with words. Your words, Brother, put on paper. Well, men who read those words killed three hundred Sioux over there on Wounded Knee Creek."

"No," Chance protested. "Some soldiers sick with the same fever you had when you sent this in to the Agency with something that had once been a man."

He brought the knife which George Sword had given him from beneath his shirt. With a sharp gesture, he stuck it into the hardened earth between them. Lane pulled it free and cleaned the blade on his naked thigh.

"You do not understand that."

"No. No decent man could."

"Because it is Indian," Beau said bitterly. "That was a Hunkpapa who was scalped out there. By a soldier. I saw many other Hunkpapas dying. Not because they had done any wrong. The fault was that they could not run away fast enough."

"I know. I went there later, as soon as I could. I helped load them in the wagons for burying. Something will be done about that, Beau."

"What?" the Dakotan demanded. "Will you bring all those dead people back? Now you talk like that Paiute who said he was the Christ. A new world, he said. Well, it is the same one, but it is no longer a world in which any Sioux wishes to live!"

He bent the good Grandmother iron of the knife across his knee with explosive force. The blade snapped and he flung the pieces from him.

"Do you know what they are saying out there in the *macoce sica?* They are saying that when a man has only enemies left and there is no longer any God, then that is the day to die. Already their spirits are dead out there. They look at this road they are being made to follow and they see nothing. It leads nowhere. Even the little children sit and do nothing. They do not talk to one another. Kicking Bear and Short Bull and a few other men keep their guns by them, but their spirits are dying, too. Well, do you know what I say to that? They are still a nation. I will not let them live half-dead!"

A fierce suffusion of color came up beneath the skin of the Dakotan's painted face.

"Brother, you do not come here for yourself. Bear Coat sent you. He thinks I will tell them that a new world is here. He thinks I will tell them all these bloody soldiers mean them well. He thinks I will tell them if they listen to Red Cloud and American Horse and all those other whining old men and give themselves up, they will be greeted as brothers.

"I told them all those lies once and they believed me. They came in and gave up their guns and they were killed when they were in Bear Coat's arms. Now bullets are better than words. That is what Bear Coat uses. This time when they die they will be men and they will not die alone. That is what I say to Bear Coat!"

"That is anger."

"It is Sioux anger. At least they still have that."

"Let them live, Beau. They are your people."

"No!" the Dakotan said with soft savagery. "Do not make that mistake. The woman who was my wife did. She turned her face from me because of that. She threw me away because I was Indian. But she was wrong. I know what I am inside. I am a white man, my friend. I found that out at Wounded Knee."

He pointed to the troopers of Easterbrook's escort.

"Those are my people. They know how to kill. So do I. Tell Bear Coat to send me many soldiers, all his soldiers, and he will see. Those are Sioux out there. Those are men. I will bring their spirits alive again. As long as I live, I will live with them. They are not going to be cattle, feeding heads-down on whatever is thrown before them on the grass of their own land. I am a white man. I cannot pay all. But I owe them that much."

Chance started to speak but Beau cut him off sharply.

"That is all! I did not come here to speak about all these useless things. I only came to tell you of a thing I found when we were fighting over there."

He pulled a small, limp bundle from the skirt of his clout. A cloth doll. A doll Chance Easterbrook had bought from a shop window in Pierre. Chance reached out. His hand closed over it. The search was done. The pursuit from Grand River, brought to an end by a pony's broken leg and the suspicion of a team of Army couriers. The enforced, uncertain wait at Miles' headquarters in Rapid City. The trip through the blizzard to Pine Ridge and the shocking fact of Wounded Knee. That long day on the battlefield, gathering in the bodies and a few survivors who could tell him nothing. Listening to Miles and Brooke, numb to their concerns and indifferent to their plans. Not really caring until he knew. And now he did.

"Let your heart bleed," Beau continued. "Hers already has. We took her away to a place of her own. She is not in that big hole they dug up there on the hill. It was for you, Brother, that we saved her from that. Now do something for me. Whenever they call that a battle out there, you remember that she ran more than three miles from that place before they killed her. Three miles, Brother! Remember that and tell Bear Coat how many soldiers are going to die!"

Lane waited a long moment but Chance had no words. He closed his hands on the stained and stiffened doll. Both of them, tightly, so that they were occupied and could not be gripped. That, as they said, was the way it had to be. He knew that, now. So, he thought, did Beau.

The Dakotan turned, ran lightly across the road, and vaulted astride his pony. His hand flung up in a gesture which could have been either defiance or farewell.

"Hoka hey!" he shouted.

The squad of picked riflemen up the road were drill-ground proficient. A single volley brought horse and rider down together.

The End

They all came in. The campaign was ended. The last Indian battle in the United States had been fought. History prepared to move elsewhere.

Chance Easterbrook walked into the post barber's stall at Pine Ridge. Suited, white-shirted, and in polished suttler's boots, he took the chair. The barber looked at the leonine hang of his hair.

"Trim, sir?" he asked.

"To the scalp," Chance ordered.

That was the way he remembered it. That, as the old men said, was the way it was.

Center Point Publishing
600 Brooks Road • PO Box 1
Thorndike ME 04986-0001 USA

(207) 568-3717

US & Canada:
1 800 929-9108